CHR. ....

THE CASE OF THE 100% ALIBIS

CHRISTOPHER BUSH was born Charlie Christmas Bush in Norfolk in 1885. His father was a farm labourer and his mother a milliner. In the early years of his childhood he lived with his aunt and uncle in London before returning to Norfolk aged seven, later winning a scholarship to Thetford Grammar School.

As an adult, Bush worked as a schoolmaster for 27 years, pausing only to fight in World War One, until retiring aged 46 in 1931 to be a full-time novelist. His first novel featuring the eccentric Ludovic Travers was published in 1926, and was followed by 62 additional Travers mysteries. These are all to be republished by Dean Street Press.

Christopher Bush fought again in World War Two, and was elected a member of the prestigious Detection Club. He died in 1973.

CHRISTOPHER BUSH

THE CASE OF THE 100% ALIBIS

With an introduction
by Curtis Evans

DEAN STREET PRESS

INTRODUCTION

THAT ONCE vast and mighty legion of bright young (and youngish) British crime writers who began publishing their ingenious tales of mystery and imagination during what is known as the Golden Age of detective fiction (traditionally dated from 1920 to 1939) had greatly diminished by the iconoclastic decade of the Sixties, many of these writers having become casualties of time. Of the 38 authors who during the Golden Age had belonged to the Detection Club, a London-based group which included within its ranks many of the finest writers of detective fiction then plying the craft in the United Kingdom, just over a third remained among the living by the second half of the 1960s, while merely seven—Agatha Christie, Anthony Gilbert, Gladys Mitchell, Margery Allingham, John Dickson Carr, Nicholas Blake and Christopher Bush—were still penning crime fiction.

In 1966--a year that saw the sad demise, at the too young age of 62, of Margery Allingham--an executive with the English book publishing firm Macdonald reflected on the continued popularity of the author who today is the least well known among this tiny but accomplished crime writing cohort: Christopher Bush (1885-1973), whose first of his three score and three series detective novels, *The Plumley Inheritance*, had appeared fully four decades earlier, in 1926. "He has a considerable public, a 'steady Bush public,' a public that has endured through many years," the executive boasted of Bush. "He never presents any problem to his publisher, who knows exactly how many copies of a title may be safely printed for the loyal Bush fans; the number is a healthy one too." Yet in 1968, just a couple of years after the Macdonald editor's affirmation of Bush's notable popular duration as a crime writer, the author, now in his 83rd year, bade farewell to mystery fiction with a final detective novel, *The Case of the Prodigal Daughter*, in which, like in Agatha Christie's *Third Girl* (1966), copious references are made, none too favorably, to youthful sex, drugs and rock and roll. Afterwards, outside of the reprinting in the UK in the early 1970s of a scattering of classic Bush titles from the Golden Age, Bush's books, in contrast with those of Christie, Carr, Allingham and Blake, disappeared from mass circulation in both the UK and the US, becoming fervently sought (and ever more unobtainable) treasures by collectors and connoisseurs of classic crime fiction. Now, in one of the signal developments in vintage mystery publishing, Dean Street Press is reprinting all 63 of the Christopher Bush detective novels. These will be published over a period of months, beginning with the release of books 1 to 10 in the series.

Few Golden Age British mystery writers had backgrounds as humble yet simultaneously mysterious, dotted with omissions and evasions, as Christopher Bush, who was born Charlie Christmas Bush on the day of the Nativity in 1885 in the Norfolk village of Great Hockham, to Charles Walter Bush and his second wife, Eva Margaret Long. While the father of Christopher Bush's Detection Club colleague and near exact contemporary Henry Wade (the pseudonym of Henry Lancelot Aubrey-Fletcher) was a baronet who lived in an elegant Georgian mansion and claimed extensive ownership of fertile English fields, Christopher's father resided in a cramped cottage and toiled in fields as a farm laborer, a term that in the late Victorian and Edwardian era, his son lamented many years afterward, "had in it something of contempt....There was something almost of serfdom about it."

Charles Walter Bush was a canny though mercurial individual, his only learning, his son recalled, having been "acquired at the Sunday school." A man of parts, Charles was a tenant farmer of three acres, a thatcher, bricklayer and carpenter (fittingly for the father of a detective novelist, coffins were his specialty), a village radical and a most adept poacher. After a flight from Great Hockham, possibly on account of his poaching activities, Charles, a widower with a baby son whom he had left in the care of his mother, resided in London, where he worked for a firm of spice importers. At a dance in the city, Charles met Christopher's mother, Eva Long, a lovely and sweet-natured young milliner and bonnet maker, sweeping her off her feet with a combination of "good looks and a certain plausibility." After their marriage the couple left London to live in a tiny rented cottage in Great Hockham, where Eva over the next eighteen years gave birth to three sons and five daughters and perforce learned the challenging ways of rural domestic economy.

Decades later an octogenarian Christopher Bush, in his memoir *Winter Harvest: A Norfolk Boyhood* (1967), characterized Great Hockham as a rustic rural redoubt where many of the words that fell from the tongues of the native inhabitants "were those of Shakespeare, Milton and the Authorised Version....Still in general use were words that were standard in Chaucer's time, but had since lost a certain respectability." Christopher amusingly recalled as a young boy telling his mother that a respectable neighbor woman had used profanity, explaining that in his hearing she had told her husband, "George, wipe you that shit off that pig's arse, do you'll datty your trousers," to which his mother had responded that although that particular usage of a four-letter word had not really been *swearing*, he was not to give vent to such language himself.

Great Hockham, which in Christopher Bush's youth had a population of about four hundred souls, was composed of a score or so of cottages, three public houses, a post-office, five shops, a couple of forges and a pair of churches, All Saint's and the Primitive Methodist Chapel, where the Bush family rather vocally worshipped. "The village lived by farming, and most of its men were labourers," Christopher recollected. "Most of the children left school as soon as the law permitted: boys to be absorbed somehow into the land and the girls to go into domestic service." There were three large farms and four smaller ones, and, in something of an anomaly, not one but two squires--the original squire, dubbed "Finch" by Christopher, having let the shooting rights at Little Hockham Hall to one "Green," a wealthy international banker, making the latter man a squire by courtesy. Finch owned most of the local houses and farms, in traditional form receiving rents for them personally on Michaelmas; and when Christopher's father fell out with Green, "a red-faced, pompous, blustering man," over a political election, he lost all of the banker's business, much to his mother's distress. Yet against all odds and adversities, Christopher's life greatly diverged from settled norms in Great Hockham, incidentally producing one of the most distinguished detective novelists from the Golden Age of detective fiction.

Although Christopher Bush was born in Great Hockham, he spent his earliest years in London living with his mother's much older sister, Elizabeth, and her husband, a fur dealer by the name of James Streeter, the couple having no children of their own. Almost certainly of illegitimate birth, Eva had been raised by the Long family from her infancy. She once told her youngest daughter how she recalled the Longs being visited, when she was a child, by a "fine lady in a carriage," whom she believed was her birth mother. Or is it possible that the "fine lady in a carriage" was simply an imaginary figment, like the aristocratic fantasies of Philippa Palfrey in P.D. James's *Innocent Blood* (1980), and that Eva's "sister" Elizabeth was in fact her mother?

The Streeters were a comfortably circumstanced couple at the time they took custody of Christopher. Their household included two maids and a governess for the young boy, whose doting but dutiful "Aunt Lizzie" devoted much of her time to the performance of "good works among the East End poor." When Christopher was seven years old, however, drastically straightened financial circumstances compelled the Streeters to leave London for Norfolk, by the way returning the boy to his birth parents in Great Hockham.

Fortunately the cause of the education of Christopher, who was not only a capable village cricketer but a precocious reader and scholar, was taken up both by his determined and devoted mother and an idealistic local elementary school headmaster. In his teens Christopher secured a scholarship to Norfolk's Thetford Grammar School, one of England's oldest educational institutions, where Thomas Paine had studied a century-and-a-half earlier. He left Thetford in 1904 to take a position as a junior schoolmaster, missing a chance to go to Cambridge University on yet another scholarship. (Later he proclaimed himself thankful for this turn of events, sardonically speculating that had he received a Cambridge degree he "might have become an exceedingly minor don or something as staid and static and respectable as a publisher.") Christopher would teach in English schools for the next twenty-seven years, retiring at the age of 46 in 1931, after he had established a successful career as a detective novelist.

Christopher's romantic relationships proved far rockier than his career path, not to mention every bit as murky as his mother's familial antecedents. In 1911, when Christopher was teaching in Wood Green School, a co-educational institution in Oxfordshire, he wed county council schoolteacher Ella Maria Pinner, a daughter of a baker neighbor of the Bushes in Great Hockham. The two appear never actually to have lived together, however, and in 1914, when Christopher at the age of 29 headed to war in the 16th (Public Schools) Battalion of the Middlesex Regiment, he falsely claimed in his attestation papers, under penalty of two years' imprisonment with hard labor, to be unmarried.

After four years of service in the Great War, including a year-long stint in Egypt, Christopher returned in 1919 to his position at Wood Green School, where he became involved in another romantic relationship, from which he soon desired to extricate himself. (A photo of the future author, taken at this time in Egypt, shows a rather dashing, thin-mustached man in uniform and is signed "Chris," suggesting that he had dispensed with "Charlie" and taken in its place a diminutive drawn from his middle name.) The next year Winifred Chart, a mathematics teacher at Wood Green, gave birth to a son, whom she named Geoffrey Bush. Christopher was the father of Geoffrey, who later in life became a noted English composer, though for reasons best known to himself Christopher never acknowledged his son. (A letter Geoffrey once sent him was returned unopened.) Winifred claimed that she and Christopher had married but separated, but she refused to speak of her purported spouse forever after and she destroyed all of his letters and other mementos, with the exception of a book of poetry that he had written for her during what she termed their engagement.

Christopher's true mate in life, though with her he had no children, was Florence Marjorie Barclay, the daughter of a draper from Ballymena, Northern Ireland, and, like Ella Pinner and Winifred Chart, a schoolteacher. Christopher and Marjorie likely had become romantically involved by 1929, when Christopher dedicated to her his second detective novel, *The Perfect Murder Case*; and they lived together as man and wife from the 1930s until her death in 1968 (after which, probably not coincidentally, Christopher stopped publishing novels). Christopher returned with Marjorie to the vicinity of Great Hockham when his writing career took flight, purchasing two adjoining cottages and commissioning his father and a stepbrother to build an extension consisting of a kitchen, two bedrooms and a new staircase. (The now sprawling structure, which Christopher called "Home Cottage," is now a bed and breakfast grandiloquently dubbed "Home Hall.") After a falling-out with his father, presumably over the conduct of Christopher's personal life, he and Marjorie in 1932 moved to Beckley, Sussex, where they purchased Horsepen, a lovely Tudor plaster and timber-framed house. In 1953 the couple settled at their final home, The Great House, a centuries-old structure (now a boutique hotel) in Lavenham, Suffolk.

From these three houses Christopher maintained a lucrative and critically esteemed career as a novelist, publishing both detective novels as Christopher Bush and, commencing in 1933 with the acclaimed book *Return* (in the UK, *God and the Rabbit*, 1934), regional novels purposefully drawing on his own life experience, under the pen name Michael Home. (During the 1940s he also published espionage novels under the Michael Home pseudonym.) Although his first detective novel, *The Plumley Inheritance*, made a limited impact, with his second, *The Perfect Murder Case*, Christopher struck gold. The latter novel, a big seller in both the UK and the US, was published in the former country by the prestigious Heinemann, soon to become the publisher of the detective novels of Margery Allingham and Carter Dickson (John Dickson Carr), and in the latter country by the Crime Club imprint of Doubleday, Doran, one of the most important publishers of mystery fiction in the United States.

Over the decade of the 1930s Christopher Bush published, in both the UK and the US as well as other countries around the world, some of the finest detective fiction of the Golden Age, prompting the brilliant Thirties crime fiction reviewer, author and Oxford University Press editor Charles Williams to avow: "Mr. Bush writes of as thoroughly enjoyable murders as any I know." (More recently, mystery genre authority B.A. Pike dubbed these novels by Bush, whom he praised as "one of the most reliable and resourceful of true detective writers"; "Golden Age baroque, rendered remarkable by some extraordinary flights of fancy.") In 1937 Christopher Bush became, along with Nicholas Blake, E.C.R. Lorac and Newton Gayle (the writing team of Muna Lee and Maurice West Guinness), one of the final authors initiated into the Detection Club before the outbreak of the Second World War and with it the demise of the Golden Age. Afterward he continued publishing a detective novel or more a year, with his final book in 1968 reaching a total of 63, all of them detailing the investigative adventures of lanky and bespectacled gentleman amateur detective Ludovic Travers. Concurring as I do with the encomia of Charles Williams and B.A. Pike, I will end this introduction by thanking Avril MacArthur for providing invaluable biographical information on her great uncle, and simply wishing fans of classic crime fiction good times as they discover (or rediscover), with this latest splendid series of Dean Street Press classic crime fiction reissues, Christopher Bush's Ludovic Travers detective novels. May a new "Bush public" yet arise!

Curtis Evans

The Case of the 100% Alibis (1934)

"What in your considered opinion carries the main stress
of a detective novel? What's the first essential, in other
words?"
"Well, the plot."
"Yes, but what is the essential for the actual plot?"
"I'd say, an alibi."

The Case of the 100% Alibis

IN MYSTERIES FROM the period between the First and Second
World Wars (the so-called "Golden Age" of detective fiction), attempting to solve the all-important question of whodunit? can
place a daunting, indeed herculean, set of labors on the shoulders of the sleuth (and the reader). Many of these tasks implicate not the intriguing question of who but rather that of how:

How did the murderer get in and out of the locked room?

How did the cyanide find its fatal way into the brandy
decanter?

How could x have committed the crime while apparently
in another location at the time?

This last question of course concerns the perpetually con-
founding matter of the unbreakable alibi, one of the key conun-
drums found in fair play detective fiction. Alibi problems lie at
the heart of British Crime Queen Dorothy L. Sayers's ingenious
novels *The Five Red Herrings* (1931), perhaps the *ne plus ultra*
of railway timetable mysteries (which concern who could have
arrived where and when), and *Have His Carcase* (1932), where
intrepid mystery writer Harriet Vane stumbles on a slashed
corpse on a beach rock and thereupon presents Lord Peter Wim-
sey with a vexing problem of times and tides. Yet in my view the
most significant of the British vintage mystery writers who made
an art out of the alibi problem are Freeman Wills Crofts (1879-
1957), extensively discussed by me in my 2012 book on superb

puzzle plotters Crofts, John Street and Alfred Stewart, and yet another accomplished spinner of detective tales, Christopher Bush (1885-1973), whose entire mystery oeuvre of 63 novels is being reissued by Dean Street Press. The mastery evinced in this challenging field by Christopher Bush made him one of the most popular and critically praised writers of detective fiction during its Golden Age, when complex timetable mysteries were, as one newspaper reviewer ingenuously confessed at the time, "a weakness even for the brightest people."

Before 1934 Christopher Bush had already established himself as a supreme alibi artisan, with such classic titles to his credit as *The Perfect Murder Case* (1929), *Cut Throat* (1932) and *The Case of the Three Strange Faces* (1933). Yet with *The Case of the 100% Alibis* (1934) (*The Kitchen Cake Murder* in the US), Bush could not have made his fascination with the alibi problem any clearer. As the title ringingly heralds, the eleventh Ludovic Travers mystery tasks Bush's brilliant amateur sleuth (who frequently indulges his hobby of murder in tandem with his friend Superintendent George "the General" Wharton but in this tale also comes to the aid of a bluff but baffled local chief constable, Major Tempest, whom we shall meet again in a later novel, and Tempest's underling, Inspector Carry) with puzzling his way through the series of intricate alibis, something rather like a set of Russian nesting dolls, that shield one of Travers's craftiest opponents. "Seldom, if ever, has the alibi problem been handled so deftly or in such an entertaining manner as Mr. Bush has done in this grade A yarn," observed reviewed Isaac Anderson in his notice of *The Case of the 100% Alibis* in the *New York Times Book Review*.

The baffling case opens (after one of the author's teasing and beguiling prologues, entitled "FOR THE INGENIOUS READER") with a cryptic phone call made at 7.13 on a Wednesday evening, March 13 to the police station at the pleasant southern coastal community of Seaborough, in which can be heard the voice of manservant Robert Trench croaking out, "Send someone here quick. There's been a murder!" When this call comes through to the police station, Superintendent Wharton, down in Seaborough—on some official business—happens to be in the cocktail bar of the Imperial Hotel with his wife, a native of Seaborough, and the Tempests, husband and wife. Soon Superintendent Wharton and Chief Constable Tempest are looking into the bizarre stabbing of the enigmatic Frederick Lewton at his domicile, Homedale, in the suburb of West Cliff.

Preliminary investigation quickly reveals that Wharton is once again enmeshed in another of those perplexing impossible crime affairs that seem constantly to plague him. A Mrs. Beece, wife of an acquaintance of Lewton's, reports that at 7.05 a placid Lewton rang up the Beece household, wanting to talk to Mr. Beece, who was in bed with a chill; yet local medico Dr. Hule states that his wife told him (he was out on his rounds) that she took a call from a highly agitated Lewton at 7.10—this merely three minutes before Lewton's manservant, Trench, called the police station stating that his master had been murdered. However, to the police Trench claims that he had been away all day in London, visiting his wife in hospital, and had only just arrived in Seaborough aboard the 7.10 train. Then there are Trench's nephew, Howard Trench, a stage actor currently performing in Seaborough the title role in Shakespeare's Julius Caesar (he will not be the last of Bush's Shakespearean thespian characters), and another Lewton acquaintance, detective novelist Raymond Rennyet (pen name of Aloysius Ringold Rennyet, popular author of *Live Man*, *Dead Man* and *Two Shots Missed*), and his devoted servant couple, the Meeks, a retired policeman and his wife--some or all of whom also may have some connection to the strange affair.

Yet proving a case against any of these individuals seems to be, well, impossible, as a disgusted George Wharton admits: "Every single person who's come to our notice at all has the most beautiful twenty-two carat, diamond-studded alibi. They're the only people Lewton ever had anything to do with and all we've got to do, therefore, is to find someone nobody's ever heard of." Adding to the challenge is the letter found at Homedale, addressed to "Uncle" and signed "Ethel," because Lewton is not believed actually to have a niece.

It all makes for a very pretty problem for genteel amateur sleuth Ludovic Travers when he arrives on the scene nearly half-way into the novel. Wharton of course is by now an old friend and "Ludo," as his family and most intimate pals know him, quickly charms Major Tempest. The chief constable takes rather a liking to "the elongated gentleman in horn-rims," sensing as he does Ludo's "delightful personality and a sureness that spoke of fine breeding." With a clever gambit Ludo will bring the case to a conclusion, though readers will judge for themselves whether justice is truly done.

There is additionally a welcome appearance by Palmer, Ludo's most capable "man" ("He was with my father when I was born," explains Travers), and an extended cameo by Wharton's wife, Jane, who genuinely contributes to her husband's investigative proceedings: "Mrs. Wharton was a motherly woman and shrewd. She was a hospital nurse before her marriage, and there had been a time when Wharton had known her definitely a cut above him. But those days were long ago. They had pulled together, and they were together—few couples more closely." A reader of detective fiction, Jane Wharton is familiar with the mysteries of Raymond Rennyet: "highbrow stuff—not too highbrow, of course....Why, you remember *Two Shots Missed*? You know, the book I told you was so good.....Very clever. He writes well too." The same could be said—and should be said—of Christopher Bush, one of the finest practitioners of the fine art of murder fiction.

FOR THE INGENIOUS READER

PROLOGUE

A PROLOGUE, as has been said before, is generally an unnecessary and even an annoying thing. In the matter of the Seaborough murder—which for want of a handier tag became known as "The Case of the Hundred-Per-Cent Alibis"—a prologue seems essential, if only to bring that tag-tide within the bounds of sense.

The circumstances connected with its opening moments were sufficiently original and startling to make that murder the most sensational for many years. And when Superintendent George Wharton of Scotland Yard saw fit to let a coroner's inquest run its full and protracted course, so that the public could follow each word of evidence and implication, it is easier to see why the affair was the main subject of popular speculation even when the inquest had long been over and the police were no wiser than before.

But the Case of the Hundred-Per-Cent Alibis was solved. That, in itself, is a contradiction. A hundred per cent is a hundred per cent, and such an alibi admits of no loophole. To say then that the murderer was caught is somewhat of a plagiarism on the old, preposterous dilemma of an irresistible force meeting an immovable object. Even the law cannot move the immovable or break an unbreakable alibi.

If, then, the murderer was caught, let it be assumed at once that it was not because of a flaw in his alibi. How then was he caught? The answer—read though it may like a further essay on the preposterous—is merely this.

The murderer of Frederick Lewton was caught for two reasons. Firstly, Mrs. Hubbard, of 33, Highway Road, Seaborough, came from the North, and Seaborough is almost farthest South. It may therefore have been unfamiliarity that made a certain Hubbard cake the unique, enticingly appetizing thing which her neighbours found it.

The second reason was the *Daily Record*. Inspired by—shall we say?—patriotic motives, it offered a prize of ten thousand pounds to the first English aviator who should fly the Atlantic, solo, both ways inside a hundred hours. That was at the end of February. Within a week, a Captain Moile made the first attempt. In spite of atrocious weather he reached Newfoundland, and immediately overhauled for the return flight. The weather was worse and the adventure nothing less than lunacy—but he started back. This Captain Moile was the son of Colonel Sir Henry Moile; at that time Mayor of Seaborough, and a noted sportsman.

Those were the two reasons why the murderer of Frederick Lewton was discovered. To drive the point still further home; if Mrs. Hubbard had not been so cocksure of her cake, and if Captain Moile had not been the lunatic the other papers called him, then the murderer of Lewton might have been alive today.

Those were the two reasons why the murderer of Frederick Lewton was discovered. To drive the point still farther home, if Mrs. Hubbard had not been so cocksure of her cake, and if Captain Moile had not been the lunatic the other papers called him, then the murderer of Lewton might have been alive to-day.

There is perhaps just one other reason—over six foot of lean figure, charming manners and all the rest of it, that went by the name of Ludovic Travers. There were the whimsical face; the immense horn rims that gave a deceptive diffidence; the patrician ease that could lure a confidence, and the money that could gratify a hobby—but those would be merely more Ludovic Travers.

PART I

CHAPTER I
THE MURDER

THAT WEDNESDAY EVENING of early March, the police-station at Seaborough was singularly peaceful. The Chief Constable—Major Tempest—had been in for a moment and then departed. The station-sergeant was looking through the six o'clock edition of the *Seaborough Evening Beacon*, and at the side table a constable was writing.

"Well, that's another damn fool gone west." He laid the paper aside. "Four o'clock at the latest they reckon they ought to have seen something of him."

"They'll never see anything of *him*," said the constable. "He's a goner; I wouldn't mind having a quid on that." He went on writing and when he spoke again it was in a more official tone. "What about that detail for West Cliff fork, sergeant? It's a tricky place now the road's up."

The sergeant grunted and his eye rose instinctively to the clock. *The time was seven-thirteen.* He had used the telephone to hold down some papers, among which were the ones that he wanted, but as his hand went out, the bell rang, and the ring was so unexpected and so strangely near, that his hand for a moment shot back.

"Is that the police?"

The voice was thick and throaty. There was more than a suspicion of asthma or catarrh about it, and it had such a definite individuality that with his inward eye the sergeant saw a man pursy, bald and slipshod.

"Yes, this is the police. What do you want?"

The voice took on an obvious agitation. "Send someone here quick. There's been a murder!"

The sergeant's eyes bulged. "Murder! Where're you ringing from?"

"Homedale, West Cliff." There was a kind of gurgling, distressful sob. "It's Mr. Lewton. I just got in and found him."

"Who are you?"

"Trench—Robert Trench. I'm his servant and I just got in—"

"Right! You stay where you are and we'll be there in no time. Homedale, West Cliff, you said? . . . Right!"

He snapped the receiver back and plugged through to the detective office across the yard. By a fifty-to-one chance Inspector Carry was there. Five minutes later the inspector was racing his car up the long slope to the suburb of West Cliff, and one of his sergeants was with him.

At ten minutes past seven, Major Tempest was standing in the cocktail bar of the Imperial with his old friend, George Wharton. The superintendent had been down on some official business, and Mrs. Wharton—who was a Seaborough woman— had come too. Mrs. Tempest was with her in the lounge, and Tempest was standing the party a dinner, after which the two women were going on to the Royalty, where a week's Shakespearean season was on.

George Wharton—or the General, as the Yard affectionately knew him—was a queer sight for a cocktail bar, unless one took him for a harassed paterfamilias who had crept apart to dull his troubles. The wrinkles at the corners of his eyes were unlaughing as he set down the glass and wiped his huge, overhanging moustache with a vast handkerchief.

"Well, John, if that's a cocktail, give me beer."

Tempest laughed. The laugh was held curiously in the air as a sound came from outside. With a "Pardon me a moment," he made for the swing doors. In half a minute he was back with a paper, and his face was all smiles. He thrust the stop-press column under Wharton's nose.

MOILE LANDED NEAR CAPE LOOP, IRELAND, 3.30.
MACHINE DAMAGED, PILOT UNHURT.

Wharton, in the act of raising his eyebrows, winced at the heavy smack of Tempest's excited hand.

"What do you think of it, eh? My God, he's a plucky devil that! What about getting hold of the *Beacon* and hearing the latest?"

As he turned, a waiter approached him.

"Pardon me, sir, but you're wanted urgently on the phone."

Wharton made a gesture of dismissal and acceptance. "I'll be in the lounge."

Tempest thrust the paper into his hand and made off. Inside two minutes he was leading Wharton aside. Another two minutes and the women were preparing to dine alone. Tempest and Wharton were in the major's car, tearing up the long slope towards West Cliff.

It was a cold night with a threat of snow. Behind and below, the lights of the town twinkled as they reached the crest, and ahead ran a warning line of red.

"What's all that?" asked Wharton.

"Road's up at the fork," Tempest told him, and slowed the car down. "That's another car just ahead. Looks as if it might be Carry."

The line of red lamps ran for a hundred yards along the centre of the main road. There was a watchman's shelter and a brazier fire, and the watchman himself peered out at them as they came cautiously through.

"Where's that other road go?" Wharton asked.

"It's the old road, back of the cliffs and out to Bicklesham," Tempest told him, eyes staring at the narrow way. "The corporation made this new road a couple of years ago."

A bare two hundred yards past the last red lamp he drew the car in to the right-hand side. The light from the street-lamp was dim and he flashed his torch at the "Homedale" on the gate. In front of his own, the inspector's car stood as if abandoned, and no sound came from the long garden before them. The dim blackness that seemed to be the house showed no spark of light.

They moved down the flagged path and a Georgian porch could now be discerned. The sergeant was there. He recognized Tempest.

"A queer thing, sir, but we can't make anyone hear. This door's locked."

"Where's Inspector Carry?"

"Gone round the back, sir."

The inspector was on them as he spoke, and his torch flashed the small group into view.

"The back door's open, sir."

"Then go in that way and open the front one while we stay here," said Wharton quietly. "Sergeant, you go with him and stay at the back door in case anyone comes out."

The two moved off into the darkness and Wharton began his apologies.

"That's all right. You take over," said Tempest. He cocked an ear. "That sounds like the other car. You stay here and I'll see."

There was a sudden gleam from the fanlight above the front door, the slipping of a catch and the door was open. Wharton stepped inside to a lounge-hall.

"Seen anybody?"

Carry shot him a look. Who he was he had no notion, but he had been with the Chief and had given orders.

"Not a soul, sir. Funny, you know, after that servant ringing us up!"

"Looks as if someone's playing a trick on us," said the sergeant.

Wharton's eyes had caught something on the plain redness of the carpet and he got to it on his knees. His finger dabbed at the tiny, dark smear, then he sniffed at it like a dog. In a second he was up again.

"One of you try that door there." His eye ran to the landing above the stairs. "You have a look up there, inspector. Turn all lights on as you go."

He made for the third door that led from the hall, and just short of it he halted. It was the way the light fell that showed the parallel grooves in the carpet, and it was the sight of the grooves that made Wharton open the door with a quick movement and then step aside. But no sound came from within, and the hall light showed merely a carpeted floor and the legs of a mahogany table. Wharton's hand felt for the switch and he stepped inside.

The parallel grooves were now continued, and they ended at the heels of the boots of Frederick Lewton. He lay there on his back, eyes fixed unseeing. Wharton's finger touched his face and it was still warm. Then gently, an inch at a time, he turned the body sideways. He got to his knees and squinted, edging the coat upwards. Everything seemed plain enough. Stabbing was the cause of death. There was the slit through the coat, the slit through the waistcoat and the discoloration that showed a faint seeping of blood. But of the knife that had done it there was never a sign.

Wharton lowered the body and stepped across it, raising it now the other way. His hand searched beneath the coat and along the line of the body, and again he let the body down. His eyes met those of the inspector, who stood by the door.

"It wasn't a false alarm, then?"

"No," said Wharton curtly and got to his feet. "Anything found upstairs?"

"Not a thing. Everything's undisturbed." He called back to the hall: "Anything in there?"

A voice came from somewhere in the other room and the sergeant appeared.

"I'd like you to have a look in here, sir. There's a safe been opened—"

"No sign of a dead man—or a knife?" cut in Wharton.

The inspector's eyes opened wide. "You don't mean *another* dead man?"

"Not necessarily," said Wharton dryly. "Only there's no sign of the servant who rang the police up, and a murderer might kill two as well as one, especially if he was of a saving turn of mind." He broke off as Tempest came in through the front door. "There's a body in there, but I wouldn't go in for a bit. What I'm worried about is that servant of his who rang up. What was his name?"

"Trench. Robert Trench," said the inspector. "And I was given to understand that he promised to stop here till we came."

Wharton nodded back at the phone which stood on a table by the fireplace. "Get hold of the one who took the message and find out all you can about this man Trench. It's queer he shouldn't be here, you know, Tempest. His master was dead and there wasn't any point in going for a doctor."

"Besides, he said he'd be here."

"Exactly," said Wharton with a shrug of the shoulders.

Then he turned and Tempest turned too, at the sound of steps outside. Two men entered, and Carry, at the phone, made a motion for less noise.

Tempest whispered an introduction. "This is Dr. Shinniford, our surgeon. They phoned you from the station, did they?"

"That's right," said Shinniford. He caught the look of polite inquiry. "This is Dr. Hule, who attends here sometimes. He was rung up to come at once."

"Rung up?" Wharton stared. "Who rang you up, doctor?"

"Mr. Lewton—so my wife said."

Wharton grabbed his arm and drew him to the living-room door. "Is that your Mr. Lewton?"

Hule looked, stared, then backed a bit. "That's him all right."

"And you mean to say he himself rang you up?"

"That's right," said Hule. "There's no possibility of mistake, and I can prove it. That man in there rang me up—or rang my wife up; it's the same thing."

"You don't know the precise time?"

"I do," said Hule. "It was ten-past seven to the dot."

"Ten-past seven!" Tempest looked incredulous. "Why, at thirteen minutes past the message came from his servant to say he was dead!"

Hule shrugged his shoulders. "Well, I'll stand by what I've said. That man in there is Fred Lewton, and Fred Lewton rang me up at ten-past seven."

He was about to add some corroboration, but voices from outside turned all eyes once more to the open door. A detective was entering with yet another man. Carry had finished phoning and came over.

"This man says he's the servant here," the detective announced to the room in general.

"I see," said Wharton dryly. "You're Robert Trench, are you?"

The man seemed surprised. "Yes, sir. My name's Trench, sir."

"Right," said Wharton. "We'd like a word with you in a moment." He looked at Tempest. "I don t think we need keep the doctor waiting. Also, you might have the print men in there, too."

He waited till the small commotion had ceased, then turned to the waiting servant. He was an oldish man with pallid face, thin, bluish lips and narrow, prominent chin. He wore a blue overcoat with a faded velvet collar, and the bowler in his hand looked none too new. There was an air of lodging-house waiter about him, and there should have been crumbs at his lip corners and stains on his waistcoat.

"So you're Robert Trench, are you?" said Wharton amiably. "And where have you been all this time?"

The man again looked startled. "All what time, sir?"

Wharton raised his eyebrows humorously and turned to Carry. "He wants to know 'all what time,' inspector?"

"Where've you been since you rung us up?" Carry asked him curtly.

"Rung *who* up?"

"Oh, my God!" wailed Carry blasphemously. Then with a large assumption of patience: "*Rang the police up.* Rang them up at seven-thirteen tonight—not twenty minutes ago—to say you'd found him dead—him in there."

A look of fright and of astounding incredulity came over the man's face. His mouth gaped, his lips pursed to speak, and when he got the words out, he was stuttering—and that was incongruous and strangely laughable, for his voice was a kind of asthmatic gurgle; a compressed utterance forced through heaven knew what wheezy, choked-up pipes.

"But it's impossible . . . I mean to say, sir . . . Well, I wasn't here, sir!"

"What do you mean—you weren't here?"

"Well, I *wasn't* here. I didn't get in till the seven-ten train, and I've only just got here. I came straight up from the station!"

Carry smiled ironically. "Here, let's get this right. Where've you been, then, if you got in by train?"

Trench raised his hand as a sort of deprecation. "It's a Wednesday, sir, and on Wednesdays I always go to London to see my wife who's in hospital there. That's where I went to-day, sir, and I got in by the seven-ten. I believe we were a minute or two late, sir; at any rate I walked straight up here." He spread his arms cringingly. "I just this moment got here—as you know."

Carry grunted. His eyes met Wharton's, then shifted as a sudden thought came.

"Just come here a minute," he said to Trench. "Wait there till I'm ready."

He took off the receiver and got the police-station.

"Oh, it's you, Jack, is it? I say, we've got that man Trench here, the one who rang up. Just listen a minute, will you, and then tell me what you think?" He beckoned to Trench. "Now then, you get this into your mind. There's supposed to have been murder committed here, and you're ringing the police. You got that? Right. All you say is, 'Is that the police?' and when they answer, you tell 'em."

Trench's hand was shaking so that the receiver wobbled queerly against his cheek.

"Is that the police? . . . Oh, it is. . . . Well, there's a murder been committed—I mean I've been told to say that there's been a murder. . . . Who am I? I'm Robert Trench. . . . Oh, I see." He let the receiver fall. "He says he doesn't want to hear any more."

"Oh, doesn't he," said Carry, and snapped the receiver to his ear. "Carry speaking."

Half a minute of nods and grunts and he was hanging up again. He turned to Wharton.

"Well, the one who took that message at seven-thirteen is prepared to swear it was the same voice he's just heard."

Wharton's eyes narrowed. He had his own ideas about Trench, and an explanation to Carry was overdue.

"Tell me, Trench," he said, and his voice was gentle as his kindly, understanding face. "I'm Superintendent Wharton of Scotland Yard, who happens to be here by chance. Your master's been murdered—and murder's a pretty desperate thing. You really assure us that what you've said is true?—that you didn't ring from here and you only got in to Seaborough at seven-ten?"

Trench drew himself up with a curious dignity. "God's my witness, sir."

Carry gave a little cough that hinted at enormous things— that the witness in question was, for instance, not likely to be called.

"I dare say, sir, the ticket-collector could give information about that."

Wharton nodded. "I expect he could. Still, you go to the kitchen and get yourself some sort of a meal, Trench—and a drink. You look pretty cold."

He watched benevolently while the old fellow moved off. No sooner had the door closed on him than his face changed dramatically. "Get hold of Exchange and find out what calls were made from here to-night. Get a list of them if you can, and exact times."

He left Carry at it and went across to the living-room door. The look of specious benevolence came to his face again as he peered in.

"I needn't warn you all not to disturb a single thing beyond the absolute necessaries. Everything all right, doctor?"

"Stabbed clean through the back," said Shinniford. "Just got the heart and no more. He might have lived a few seconds—and he might not."

"And when was it done?"

Shinniford looked at his watch, frowned, and worked it out. "At about ten-past. A minute or two either way for luck."

"That's what I made it," said Wharton. "Anything important in his pockets?"

"Nothing worth a damn," said Tempest.

Wharton cut short his recital of trivial contents. "Might I have a word with Dr. Hule?"

They went apart to the far corner of the bow window that overlooked the front.

"About that message you got," said Wharton. "I wonder if you'd be good enough to tell me all about it. The time, and why your wife knew the voice and so on."

"Well, it's all very puzzling," said Hule. "I was out on a case and my wife took the message. I ought to say that a clock hangs just above the phone, and that's why she knew the time was ten-past seven. She thought Lewton was drunk—or something."

Wharton's eyebrows rose in a non-committal interest. His look stayed for a moment on the decanter, the siphon and the two glasses on the table by the still glowing fire.

"What was the message exactly?"

"Well, it was Lewton speaking—there wasn't any doubt about that. He was a bit of a hypochondriac and he was often ringing up. Also, he got to know my wife through her voice, just as she knew his. Ever listen to that chap Putts on the wireless? Well, that was Lewton's voice to the life—squeaky and high-pitched. Only what he said to-night was rather a muddle as far as I could make out. He said he was alone in the house and feeling pretty queer, and he'd just had a shock. He said he was afraid and would I come on at once. My wife tried to question him tactfully to see what he meant—what he was afraid of, whether it was his heart, and so on—and then she heard some kind of a grunt and the receiver was hung up."

"It wasn't the sound of a struggle?"

Hule pursed his lips. "My wife didn't know what to think. She had a kind of idea he was drunk—he used to tip the bottle a bit, you know. Then she didn't know what to make of it. Sort of wondered if she should call up the police. Then I happened to come in, and as soon as I knew I popped up here."

"Thank you, doctor," said Wharton abstractedly. "I'm much obliged to you. Just hang on a few moments, will you? We won't keep you long."

He went out to the hall, where Carry was bursting to tell the news.

"Just had a bit of luck, sir. I'll tell you how later, but we've found out from Exchange operator that that call to the police *was* from here, sir. So was the one to the doctor. At five-past seven there was another one—to a Mr. Beece; number's one three."

Wharton lifted the receiver and asked for one three. Inside a minute a woman's voice was heard.

"May I speak to Mr. Beece?" said Wharton, and, "In bed with a cold, is he? Sorry to hear that. . . . Oh, I'm a friend of Mr. Lewton. He's just died very suddenly. . . . Yes, very suddenly. A great shock to us all. . . . Well, the real point's this: we wanted to know who saw him alive last. . . . No, I'm not referring to Mr. Beece. You just told me he'd been in bed all the evening with a chill. All we want to know now is what Mr. Lewton said to Mr. Beece when he called him up this evening. . . . That's right. We know he rang up Mr. Beece, and we'd like to know if anything he said can throw any light on his death. . . . Well, if you want it perfectly bluntly, he was murdered!". . . There Wharton squinted round at Carry with a prodigious raising of eyebrows. "Oh, yes, I'll hold on."

And exactly one second after that remark, Wharton gave a start. His eyes stared as if he strained to listen—but no sound came. For a good two minutes he stood there straining and rigid, then the tension relaxed as the voice came again.

"Just a trivial matter? . . . I see—fixing up a kind of appointment. . . . Yes, thank you. I understand, quite . . . Good-bye."

Wharton replaced the receiver and blew out a breath.

"Well, that's that. At five-past seven Lewton himself—Mrs. Beece is dead plumb sure—rang up in a normal voice mentioning some tolerably unimportant meeting. You get that, inspector? Normal voice and unimportant topic. Yet by ten-past, Lewton's scared stiff of something, and while he phones Mrs. Rule, he's murdered. Three minutes later, Trench finds him and calls the police—and calls them from this room. *And Trench at that time was over a mile away at Seaborough station.*"

"So *he* says, sir."

Wharton shrugged his shoulders. "Well, I'll bet you the sum of one ha'penny he's telling the truth." He shook his head perplexedly. "You got any ideas—other than that Trench may be a liar?"

"I don't know that I have, sir," said Carry, "except that there seems to have been a lot of telephoning. I might say, the hell of a lot of telephoning."

Wharton gave a wry smile. "Say it by all means. It's just what I've been thinking myself."

CHAPTER II
THE FIRST ALIBI

WHARTON CAST his eye round the living-room and let his mind record its own impressions of the spot where the dead man had spent a good many of his hours. The furniture was mahogany and massive, on the walls were cumbrous, mediocre prints, and the general atmosphere was one of frowstiness. A bureau-bookcase stood on the left. Facing it was the pretentious marble fireplace. Due south was the window with its stand and palm in pot, and opposite that was a huge sideboard which the finger-print men were at that moment examining. To the right of the fireplace was a cheap card table, on which stood decanter—about an eighth full—two empty glasses and an almost empty siphon.

"Is that whisky?" Wharton asked.

"Yes, that's whisky, sir," the sergeant told him. "Both glasses have been used."

"What about the house, Tempest? Got the back under observation?"

"Back and front—both," said Tempest.

Wharton nodded. Another thought struck him. "Would I be right in saying the back opens on what you called the old road?"

"That's right," said Tempest, and spread two fingers apart. "It's like this. This is the new road which we came on after we left the fork. It runs right along the coast—or it will do when it's finished. The other one's the old road that goes out to the country. Where my fingers meet is the fork, and this house where we are has the new road at the front and the old road at the back."

Wharton nodded and relapsed into another abstraction. Now his thoughts moved carelessly about the dead man himself. About sixty-five he looked—or maybe a hardy seventy. His face was fleshy and purple-hued with good living. His grey beard was foppishly trimmed, and some tenuous, straggly hairs had been drawn across the bald skull as a camouflage.

"Tipped the bottle, did he?" said Wharton, as if to himself.

"He did that," said Hule. "Take him all round I'd call him a bit of an old rip. He actually tried to get skittish with my missis on the telephone. That's how she knew his voice so well."

"And his pockets had been gone through?"

"Well, there's nothing in 'em except this rubbish," said Tempest. "And look at this chain. That swivel's had either a watch on it or a bunch of keys."

The sergeant gave Wharton a look that was a deferential reminder, and an admonition. "There's that safe in the other room, sir, what's been gone through."

"A wall safe is it?" asked Wharton with a twinkle.

"That's right, sir."

"Capital," said Wharton. "Then it won't run away. Now if you've finished with him and got his prints and everything, you might get him to the mortuary."

The ambulance was waiting, and the body of Frederick Lewton was carried out. Hule picked up his bag and prepared to go. He was a youngish man of easy-going, confident manner. Brainy enough, thought Wharton, but little breeding. One of the lads, maybe, of the Seaborough village.

"You say you attended here, doctor?" Wharton asked him.

"Yes, quite a fair amount. Lewton himself, and Trench and his wife."

"Anything the matter with Lewton's heart, was there?"

Hule laughed. "Not a thing. His heart was sound as a bell."

Wharton nodded. "And what's the matter with Trench's throat?"

Hule gave a little shrug of dismissal. "After effects of gas. I don't think it'll ever get any worse."

Wharton was surprised. "In the war, was he? I didn't think he was young enough."

"Maybe he wasn't—officially." Hule spoke with no intention to reprove, but Wharton was suddenly annoyed with himself for jumping so complacently to conclusions.

"His wife's in a hospital in town," went on Hule. "Trench goes up every Wednesday to see her. I believe old Lewton was quite fond of Trench—in his way."

"The Trenches were what they call a 'married couple'?"

"That's right," said Hule. "Wife—cook and so on; husband—general man. Hundred a year all found sort of thing."

Wharton caught his eye. "Trench absolutely reliable?"

Hule shrugged his shoulders again. "It's a matter of opinion. I may be prejudiced, but I can't say I'd trust him very far. Not that I can give you any reasons."

Wharton nodded. "I see. Just general impressions. And now about Lewton. What do you know about him precisely?"

Hule smiled. "Precisely—nothing."

Wharton returned the smile roguishly. "That's not bad. Still, joking apart, what do you know? Anything whatever will do."

"Well"—Hule frowned in thought—"I gathered he'd a private income of sorts. I know he never did any work, or went to an office or anything like that. I don't know if he was ever married, but I've always looked on him as a bachelor. I believe he took this place on just after the war when his father died; at least, that's what I've understood. Also he had about the best collection of smutty yarns it's been my pleasure to listen to."

Wharton gave a man-of-the-world nod. "Any relatives, do you know?"

"I've never heard him speak of any."

"I see." Wharton rubbed his chin, then all at once shoved out a hand. "Well, we're very grateful to you, doctor. Later on perhaps we may need you again."

Tempest added more thanks and showed Hule out. He came back in time to follow Wharton and his retinue into that other room, which was a museum representation of an Edwardian drawing-room. The General stood for a moment letting the atmosphere sink in, then looked back at the sergeant.

"And where's this famous safe?"

The sergeant showed it at once. A table stood by the left-hand wall, and on it was a tall case of stuffed, gaudy birds. But that case was a blind. It swivelled out on hinges, and behind it was the safe—let into the wall.

"Oh-ho!" said Wharton jocularly. "Now this is really interesting. Hidden safe, eh?" He turned to the showman. "How'd you find it?"

"Well, sir, it was not properly closed," the sergeant confessed modestly—and drew the case out a little in illustration.

"Your prints been taken?" Wharton asked, genially heavy. "If not you'd better see to it—and send those finger-print people in here."

He had a look inside the empty safe, holding back the door with a careful finger-tip.

"Cleaned it out properly, didn't he? And didn't bother to take the keys."

"Why *he*?" asked Tempest quietly.

Wharton gave him a droll look. Here was a situation after his own heart. "Well, I called him a he because I've a pretty shrewd idea I know the man who did it."

Tempest stared. Carry's eyes bulged.

"What! Trench, sir?"

"Oh, Lord, no!" said Wharton. "What's more, I'm answering no questions. All the same, when the time comes you might remember what I've told you."

He turned his back on the safe with the same amiable twinkle, and left the room to the sergeant and the finger-print men. Back in the hall again he dropped into an easy chair with a portentous shake of the head. Then he drew another chair in handy.

"Inspector, bring in Trench again, will you? John, you sit somewhere handy, and if you think I'm leaving anything out, don't be nervous about chipping in."

It was typical of the manner and appearance of Trench that nobody could treat him with unforced courtesy. As he sat in the chair, well in the light and with Wharton's eyes searching him, there was in his grey, deep-set eyes a definite furtiveness that went beyond mere shock or natural nervousness. Besides, he had had a meal and now there was some colour in his cheeks, that showed the man more of his normal self.

"And how did you find your wife?" began Wharton.

A slow, unexpected smile came to Trench's face. As he croaked the words out Wharton thought of a frog. "A little bit better, sir, thank you."

"Capital!" said Wharton. "But you must have been feeling in good form yourself to-night to have walked all the way from the station when a corporation bus passes the door?"

"Well, there wasn't one, sir, and it was a fine night so I thought I'd walk. Then when one did pass me I thought it wasn't worth while."

Wharton nodded understandingly. "The ticket-collector could identify you all right?"

"I think so, sir. I'm sure he could, sir."

"Good," said Wharton, and turned to Carry. "Get hold of the railway people and arrange for the collector to come here at once. Let him take a taxi if necessary." His own voice now lowered to almost a whisper while Carry's voice made a background. "You didn't meet anybody you knew?"

Trench shook his head, then his face brightened. "Only the watchman, sir. I spoke to him and said it looked like snow, and he said it didn't."

"What watchman's that?"

Tempest intervened. Trench no doubt referred to the night-watchman at the fork; the one who was minding the lamps where the road was up.

"Right," said Wharton. "We'll attend to him later. And now about yourself. How long have you been here?"

"In this job, sir? Over twelve years now."

"How'd you and your wife get the job? Answer an advertisement?"

"Well, no, sir. We got it through an agency."

"I see. And who was here before you?"

"Nobody, sir. We got here just after the—Mr. Lewton did. His father had just died, sir, so I understood, and the house was empty when he got here—except for furniture and things—so he engaged me and my wife."

"Where'd he come from?"

"That I don't know, sir. I have heard him speak about Canada a good deal. And I do know he was somewhere abroad so that he didn't get here till his father was dead and buried."

"Quite," said Wharton, and nodded as if the information were of tremendous moment. "And what relatives has he got?"

Trench looked surprised. "Relatives, sir? Not one that I know of."

"No relations at all!"

"No, sir." Trench shook his head emphatically. "I've heard him say so himself."

"And what about his wife's relations?"

Trench smiled tolerantly. "He never was married, sir—not that I ever heard."

Wharton's smile accepted the defeat. "Well, we'll try another tack. Who were his friends? Who came round here regularly and spent an hour or two and had a drink?"

Trench rubbed his lean jaws. "I don't know that he had any friends, sir. The only one who came round fairly regular was a Mr. Beece, and he used to come and have a game of cribbage."

"Mr. Beece a teetotaller?"

Trench smiled. "Not him, sir!"

"And no other friends?"

"Well, there was a Mr. Rennyet who called once or twice recently. He's a gentleman—a writing gentleman—from Bicklesham."

Wharton wrote that down. "And no other callers whatever?"

"Not that I know of, sir."

Wharton grunted. "Then what did your late master do with his time?"

"That I can't say exactly, sir. I know he used to go and watch the bowls a lot in the summer, and go to the pictures. He used to go out of evenings—the pictures, I expect, sir, and to have a drink somewhere. Sometimes he used to play patience, or read the paper."

Wharton grunted again. Then he leaned forward. "Doesn't it strike you as very funny that only one man ever came in to stay any time, and yet to-night that very man—Mr. Beece—has definitely not been out at all, but has been in bed with a chill? Yet there're two glasses that have been drunk out of in that room there."

Trench looked duly puzzled. "I don't understand it, sir—unless that Mr. Rennyet called."

Wharton turned to Carry. "Everything all right?"

"He's coming up now, sir," Carry told him.

"Good. Then look up Mr. Rennyet's phone number." He turned to Trench again. "And nobody else has called except tradesmen?"

A slow, queer smile spread over Trench's face. "Not unless my nephew happened to call, sir."

"Your nephew? Who's he?"

Trench's modesty revealed nothing so much as his pride. "He's an actor, sir. Howard Trench." He gave a little sideways look that expected some response. "He's here this week, sir—playing at the theatre."

"Really?" Wharton was interested and gratified. "What sort of parts does he take?"

"Take, sir?" He fumbled in his pocket. "Here you are, sir. Here's the full programme for the week."

Wharton took it. Tempest came over and had a look.

Carry's voice came in. "There's no one called Rennyet on the phone, sir."

"Never mind," said Tempest. "Bicklesham's only six miles away. We can always slip over there."

Carry went out to meet the collector's taxi and Wharton resumed his inspection of the programme. Through his mind, and Tempest's, flashed the scene when they had stood that afternoon with their wives before the theatre front, and the women had prattled about the handsome profile of one of the leading actors, whose photograph was lavishly displayed.

"So Howard Trench is your nephew, is he?" said Wharton with a delightful smile. "And *Julius Cæsar* to-night, eh? My wife's in the Royalty at this very moment. And he's playing Caesar himself. You see the point, John?"

"I can't say I do," admitted Tempest.

"Well, if he's Caesar, then he's dead before the show's half over. If we should happen to want a word with him, he ought to be available." Another smile at Trench. "And what made you think your nephew might have been here to-night?"

Trench shuffled a bit. "Well, I don't think he has, sir I mean I'm not sure. He came to see me last night, sir, and he said he'd come again to-night to hear how his aunt was. He might have mistook the time and thought I'd be back earlier than I was."

"Well, we'll soon make sure of that," said Wharton. He looked round to see the sergeant holding out a sheet of paper.

"We just found this in there, sir. Found it under one of the chairs. Looks as if it was dropped out of the safe."

Wharton took it gingerly by the corner. Various finger-prints stood clearly on it where the powder had been puffed, and on the underside was such a perfect set that Wharton saw the sheet as the bottom one of a pile of papers, held in both hands as it was lifted from the safe. With definite deliberation he got out his case and adjusted his antiquated glasses. Tempest peered over his shoulder.

ASSISI,
Feb. 27th.

DEAR UNCLE,—Everything is very nice here and I have seen Albert. H.M.G. has told me to have two days home but Albert knows. C.R. has been in twice but I had to go to the pictures but A. was there. He will write next time if you want him.

Love from your loving niece,
ETHEL.

Wharton read the letter twice, then peered amiably across at Trench. There followed a playful beckoning and a finger on a word beneath the man's nose.

"No relations, eh? What about that?"

Trench saw two words only, but they were enough to bring a look of natural surprise.

"He's got no niece that I know of, sir."

"Very well," said Wharton graciously. "We'll take it the letter refers to another uncle. And what's all this?"

The sheet of paper had been torn from a block of moderate quality, and the writing occupied little more than a third. But in the bottom right-hand corner, written diagonally in quite another hand, were the following words:

> Little fish may be sweet but what about this for a
> middle cut of salmon!

"Quite a nice little joke," said Wharton, and beamed at it with a good deal of nodding. "What it all means, I don't know—still, it strikes me as funny. And what's this other scribbling?"

R.C. 105
B.C. 33

The figures were pencilled in the bottom left-hand corner, and they might have been in either of the other hands. Wharton made a face at them and handed the sheet back.

"Found out anything about the prints?"

"Yes, sir." The sergeant grinned. "That set on the other side is the same as the ones on the safe door."

Wharton's face fell. "What about those on the other glass?"

"They're different altogether, sir," the sergeant said.

Wharton nodded. "Right. Put the letter with any other exhibits and carry on. Have a good hunt for the knife." He turned to Trench again. "Well, I don't think there's any more you can tell us for the moment. Was Mr. Beece here recently?"

"Mr. Beece, sir?" Again he rubbed his chin, and Wharton could have sworn he took the question at more than its surface value. "Yes, sir. Monday evening he was here."

"And Mr. Rennyet?"

"He came yesterday evening, sir." There was no hesitation about that. "His man was with him, sir, because he brought his car." A little cough. "The man came in with me, sir, while his master was with Mr. Lewton."

There was a sound of steps outside. Tempest opened the door and Carry came in with a man who was obviously the ticket-collector. Trench rose somewhat nervously. Wharton held out his hand with considerable effusion.

"Good evening, Mr.—?"

"Abel, sir. Henry Abel."

Wharton nodded graciously. "Well, Mr. Abel, we know you're a man of discretion, and you'll keep this to yourself till the news gets out, but circumstances make it necessary for you to say if you saw Mr. Trench here come off the seven-ten from London to-night. This is Mr. Trench."

Abel had a look at him. "I think I remember the gentleman, sir."

"He was wearing a dark overcoat and bowler at the time," said Wharton. "Perhaps that may help you."

Trench moved a step forward. "Don't you remember, I dropped my ticket. You remember; just when—"

A light had dawned on Abel's face as soon as Trench had wheezed a couple of words. "Of course I remember. You was coming through the barrier and you sort of slipped."

The two beamed at each other. Wharton beamed too.

"Well, that's all, Mr. Abel, thank you. We're sorry to have troubled you." Then his ancient joke. "Next time you're in jail, send for me and I'll see what I can do to make you comfortable."

Abel was shown out, and Trench was dismissed once more to the kitchen. Wharton kept his own counsel till Carry got back again, and it was the inspector who showed which way he thought the wind ought to be blowing.

"Pretty fishy, wasn't it, sir? I mean that business of dropping the ticket? Don't it seem as if he deliberately called attention to himself?"

"Suppose he did," said Wharton. "What are you assuming? That he might have got down there somehow to the platform and pretended he'd come off the train?"

"Why not, sir?"

"It certainly looks a bit glaring to me," said Tempest.

"So it does to me," said Wharton. "All the same, the fact remains that he *was* seen at seven-ten or just after, and at that very time he was presumably phoning the police from here to say a murder had been done!"

"Yes," said Carry dubiously. But he nodded viciously for all that, like a man who has his own opinion. "And one other thing," he went on. "Suppose he really has an alibi. Make it a hundred-percent alibi—the tighter the better. Then if he didn't phone, someone else did who knew his voice well enough to imitate it."

Wharton smiled dryly. "I confess I've had some idea of that sort myself."

Carry nodded. "Well, let's say someone did imitate his voice. Doesn't it strike you, sir, that it's a remarkable thing that he has a nephew who's an actor—*the very man who could imitate his voice*?" Wharton smiled still more dryly. "Not only does it strike me, but I was just about to suggest that you ring up the Royalty and ask Mr. Trench to come here at once. Caesar's dead by now and they'll have a dummy for Mark Antony to slobber over." He nodded to Tempest. "Pardon me a moment while I jot a few things down."

Wharton wrote on and Carry's voice was apparently unheard. Then a note of surprise came in and the General looked up. Carry hung up the receiver.

"He *was* here, sir; what do you think of that? He says he left just after seven—and he can prove it."

"Excellent!" said Wharton. "Proof's a capital thing in our line of business. When's he coming here?"

"Now, sir. He's taking a taxi straightaway."

"Splendid!" said Wharton. "We'll ask him to do a few imitations."

He settled again to his scribbling, and then all at once there was a minor commotion from the drawing-room and the door burst open.

"We've got the knife, sir!"

"The devil you have," said Wharton, and got to his feet.

"It's in here, sir," said the sergeant. "They're just going over it for prints."

The three went in at once to watch.

"Where do you think it was, sir?" the sergeant asked. "Up the chimney, there. Resting behind the register. And the real funny thing is, we think whoever put it there saw he didn't leave any prints on it—only he was too clever. He left quite a decent set while he steadied his hand under the mantel-piece!"

Wharton gave him an appreciative nod. "That's good work. Now we ought to learn something."

He cast his eye over the knife while the two men fussed with the prints. It was a triangular-bladed affair with black handle; the kind of thing that is found in most good-class kitchens. The blade was a good five inches, and tremendously strong.

"It's rather a tricky job, sir," one of the men said, "what with the soot and the stain."

"Take your time," said Wharton phlegmatically.

"I'm sure enough now, sir," he was told. "There isn't a print on it."

"And what about those on the mantelpiece?"

In a couple of minutes Wharton had verified results for himself. The hand that had hidden the knife was the one that had rifled the safe.

"Put the knife with the other things," said Wharton, "then go on hunting round." He moved back to the lounge.

The sight of that knife had given Tempest a queer sort of feeling, and out of the quick nervousness came the desire to pull Wharton's leg—or draw him out.

"I suppose you don't know who put the knife there, George?"

"I think perhaps I do," said Wharton.

"You mean the one who rifled the safe?"

"Maybe," said Wharton laconically.

"Well, if it wasn't Trench, who could it have been?" persisted Tempest.

And hard on the question, Carry suddenly stiffened. There was a sound from outside, and his words might have been an answer or an omen.

"Howard Trench for a fiver."

CHAPTER III
USES OF A NIGHT-WATCHMAN

"WE'LL SEE HIM in the dining-room," said Wharton, "and, inspector, you send someone down with that knife so that Shinniford can make sure it was the one that did it. And just one other thing. You don't happen to know how many houses face this one?"

"I can't say I do," said Carry. "They're high-class houses the other side of the road, and there wouldn't be more than three."

"Well, get a canvass going," Wharton told him. "Your sergeant might do it. Find out if anything unusual was seen, especially from upstair windows. Then you'd better come in and listen to—you know who."

The pseudonym was for the benefit of Howard Trench, whom Tempest at that moment was ushering into the dining-room. Wharton recognized him from his photographs. He was a man of close on forty; of easy bearing; just under six foot, dark haired and with aquiline features. There was nothing of the actor of caricature about him, though his jowl was blue and his gestures had a touch of the flamboyant.

It was the way he unsnobbishly spoke that gave him status. Tempest, who owned afterwards that he had anticipated someone well below the salt, knew himself in the presence of those indefinable qualities that give a sense of inferiority. There was the same dignified simplicity when he answered Wharton's questions about himself; how he had started from nothing and been helped by many a lucky chance. Now he was apparently the star turn of the Langhorn-Trewitt Shakespearean Company, and was booked for a world tour beginning in August.

"That's one reason why I was so glad to be in Seaborough where I could look my uncle up," he said. "You know what our life is—hardly a minute to spare. It's two years since I saw him, and if I hadn't seen him now it might have been two more."

Wharton got a wink across to Tempest, who went out in search of old Trench. Wharton made play for a bit.

"It was lucky for us that you died in the middle of the play," he said, "or we shouldn't have had you here so soon."

"You oughtn't to have had me now," Trench told him. "I'm supposed to be present in the ghost scene."

When Robert Trench was in, Wharton began his questioning. As he told the actor, the things that had happened with the dead man and himself were the most vitally important from the coroner's point of view as well as from that of the police.

"As far as we can judge," he said, "you were the last to see him alive. His voice was then heard over the telephone, and after that—nothing."

Howard Trench explained. Somehow he had got into his head that his uncle was due back at six-ten.

"I don't know how you came to make that mistake," his uncle told him. "I'm sure I said *seven*-ten."

"Never mind," said Wharton. "It's the luckiest thing in the world the mistake was made. Go on with your story, Mr. Trench."

Trench said he had knocked at the back door, and when it was opened had been surprised to see Mr. Lewton. But as soon as Lewton knew who he was he asked him in.

"I'm afraid Uncle Robert there had been telling him some rather flattering things about myself." Howard smiled across at his uncle. "At any rate we came into this room here and sat yarning for a pretty good while, and we had a drink. I had one long one and a very tiny one, and he had two or three—no more. For all I know those may be the very glasses we used."

"They are," said Wharton—and then gave a curious chuckle. "However, in case we take any more things for granted, perhaps you'll let us have your prints for the mere matter of comparison."

Carry, who had just sidled in, fetched a fingerprint man, and the comparison was made. Wharton took pains to explain the performance and instil a little romance. Then he handed over the sheet on which the official prints had been taken.

"It's a gruesome sort of souvenir, Mr. Trench, but you may like to keep it. And what sort of things did you talk about?"

The actor shrugged his shoulders. "Most things, I think. He got me talking about myself, and he talked a bit about Canada. I took it he'd spent some time there, and I'd happened to say I was going there myself."

"And what time did you leave?"

"Seven o'clock, and by the front door," smiled Trench. "Just after seven it'd probably be."

Wharton's face assumed a look of the most tremendous seriousness. "Now think most carefully, Mr. Trench. First I'm going to inform you that just after you went, Mr. Lewton rang up his doctor in a state of considerable agitation. He said he was ill and frightened. You got that? Now then, had you any reason to think he was either unwell or frightened when you left him?"

The actor's face had already given the answer. "Why, it's extraordinary! I mean, he was laughing and joking when I left him. And ill! Why, he was absolutely fit as a fiddle."

Wharton grunted. "I see. No complaints about his health?"

"Well, he did happen to say he wasn't any too fit, and when I looked surprised, he dug me in the ribs and laughed—you know, to show he'd been trying to pull my leg."

"You mean he was really trying to tell you he was very fit indeed, or—if you'll pardon the slang—that there was many a good kick in the old dog yet."

"The very thing. Also I remember he followed it up by saying he'd done a good stroke of business to-day. He didn't say what sort."

Wharton grunted. Then he switched round. "You know anything about that, Mr. Trench? What business he was referring to?"

"I haven't the faintest notion, sir," old Trench said frankly, and Wharton, who had caught his eye, could once more have sworn that the very finality of the answer was only a refuge from more questioning.

"Now the time when you left here." Wharton turned to the nephew again. "We hope you'll take it the right way, but what it really amounts to is helping to fix the time of the murder—and establishing your own alibi. A blunt way of putting it, Mr. Trench, but we're both sensible people."

"I understand perfectly," Trench told him. "You can bet your life I'm only too glad to prove an alibi—and I'm glad to say I can do it." A slight doubt seemed to cross his face. "What time was it when he telephoned?"

"Ten-past seven."

Trench smiled. "If you'll be so good as to come as far as where the road is up, the night-watchman will prove where I was."

Wharton got up at once. "No time like the present—also we mustn't keep you any longer tonight. Perhaps in the morning we can see you again if anything turns up. Later, of course, there'll be the inquest. I'll go down with you if you'll wait for just one moment."

He beckoned to Carry, and while the various good-nights were being said, went out to the lounge.

"Get a man in and take his prints again. There's a bit of paper on the table he was fiddling with." A quick look round. "And try and have that information ready for me—if there is any."

Howard Trench's taxi had not waited, and he and Wharton stood irresolutely for a moment on the pavement outside the house. Then Trench said it was a fine night, and Wharton said he would rather walk the few yards, and off they set. By Wharton's watch it took just two minutes to reach the watchman's shelter.

"He's a queer old fellow—the watchman," Trench said. "I had a chat with him last night. I think he'll rather amuse you."

"A bit of a character, is he?"

Trench smiled. "Yes—a philosopher. Oh, by the way, I ought to have told you that when I left there this evening we didn't know if the clock was dead right, and we'd been yarning long after I'd intended to stay. I ought to have been at the theatre at a quarter past."

The night-watchman—Juker by name-—sat in his shelter. He looked a mournful soul, with long face and bushy moustache. All the stage appurtenances were there—a bowler hat, red neckerchief and corduroy trousers fastened below the knee; and what with the cheerful fire in the perforated pail and the line of red lamps, the setting was incongruously festive. His voice was slightly Cockney and most deliberate.

"Been something going on up there, ain't there?" He pointed vaguely up the hill. "Seen some of the police about."

"A burglary," announced Wharton. "A house up there on the right."

"A burglary, eh?" He was proceeding to think that over when Wharton aroused him with an assumption of jocularity.

"I suppose you're of a sporting turn of mind?"

"Me, guv'nor?" He gave a mild look of inspection, then his eyes fell to the fire again. "Maybe I am—maybe I ain't."

Wharton's ardour was undamped. "I asked you that because my friend and I here have a little bet on, and we want you to settle it. He says he came past here to-night and spoke to you just after seven o'clock. I say it was just before seven o'clock."

"Then you say wrong, guv'nor," said Juker meditatively. "Five minutes past to the dot it was."

Wharton shot a look at him. "What makes you so sure?"

"What makes me sure?" He spoke with the deliberation of one who thinks much in lonely places. "I'll tell you. See this watch? The best in the country, that is. Never varies a minute a month. I got it from my brother what was killed in the war, and he had it off some toff." He held it out for inspection. "That watch knows me, guv'nor. It's what I call a companion. It's company, see? When everybody's in bed, him and me talk to each other—only it ain't talking, it's ticking—see?"

The watch was replaced in the trouser pocket.

"Five-past it was, to the dot. This gentleman asked me if I knew a short cut to the town as he was late, and I told him one—and I see him take it. And if you was to come to me in a month's time I could tell you that, the same as I'm telling you now." His voice took on a definite pride. "People know me, guv'nor. They try to catch me out—but they don't."

"I can quite believe it," Wharton told him. "By the way, do you remember speaking to-night to an elderly man in a dark overcoat with velvet collar, and bowler hat, who was going up the new road there? I believe he said it looked like snow and you said it didn't."

"I remember the gent what you refer to," said Juker, "and I remember the words what was used. Half a minute short of five and twenty to eight that was."

Wharton laughed. "You're a holy terror!" He slipped across a half-crown. "Perhaps as a favour you'll drink our very good health."

"Thank you, sir." Juker spoke with more briskness than he had hitherto shown, and he spat deftly on the coin before stowing it away.

Wharton and his companion were already on the opposite pavement.

"This was the short cut I took," Trench said. "I'd like you to come down with me if you will, because I have another alibi at the other end."

The going was downhill, and in ten minutes they came out by the centre of the town. Opposite the war memorial was the tobacconist's shop—now closed. But there was a side door and the man they wanted came out. He remembered the gentleman very well indeed. He even knew who he was, since from his door he had those enlarged photographs beneath his eye. The gentleman had entered at a quarter-past seven. He had asked if the clock above the counter was correct—and it was. His purchase had been twenty cigarettes, and he had gone straight from the shop to the theatre across the road.

"It just shows you how curiously the mind works," Trench said, when he and Wharton had themselves crossed the road. "There was that clock staring at me"—he nodded up at the clock tower that formed the memorial—"and I didn't see it. Yet I saw the clock in the shop as soon as I walked in."

"The mind works that way sometimes," said Wharton sententiously, his own mind on other things. "Where are you going now?"

"Inside, I think," said Trench. "I've got one or two things to collect."

"I'll come in too," said Wharton. "I want to see my wife when she comes out, and I may as well wait in the warm as anywhere else."

It was almost an hour later when Wharton made his way towards West Cliff again. This time he took the new road, and as he came abreast of Juker's box the watchman must have heard his steps, for his head peered round.

"What's the time now?" asked Wharton jocularly.

"Time, sir?" He lugged out the watch. "Three minutes to eleven, sir." He replaced it with the same slow heaving, then, "I've been looking for you, sir."

"Oh?" said Wharton, and came over. There was an upturned box in the lee of the wind and he took it.

"I reckon you're to do with the police." It was half statement, half question, and a cautious look went with it.

"I am," said Wharton bluntly.

"So I've been thinking," said Juker, and for a moment or two thought some more. "What time might this burglary have been?"

"About a quarter-past seven," Wharton told him.

"Quarter-past seven." He chewed on that for a bit. "Early for a burglary, ain't it, sir?"

Wharton smiled. "No time's too early if you can do the job and get away with it. You see, burglars don't work to union rules."

The merest flicker showed that Juker appreciated the heavy humour.

"Well, the one I had in mind must have been high up in the union, seeing as how he come by motor-car."

Wharton's face straightened and he was all ears. Juker's story was this: At precisely a quarter-past seven a man had come up in a saloon car—maroon in colour as far as Wharton could make out. Juker himself had blocked the narrow entry at that particular moment, and the man had drawn the car in behind the shelter, with the statement that he hadn't far to go in any case, and would Juker keep an eye on the car for a bit.

"It was twenty-two minutes past, and two cars come through," Juker was going on.

Wharton interrupted. "That's right. I was in one of them."

"Well, be that as it may, no sooner'd they gone than I cast my eye up and there was the man who'd left the car coming down the old road there as hard as he could tear. Soon as he got to the corner there, he sort of dropped to a walk and he come across, right behind where we're sitting now, and I could hear him breathing heavy. Well, I waited a minute, thinking he'd say something, and then—blow me if I didn't hear him turning the car round and driving off without a damn-your-eyes or a thank-you or nothing."

Wharton nodded. "When he left the car he went up the new road, and when he came back he came by the old."

"That's right," said Juker. "It'd be about twenty-three minutes past."

"What was he like?"

"Like? Well, a stiffish-built feller. One o' them little white beards." He stroked his chin by way of illustration. "Be about sixty I should say."

"You'd know him again?"

"Know him anywhere," said Juker contemptuously.

Wharton thought for a bit. "What time do you go off duty?"

"Seven in the morning—if I'm lucky."

"Well, keep what you've told me under your hat," said Wharton, putting back the box. "If I want to see you to-morrow, where can I find you?"

He took the address, hinted at a reward, said good night again and moved on up the short slope. The blinds were drawn at Homedale and the house might have been deserted. Tempest opened the door for him.

"Anything happen?"

"Nothing special," said Wharton. "But what's this news you're bursting to tell me?"

The news was not particularly startling, but it helped to fit in. Those houses that faced the new road and backed to the sea had been visited, and only the middle one—Highcliffe—could give any information. There, the lady of the house had gone out at twenty-past seven to post a letter. The time was fixed because the post left at half-past and she had glanced at the clock as she went out. The clock was right, moreover, by wireless time. As she came out of the front gate she noticed the light above the porch of Homedale, and she noticed it particularly because she thought for a moment it was the moon—shaped and rounded as it was by the boughs of overhanging trees. And just as she realized it was not the moon, out the light went.

"That'd be about twenty-one minutes past," said Wharton, and made a note in his book. "This is all fitting in like a jigsaw."

The other item of news originated from Carry's own restlessness and initiative, since he had had the idea of questioning the two houses that bordered the garden of Homedale. At the west one he learned that that morning a fine car had drawn up in the old road—really little more than a quiet lane—and a lady had got out and gone to the back door of Homedale. There was no chauffeur in the car, and she had stayed for a quarter of an hour. The term "lady" had been insisted on; her clothes and bearing had proved her status to the satisfaction of the informant.

"What we've been thinking is this," said Tempest. "It was curious she should come the back way, and that it should happen on the day when Trench wasn't there to answer the back door."

"Yes," said Wharton, and pursed his lips. "All the same, we've got to keep a sense of proportion. For all we know she might have been collecting for hospitals or something."

"We thought of that," Tempest told him, "only, you see, she went nowhere else but here. Therefore she wasn't going from door to door."

"And which way was the car heading?"

"For the fork," said Tempest. "I admit that shows she didn't deliberately choose the back road. She must have come in from Bicklesham way."

"Bicklesham," repeated Wharton and frowned. "That's where Rennyet lives. Still, we'll talk about that later. Let's go inside and see how we stand."

Trench found some cold meat and made a pot of tea, and over the scratch meal the three argued. And no sooner had Wharton finished the story of his inquiry into Howard Trench's alibi, than Carry had to ease his mind. Uncle and nephew might be out of it, and yet he was reluctant to part with that magnificent and spectacular theory.

"Well, sir, you've said we're to speak our minds without fear or favour, and I'll speak mine. You can say what you like, but all I know is that I'm plumb sure that actor had something to do with it. Why should he go speaking to that watchman if he wasn't impressing on his mind what the time was? *He wanted him to know it was five-past seven.*"

Wharton shrugged his shoulders. "That means he doubled back here again, and he hadn't even a second to do it in. And if he assumed his uncle's voice and phoned to the police, how on earth could he have been at the war memorial at a quarter-past?"

"That remains to be seen," said Carry obstinately. "But about that war memorial, sir. You can see that clock no end of a distance off. Only, *if you see the time by a public clock, you see it alone.* If you go to a tobacconist's, where you know there happens to be a clock, *then you have someone to support your word.*"

Wharton was impressed, as his face showed. "There's some good thinking behind what you say, Carry; all the same, I'd rather leave it for a night's chewing over. It's too involved for me at the moment. You want a chess board to work it all out. I suppose, by the way, you're taking the uncle as a sort of confederate?"

"Why not, sir? There's that little matter of the dropped ticket. And why should the nephew have made that mistake about the time old Trench's train got in?"

Wharton waved his hand. "Don't hurl any more at me. Let me think it out to-night for myself." His eye fell on the now open bureau. "If you get me a sheet or two of paper, I'll show you the way the times fit in."

He made out three sheets, and each item remained unchallenged.

7.03. Howard Trench leaves.

7.05. Lewton phones Beece.

Allow three minutes for the phoning and two minutes are left for the something to happen which frightened Lewton.

7.10. Lewton phones Hule.

7.12. Lewton is stabbed.

7.13. Police are called.

Allow eight minutes to rifle the safe and at

7.21. Light goes out, showing murderer-burglar has left the house.

"Now I call your particular attention to something else," said Wharton. "Take the man with the car whom Juker put up as the burglar—and I leave out *murderer* advisedly. Let's check his times."

7.15. Man in car arrives.

7.17. Man reaches house by new road.

7.21. Light goes out and man leaves house by backdoor, which was found unlocked.

7.23. Man reappears at Juker's shelter, and is out of breath.

"You see the implication?" asked Wharton. "If he's connected with the affair at all, he's not the murderer, for he didn't arrive till the murder was over. In other words, he may be the man who rifled the safe and hid the knife, but he certainly isn't the one who did the killing."

"That's sound enough logic," said Tempest. "It's up to us for a start to try to get hold of this man with the white, torpedo beard and maroon saloon car. Even if he wasn't the actual murderer, he must have known something about it."

"Damned if I know," said Wharton. "The more I think, the more I'm muddled. If he had anything to do with it, why did he leave the car by Juker's shelter, where he knew both it and himself would be identified?"

"What do you suggest we ought to do, sir?" asked Carry.

"Well, I'm not here officially—as yet," Wharton told him. "What your Chief Constable decides will be his decision entirely, and there's the matter of my own superiors. Not that I don't think we three can't handle this case if they let us. Still, it's up to us to get on with it. And if you want my advice, here it is. You'd better get another sheet of paper and write it all down."

Wharton's suggestions took up the sheet, and mysterious though some of them were, he refused for the moment any amplifications.

(*a*) Find out contents of dead man's will. Solicitors to be found from search of bureau.

(*b*) Beece's house to be kept under observation from midnight.

(*c*) Tempest to find out from telephone authorities the exact position of Beece's telephone and if extensions existed.

(*d*) Information of murder to be rushed to local and London press, and special request to be made for relatives of dead man to come forward.

Wharton got up with, "That's enough to get on with. First thing in the morning I'll be along to hear developments, and I may have another idea or two myself then. Also I'm proposing to go to Bicklesham to see this man Rennyet. Who's spending the night here? You, Carry?"

"Yes, sir; me and my sergeant."

"Good," said Wharton. "I'd keep an eye on that drawing-room if I were you. That dropped letter may be important and it may not."

Carry's eyes opened. "You think he may come back for it?"

Wharton shrugged his shoulders. "I'm merely suggesting precautions. And if you should want me, I've got a telephone by my bed." He bestowed an arch smile on Carry. "Running water and telephone in every room. The Seaborough Corporation pays—till to-morrow. And if I weren't a married man—and officially unemployed—I'd stay here and keep you company. You coming, John?"

"Not for a bit," the major told him. "But you take my car and run yourself down."

"Not a bit of it," said Wharton from the door. "Besides, I've half a mind to put in a few minutes with my philosophic friend Juker."

CHAPTER IV
RUSTIC REVELS

WHARTON WAS by no means the quitter he seemed. in the curious maze that the case already presented, he had discerned one clear track, and now, before that one track was obscured, he felt the need to survey and map Homedale, and the company of Carry and Tempest, were distracting things to a man who had need of clear thinking, and Wharton already had prejudices enough of his own without having to take into consideration the hunches and brain-waves of others.

Mrs. Wharton was used to his ways, and while she slept her husband sat at the dressing-table with the electric fire on. First he collated his notes, with clear divisions into facts and deductions. That done, he opened the window a little farther, got his pipe going, and drew up his chair to think a few things further out. His mind now visualized the house as it was at ten minutes past seven. He saw Lewton take up the phone to call the doctor—and at once Wharton found a problem urging solution.

Why, precisely, the doctor? If it had been his heart of which he was afraid, then—hypochondriac or not—he should have had a something or other which Shinniford would have discovered at the post-mortem, and of which Hule, as his regular doctor, should have been aware. But as Wharton interpreted the message which Mrs. Hule had taken, it was rather a case of physical or moral fear—the fear of mortal human danger.

Very well, then, said Wharton to himself, let it be assumed that Lewton was aware that an enemy was threatening. Perhaps he had seen his face through the window; perhaps he was even in the house. Lewton had shut himself in the lounge, therefore, and had called the doctor, and the only reason why he had called the doctor was that a doctor would come quickly—and *he himself had been afraid of the police.*

Wharton gave a little pleasurable wriggle when he thought of that, and his mind ran on to the actual telephoning. How the murderer had entered the lounge was yet to be ascertained, but he had waited till the telephone message was practically over, and then he had stabbed hard and true. It had been the thrust of a man of ice-cold nerve; the man who had then deliberately assumed the voice of old Trench and summoned the police, and— Wharton wriggled again in his seat—summoned them with a kind of cynical disdain, to come and clear up the mess he had made and the unsolvable problem he had set.

Then he had seized the dead man by the collar and dragged him into the dining-room, as the groove of the heels had plainly shown. That would have been at just after a quarter-past, and perhaps by then his confederate—the man in the car—had joined him. The man in the car had not expected anything so drastic as murder, and that was why he had been indifferent about Juker. But when he entered the house he had been incredibly shocked. Yet the safe had had to be ransacked for something that was in it, and then had come the desperate escape—the murderer going one way and the man back to his car. A second or two later the police had arrived.

But in the very middle of his gratification at having reconstructed so admirably the steps in the tragedy, Wharton was aware of a detail that presented the biggest problem of all. *Why had the knife been taken from the body?* Surely not because the murderer had found it an impediment when he dragged the body? And if it had been the murderer who removed it, why had his confederate hidden it up the chimney? The knife had no distinguishing marks. The ironmongers' shops of Seaborough had many a gross like it, and the scores of hotel kitchens had hundreds more. Why hide it at all? And why up the chimney?

Then about that last, Wharton had a sudden, tentative idea. It was a solution that was not too satisfactory—and yet it began to fit in with other things. It had been placed in the chimney because it might be recovered. A ridiculous idea—and yet Wharton liked it. The confederate, or the murderer himself, might have taken the knife away—but he didn't. For that there must be some reason, and Wharton stirred restlessly in his chair as his brain began to pry this way and that in search of it. And then the telephone bell rang.

Wharton was over at once. Mrs. Wharton stirred, moaned, and woke. Wharton raised his hand for silence and stuck the receiver to his ear. It was Carry speaking.

"What you said has happened, sir—or something like it. A man tried to make an entry but he was spotted from outside. How'd he get in? Oh, through a neighbouring garden, we think. We'll look for footprints as soon as it's light. He got as far as the drawing-room window. The sergeant was in there, and I was having a nap in the dining-room."

"Could you identify him?"

"Too dark for that, sir. Only, we heard him making off, and one of the men chased him out the back way. You know what it'd be like in the pitch dark. Which way? The back road, towards Bicklesham. The man says he got reasonably close to him and then he heard him roar off in a car he had hidden down the road. A little, squat racing sort of car it was."

"Not a maroon saloon?"

Carry gave a little laugh. "I asked that particular, sir. Nothing like it. The man says he'd almost swear it was lightish in colour, and he got within twenty yards of it when it suddenly roared off. Snarled off, he described it, like a racer."

"Beece's house been under observation?"

"Yes, sir—at least, the Chief gave the order."

"Right. Find out at once if anything was stirring there. I'll wait till you get me word. And first thing in the morning, find out if Beece has a car, and what sort and colour."

Wharton hung up, and his eye regarded his wife with an anticipation of the words he knew would come.

"Whatever is the time?"

"It's early yet," said Wharton. "You get off to sleep again and I'll put out the light."

He drew his chair to the fire again and sat thinking things over in the comparative dark. Some mystery, tortuous and underground, had been centred about the apparently quiet life of the murdered man. Old Trench knew something of that life and was determined his jaws should not be prised open. If he could be made to speak he might disclose why there had been a camouflaging of the safe behind the case of stuffed birds, why that safe had been ransacked, and why its contents had been of such importance that murder had been done in order to get hold of them.

Wharton's mind played about those tentative ideas and found little anchorage. At one moment the case had its simple aspects, and then from the very simplicity there would emerge something that contradicted and baffled. Why had the knife been hidden? Why had it been removed from the body? Why had somebody come back for that one letter? Or was it the knife that the new burglar had hoped to get? And who was that somebody in the sports car who had come in from Bicklesham way? Of what had Lewton been suddenly afraid? Why had old Trench's voice been impersonated? Or had it not been impersonation at all, and had old Trench discovered the secret of a perfect alibi and profited by it to commit a sure murder?

The telephone bell went again, Carry ringing up once more.

"There's been nothing stirring at you-know-where," he said. "The house has been under observation since before midnight and the garage is locked up. Our man flashed his light through the window and he knows it's a saloon—and he thinks it's some sort of red, but he isn't sure."

"First thing in the morning find out definitely."

"That'll be easy," Carry said. "We know where he gets his petrol and stuff. And about you-know-who himself, sir, we've found out a thing or two. He owns an employment agency in the town—the Seaborough and Southern Counties Employment Bureau, it's called. They've a fine big office near the pier. A very flourishing concern, so I understand."

Wharton, with the happy facility for sleep that resembled Napoleon's, turned in at three and woke at half-past seven. At half-past eight he and Tempest were at Homedale to hear the latest.

"It's a maroon car," Carry said. "He hasn't stirred yet himself, and the garage is still locked."

"All right," said Wharton. "You see I have that information about the telephone when I get back from Bicklesham. I suppose you haven't found any footprints after last night's affair?"

Carry shook his head ruefully. "It was too hard a frost, sir. We know where that sports car was parked down the lane because there happened to be a spot or two of oil, but we couldn't get a tyre mark."

Wharton saw a busy day ahead and was minded to get to Bicklesham as soon as the decencies permitted. The sergeant, who knew the countryside, was accompanying him in Tempest's car, and the General had her head set for Seaborough so that he might turn by the fork. The road was now swarming with navvies, and there was no sign of Juker as they made the quick, left-hand cut-back. The difference in the two roads was remarkable. The corporation's wide, palatial turnpike was left for what was only a country lane, with steep banks, overhanging trees and little more than twelve foot of metalling.

Wharton let the car dawdle for a bit while his eye took in the left side of the road that ran past the back garden of Homedale.

"Nice quiet, handy way to approach the house," he remarked to Polegate, the sergeant. "Quiet road, too, if you wanted to draw in. Handy to remove the swag."

Then all at once the lane fell steeply and swerved inland. The line of cliffs was left behind and the country was nothing but chestnut woods and damp pasture. Then they climbed the opposite slope by the edge of a hamlet and came out to a ridge road with a view out to the Channel. Then came another valley across which could be seen the red roofs of houses and a church spire.

"That's Bicklesham, sir," said Polegate.

"Short six miles, isn't it?" remarked Wharton.

"We're not there yet, sir," Polegate told him quietly.

They dropped to that last valley and began to climb again. Almost at the top of the long incline was a pleasant, timbered house, and then came yet another ridge road and, a quarter of a mile on, the first houses of the village. Wharton drew the car up.

"Hop out and ask our man's whereabouts," he said to Polegate. "We'd look a couple of fools if we'd come too far already."

Overshot the mark was precisely what they had done. Rennyet's house, now hidden by a bend or two, was the ancient one already passed, so the car was turned round and back they went again. As they came slowly along the low hedge that separated the kitchen garden from the road, Polegate suddenly gripped Wharton's arm.

"Hold hard a minute, sir. There's someone I know."

A man with his back to them was contemplating a rubbish fire, and Wharton thought it curious that the sight of a back should recall a face.

"That's Tom Meek," explained Polegate, as Wharton pulled up the car just beyond in the shelter of a holly tree. "I really took over from him, sir. He was taken a bit ill a couple of years back and had to retire. I knew him and his wife had got a job somewhere out this way, but I never had a thought it'd be here."

"An old detective-sergeant, eh?" said Wharton. "That's a bit of luck for us, isn't it?"

"It is that, sir," agreed Polegate. "He's a good sort is Tom. So's his wife. I know 'em as well as I know anybody."

Wharton, always ready for a stratagem, was thinking hard. "Tell you what, sergeant," he said. "We'll go on a bit and turn round again, and you pretend to see our friend in the garden. I'll tell you what to say."

There was a tiny side road a hundred yards on and there they reversed. The car dawdled once more till they came to the kitchen garden and then Polegate gave a holler.

"Do you happen to know if—" The words trailed away artistically into a profound and speechless astonishment.

Meek's face lighted up too as he stuck his fork into the ground.

"Hallo, Jim! What are you doing this way?"

Polegate grinned. "Just out for a ride. And what are you doing here? This is my friend, Mr. Ward, by the way."

The two shook hands and Wharton beamed amiably. "Nice little place you've got here, Mr. Meek?"

"It's not mine," said Meek. He was a tall, clean-shaven, good-humoured-looking fellow with a quiet, pleasing smile. "My wife and I are sort of housekeeper and gardener here."

"Good job?"

Meek gave a kind of wink. "Money for nothing. Damn good master, and we live like fighting-cocks."

"So that's why we never see you in Seaborough nowadays?"

Meek smiled rather curiously. "I don't know if you'll understand what I mean, Jim, but somehow Seaborough always gives me a kind of a queer turn after—well, after that illness of mine. It sort of brings it back. I like it out here—quiet, not much traffic, and plenty of good air. I sleep like a top now, and you know how I used to be once."

Polegate nodded sympathetically. "And what's your guv'nor do for a living?"

A suggestive smile flitted across the ex-detective's face. "He's an author. Writes detective stories. That's why I got the job, I reckon."

Polegate's laugh faded to something serious. "That's funny, Tom. It's something of that sort that brought us round this way this morning, though we never expected to run across you here. Do you know there was a murder in Seaborough last night—and someone we think your guv'nor knows?"

"A murder? Who was it?"

"A chap called Lewton. Lives up at West Cliff."

"Lewton?" Meek stared incredulously. "Why, I know Lewton—least, I've seen him. My guv'nor went there once or twice and I went with him. I used to pass my time with that man of his—Trench." He stared again as the thought came. "Don't say old Trench did him in?"

Polegate shook his head. Then Wharton thought the moment ripe for taking a hand.

"I'm connected with the police myself," he said modestly, "and the Chief Constable thought it wouldn't be a bad idea if we saw your master about giving us some news. You see, as far as we can make out, the dead man hadn't a friend in the world or a relation, and we hoped he'd let something fall about his past history so that we could get into touch with people who knew him."

Meek nodded. "Yes, but how was he murdered? I mean, it sort of staggers you when you hear somebody you knew is dead like that."

Wharton gave a prosaic account, from which all mystery had been skilfully skimmed. The one vital fact he allowed to emerge was that of the time.

"That's a funny thing," said Meek, and looked almost perturbed. "The guv'nor did happen to be in Seaborough last night." He thought for a moment, then shook his head. "He didn't see Lewton, or he'd have said something. Besides, he only went in to post a letter."

"A long way to post a letter, isn't it?" smiled Wharton suggestively.

"It isn't that," said Meek. "You see, our post leaves at five-thirty, and sometimes there's a letter the guv'nor wants to go, and so we take it into Seaborough. I know he did have an important one last night. Him and me were working out here all the afternoon on that pergola you see there, and he forgot about it."

"What time was it when he went in?" asked Wharton, with a shade too much carelessness.

Meek's smile showed he had spotted the innuendo. "You needn't think of him that way. He was back long before seven. Besides, he always has dinner at seven, and he had it last night as usual." Another thought came. "Why not come in a minute or two, Jim, and have a word with the missus? She'll be surprised to see you, you bet."

The three went round to the back door by a side gate, and as they approached, a woman came out rubbing her hands on her apron. She was a buxom, friendly looking soul, with dimples and plumpness that spoke of a contented mind. Her eyes opened wide at the sight of Polegate, but not so wide as Polegate's opened at the sight of her. He smiled, too, with an amusement in which was something of affection.

"Why, bless my soul! I shouldn't have known you. You do look well." He had another look. "Never saw such a change in anybody in my life. I'll bet you don't go pillion-riding now!"

She smiled, too, rather shyly in the presence of the stranger. "Yes, I keep telling Tom I shall have to do something about it. None of my old dresses fit me now."

For a minute there was nothing but inquiries and exchanging of news, then the party entered the comfortable, brick-floored kitchen.

"It's too late or too early to offer you anything, I suppose," said Meek, and to his wife—rather more loudly, because she was the least bit deaf, "Something serious happened in Seaborough last night."

He and Polegate between them explained all about it. Mrs. Meek was incredibly shocked. As she said, one often read about murders, but to know the murdered person made it all the more horrible.

"What time did the guv'nor get back from Seaborough last night?" her husband asked.

She frowned, then gave a little laugh. "I don't seem to be able to think clear this morning. It was Mr. Rennyet's birthday yesterday, and he made me and Tom have a glass of special port after dinner, and it always makes me muddled. What were you saying, dear?"

Meek smiled patiently. "I just asked if you knew what time it was when the guv nor got back from Seaborough."

"Well"—she thought—"it would be about five or ten to seven. He only went straight in and back again, you know."

"Dinner wasn't late, was it?"

She looked surprised. "Of course it wasn't. Seven o'clock it was—same as it always is."

And Mrs. Meek should have known, thought Wharton to himself, for one clock stood on the kitchen mantelpiece and a grandfather ticked by the far wall. Wharton cleared his throat.

"I wonder if you'd mind asking Mr. Rennyet if I might have a word with him? I won't keep him a minute. Tell him the name's Ward."

Meek went off to the study, and inside a minute he was showing Wharton in. The room was somehow like its owner—compact, tidy, and well-ordered. Rennyet looked about forty, and with the tiny side-whiskers as much like a Spanish lawyer as anything else. His smile had charm, but to Wharton's mind there was some subtle irony in his manner that hinted at complacency, or was the outcome of some cynical philosophy.

"Do sit down, won't you?" he said. "I don't know what you want, but I take it you want to see me."

"That's right," said Wharton, slightly irritated already. "You haven't seen the paper yet this morning?"

"I'm afraid not," smiled Rennyet. "We don't get them delivered till almost midday. That's the result of being the last house in the village."

Wharton smiled grimly. "Well, when you do see them, you'll see that a friend of yours was murdered last night. A Mr. Lewton of Homedale, Seaborough."

Rennyet's mouth gaped blankly. His lips shaped words that wouldn't come. He gave a foolish kind of smile and then got something out.

"Lewton murdered?"

Wharton gave once more the skimmed, prosaic version. And he added that the murder was known to have been committed at a quarter-past seven.

"Good God!" said Rennyet. "Why, I was right past the door at half an hour before!"

He explained the circumstances, and the letter which had to be that morning at Westerley's, his publishers. He had actually passed the back of the house twice, he said—though it was that last time that must have been at about a quarter to seven.

Wharton gave a smile that was grovellingly apologetic. "Of course, Mr. Rennyet, we're not thinking of you as anyway connected with last night's crime—"

Rennyet gave a dry smile. "You mean you're satisfied about my alibi,"

"I didn't come here to test an alibi," said Wharton, with less imperturbability than he intended. "All I'd like you to do is to tell me what you know about the murdered man."

"That's done in a couple of seconds," said Rennyet. "I know nothing at all."

"But surely!"

Rennyet's wave of the hand accepted the protest. "You know what I mean. I know nothing at all. What I might assume is quite a different matter." He hesitated for a moment. "The fact is I've only known him for a week or two. I was given to understand he'd lived in Canada, and I happened to want some local colour, so I ventured to see him."

It was on the tip of Wharton's tongue to ask who had been the intermediary, but the curiously ironic smile that came over Rennyet's face took his mind from the question. Rennyet caught his eye.

"What I discovered was that Lewton was a delightful liar," he said. "I don't believe he was ever in Canada at all." He laughed. "I know he talked a lot, but it didn't convince even me. Besides, he hadn't a trace of accent, and everybody picks up something of that."

Wharton nodded. "He was just a bluffer."

"That's it," said Rennyet.

"And why?"

"Well, speaking as a writer of detective novels, I'd say he set himself deliberately to the pose—public and private—of having been in Canada to conceal having been somewhere else."

Wharton nodded again. "That's a shrewd deduction. And"—with a smile of some wariness—"all that talk about Canada occurred the first time you saw him?"

Rennyet thought hard for a moment, then he laughed gently. Once more there was something of ironic complacence.

"I think I see your point—and I'll answer it. I admit that I saw his bluff the first time I saw him. Only, it happened to amuse me. It amused me so much that it gave me the idea of writing a book in quite a different vein from my normal ones. It was to be a sort of Munchausen, Tartarin affair. You know—the hero a sort of liar and pleasing rogue. That's why I saw him again—and why I'm extraordinarily sorry he's dead." Another wave of the hand. "Not that murder—in real life—isn't a damnable thing."

Wharton rose. "Well, I won't take up any more of your valuable time, sir—"

Rennyet rose too, and on his face was that ironical, superior smile that had irritated Wharton from the first. "Oh, but you'll let me call my people in? I'd like you to test that alibi of mine." Another dry smile. "You see, I don't want you people sitting on my doorstep."

"We have tested it already," said Wharton, with something of the same dryness. "You were just one happy family here from seven o'clock onwards, birthday celebrations and so on."

"We were," said Rennyet, and there seemed some peculiar satisfaction that left the other's irony unchallenged. "I think I finished my meal at a quarter to eight, then I worked for a bit, and that's the lot. Rather a long meal, but I was questioning my man about the ways of the law. For a book, naturally. He used to be a detective, you know."

"So I believe," said Wharton, and wondered why he suddenly hated the sight of Rennyet and his implied patronage. But he held out his hand. "Well, good day, sir, and thank you."

"The pleasure's been my own," said Rennyet. "All the same, I wish you'd tested my alibi."

"When a thing's a hundred-per-cent genuine, it doesn't need testing," said Wharton, and knew somehow the words were hardly the apt and staggering retort he would have liked to make.

Two minutes and the car was headed for Seaborough again, and Wharton was rather taciturn.

"Find out anything else?" he asked Polegate.

"Not a thing, sir," the sergeant told him. "Tom Meek seems to have a good job, and his guv'nor seems to make a lot of him as far as I could gather. Tom reckoned he best part of wrote one of his books for him if you know what I mean; you know, sir, giving him the inside information."

"You think they've all got good alibis?" asked Wharton, and the surprise on the man's face made him follow with an addendum. "You know, we don't want to have to come trotting over here every five minutes."

"If I was up for murder I hope I'd have one as good," said Polegate, with a shake of the head. "The whole three of them were in that house from seven onwards, and they'll all swear to each other."

Wharton nodded with heavy irony. "Funny, isn't it, when you come to think it over? There's that actor—the very man for the job—and he's got a hundred-per-cent alibi. So's his uncle. Then we get a writer of detective novels, and he's got one too. His man's an ex-detective, and he's got the same hundred-per-cent alibi—just to be in the fashion."

"And that Mr. Beece, too," said Polegate. "He was indoors all the evening with a chill."

"Yes," said Wharton, "only I don't count chills—when they're reported by your wife." He changed the subject quickly. "What about Rennyet's car? What sort is it?"

"A big blue saloon," the sergeant said. "They know nothing about a light-coloured racer."

Wharton smiled wryly. "If they did, it'd be sure to have a hundred-per-cent alibi."

CHAPTER V
THE FINAL ALIBI

"How'd you get on, sir?" asked Carry, and beneath the question was an optimism that showed things had not gone so badly for himself.

"About as well as I expected," Wharton told him. "Rennyet's got a rock-bottom alibi. We ran across someone you know, by the way."

"Tom Meek," said Polegate, accepting Wharton's glance to do the explaining.

Carry was very interested—and pleased. "I'm glad he's got a damn good job," he said. "He was always a good chap, was Tom."

"What was that illness he was hinting at?" asked Wharton.

"Worry, I think," said Carry. "There was some family trouble and he took his work too seriously, and then he couldn't sleep. He was heading for disaster if he hadn't thrown his hand in. It was pretty lucky for us, by the way, sir, that we had a good witness on the spot."

"Yes—or for Rennyet," said Wharton. "But about this old sergeant of yours. He was a really good man?"

"An exceptionally good man," said Carry emphatically.

Wharton grunted. "I reckon Rennyet found that out when he interviewed him for the job." He gave Carry a shrewd look. "Suppose you had a job of dirty work to do, wouldn't you be amazingly glad to have somewhere handy a man like Meek to back your alibi with his old colleagues?"

"Like that, you think then, sir?"

"I don't," said Wharton ruefully. "I'm merely putting hypothetical circumstances. Also, still pursuing the same idea, wouldn't you be glad of somebody so trustful and good-natured as your old friend, Meek, who'd never believe ill of you, and could put you up to all the tricks of the trade?"

"You mean that this man Rennyet might have been making use of him for his own ends?"

"I mean nothing," said Wharton dryly. "I liked Meek and I didn't like his master. Neither seems remotely connected with sticking knives in people's backs, or with the fast, sporting cars used by burglars."

And in the middle of that spontaneous outburst of humour, Wharton's face gradually began to straighten, till by the time the sentence was completed, he was positively scowling at Polegate.

"You heard what Mrs. Meek said about the special port that made her sleep last night, and made her still a bit fuddled this morning?"

"Yes, but I told you all about Rennyet's car, sir," protested the sergeant.

"I know you did," said Wharton. "But why shouldn't Rennyet have borrowed or hired one? His two faithful servants are sound asleep, his own car hasn't been used—"

"Pardon me, sir," broke in Carry, "but just why should Rennyet have anything to do with the murder or the attempted burglary last night, except that he's happened to have called at the house once or twice?"

"Why?" Wharton stared. Then he smiled. "You've pricked the bubble. There's no reason whatever—except that he happens to be a writer of detective novels—and England's lousy enough with them, in all conscience. Still, let's get back to good hard sense. Anything about Beece's telephone?"

There was. The telephone stood in Beece's tiny lounge-hall, and there was no extension to another room. And while Wharton was beginning the first delighted rubbing of his hands at that piece of brave news, their own telephone went. Carry took off the receiver and said it was for Wharton.

Tempest was speaking, and from the solicitor's office. He would be along in a few minutes, but he thought the news might be of immediate interest. Lewton had been pretty well off, having owned a lot of local house-property, which was managed for him by local estate-agents. Beece was sole executor of the will, and received two thousand pounds. Trench and his wife got five hundred and Homedale with contents—in consideration of faithful service and so on. The balance of the estate was to go to the Seaborough Corporation on condition that they purchased a plot of ground within the borough boundaries, and made it into a public park to be called after the testator. If the Corporation declined, the money went to a specified list of charities.

"Nothing much there to bite on," said Wharton when he'd passed the news on. "Still, it's a pity I was born with a suspicious mind. What salary do Trench and his wife get?"

"A hundred a year," said Carry. "They used to get ninety."

Wharton nodded. "That's ten pounds below the usual figure. And I don't know what Mrs. Trench was like, but I can't imagine anyone of the calibre of Lewton leaving a two-thousand-guinea house and five hundred pounds in grateful acknowledgment of what his servants did for him. Also, there are two of them."

Carry was puzzled. Wharton was much given to little obscurities like that.

"Two of what, sir?"

"Two Trenches," said Wharton. "Man and wife. If one dies, the other can still talk."

Carry was still puzzled. "Yes, but it wasn't either of them who died, sir; it was Lewton."

Wharton raised his eyebrows. "Yes—I suppose it was. Now about our friend Beece. We oughtn't to let the morning pass without some little courteous inquiry after his health."

He sat down by the table and took off the receiver. At times like that Wharton was in his element. It's a poor showman who has no audience, and now there was the added subtlety that Wharton had himself to convey to his listeners the gist of the unheard words from the other end of the line. And he did it all perfectly. He greeted Mrs. Beece with the grave kindliness of a very old friend; mentioned his own ailments and got to chills in general; pooh-poohed the idea of any mystery in Lewton's death; hinted at suicide and then hinted still more vaguely at a burglar caught in the act; wheedled and coaxed, pleaded and grovelled, till as a mark of tremendous favour he induced the good lady to persuade her husband to wrap up and come to Homedale for just a minute or two, where his counsel and advice as the dead man's executor would be most gratefully welcomed. The Chief Constable's own car should certainly be sent for Mr. Beece, whose own car was temporarily out of order.

The histrionics were over and Wharton hung up. Then he got into action.

"This is where Juker's to be found. Have him here at once— and find somewhere to put him so that he can have a good look at Beece. When Beece gets here, put him in the drawing-room;

then make an excuse to leave him alone for a minute and keep him under observation nevertheless. And get your best finger-print man here at once."

He strolled off towards the kitchen in search of Trench. The old chap was sitting by the range fire and he got wheezily to his feet as Wharton entered.

"Good morning, sir. Anything I can get you, sir?"

"A cup of tea, if you'll be so good," said Wharton. "And how're you feeling this morning, Trench?"

"A bit clearer in the pipes than usual, sir. The kettle's just on, sir. I was going to have one myself." He stopped Wharton in the act of sitting down. "Let me dust that for you, sir. There might be something on it."

Wharton watched the wiping of the chair with a faint irritability that Trench should be so humble and thoughtful. There was something of the same feeling when Trench looked up, duster still in hand, with a deferential:

"Would you mind if I asked you a question, sir?"

"Depends what it is," said Wharton.

Trench straightened himself. "Well, sir, why should anyone want to go using my voice and making out I was in the house last night when I wasn't? It's worried me, sir—worried me a lot."

Wharton sat down. "Perhaps you've got an enemy who wanted to plant the murder on you." He gave a roguish leer. "Somebody's found you out—and tracked you down."

"Found me out?" There was distinct alarm for a moment, and then as he caught Wharton's eye it faded to an absurd kind of smile. I don t think I've got anything of that sort—I mean I don t think there's much to find out about me, sir.

"You haven't got any enemies, then?"

"Not that I know of, sir."

"Got any friends, then?"

"One or two in the town, sir, that I've made in my humble sort of way."

Wharton gave his usual grunt.

Trench took down the caddy and got the teapot ready. Now and again he wheezed alarmingly, and he seemed to take the infliction with the indifference of long sufferance. The tea was made, and it was not till Wharton's cup was filled that the talk was resumed.

The General put in a liberal dose of milk and then raised the cup. "As it's really your own tea I'm drinking, Trench, I'd like to drink your very good health and wish you long life to enjoy your good fortune."

"Good fortune, sir?"

"Yes," said Wharton. "Didn't you know your master left you five hundred pounds and this house and all that's in it?"

Trench's face was a curious study. Wharton read in it so many things that he feared to give them a name, but he could have sworn to some disappointment and a grievance, and the surprise and gratification were certainly forced.

"That's a lot of money, sir. And the house as well. Not that I'd ever dream of living in it!"

"You can sell it, can't you?" said Wharton ironically. "You and your wife—when she comes out of hospital—won't have much to worry about the rest of your days."

He finished the hot tea at a gulp, and got to his feet with the new idea that had come to him. A word of thanks and he was out in the lounge again. One of Carry's men was on duty, and Wharton beckoned him across.

"There's a cup of tea going in the kitchen. Keep in there with Trench for a bit, and if you should happen to hear my voice, come out and let me know."

He took off the receiver and asked for an urgent call through to Scotland Yard. Tempest, he learned, had already been in communication there, but that was not the business about which Wharton was at the moment particularly anxious. There were two things that he wanted done, and each needed an explanatory preface. Firstly, Westerley's were to be discreetly questioned about the real urgency of a certain letter they should, that morning, have received from one of their authors, and secondly, a very competent and tactful questioner was to go to St. Wilfred's Hospital to induce a Mrs. Trench to give helpful information about her late employer.

It was twenty minutes before Wharton hung up again, and Carry was entering the room with Juker. The night-watchman touched his forelock at Wharton with a mild look of recognition as the inspector showed him into the living-room. The finger-print man was already there, and Tempest was coming down the path. The stage was set, and all that was needed was Beece himself. Then, before Wharton had time for half a dozen words, the car drew up, and there was a kind of scurrying for shelter. Juker took the slit by the partly opened door of the dining-room, and Wharton bolted for the cloak-room and his own private slit. Carry remained in sight as reception committee.

But what disturbed Wharton was that Beece, buttoned up to the ears as he was, answered Juker's description to a nicety. Somehow that seemed scarcely right. It was all too obvious, and Wharton hated the obvious when cool reason asked for the mysterious. But he had no particular liking for what he saw of Beece's face—which had more than a touch of the common about it; and his voice was common, too, with some hesitation about the aitches. A self-made man, thought Wharton, and if I let him, he'll be telling me that he doesn't hold with education—or too much of it—and pointing to himself, with false modesty, as to what common sense and hard work can really achieve.

The door of the drawing-room closed on Beece and Carry. The finger-print man pounced on the newspaper which Polegate gave him, and Wharton did a quick and silent sprint to the dining-room.

"Is he the one?" he asked Juker.

"That's him—or else his twin brother," said Juker. "Only he don't seem so spry, somehow, like he did last night."

"A guilty conscience," Wharton whispered hoarsely. "Wonderful how it puts a man off his feed. Now you sit here for a bit, Juker, in case we want you again."

The finger-print man was working with tremendous concentration at that newspaper which Beece had held in his hand. The prints had already been verified, but he wanted to make doubly sure.

"It's absolutely certain, sir," he said. "These are the ones on the mantelpiece and on the back of that letter and the safe."

The door opened and Carry nipped in. He whispered to Wharton just the few words before he nipped out again.

"He went to the fireplace as if he wanted to look—only he didn't dare!"

"Right!" said Wharton. "Now I'm going to do something which I'd have the coat off your back for doing."

Carry's eyes opened. "Something illegal, sir?"

Wharton shrugged his shoulders. "Maybe. I'm going to turn Beece inside out and then put him back again—rulings on evidence or no rulings on evidence."

The great moment had come. Carry's man remained with Juker, and Tempest and Polegate entered the drawing-room at Wharton's heels. Beece was sitting in an easy chair in the centre of the room, and the air struck chill.

"You shouldn't have allowed Mr. Beece to come in this cold room," said Wharton reprovingly. "No, don't get up, Mr. Beece. We know how you're feeling." He pulled himself up a chair and sat down. His smile had the same paternal, humorous reproof. "You know, Mr. Beece, it was most indiscreet of you going out last night."

Beece looked at him. "Going out, sir? I don't know what you mean."

Wharton gave a shrug of the shoulders, appeared to think for a moment, then thrust out his chin with a look so aggressive that Beece's mouth gaped with the surprise of it.

"Mr. Beece, we've got no time to waste in proving to you one by one that the various things you're going to tell us are lies. We're going to tell you here and now that you're in as dangerous a position as a man can be in. Your chance is to tell the truth, and God help you if it isn't the truth." He drew back, and his face was set in a hard sneer. "Come on, now; out with it—and no lies. Begin at when Lewton rang you up at five minutes past seven, and go on from there."

Beece licked his lips and cast a nervous look around. He shook his head with a sort of haggard weariness, then he tried to speak. His eye caught Wharton's and he turned his head away.

"I don't know what you're getting at, gentlemen, but you're all wrong somewhere. My wife can prove that I didn't stir out of my house last night."

The words gave courage and he met Wharton's look.

The General shrugged his shoulders with the supremest indifference and got to his feet. "Take him away," he said to Tempest. "Get him in front of a magistrate at once and have him held."

Beece half rose, fingers fumbling at his thin, torpedo beard. "Here, you can't do that."

Wharton's back was still turned. "And take with you," he said to Tempest, "the man who saw him leave his car and come back out of breath. And you'd better have the finger-print man to swear to his prints when he hid the knife. And don't forget to mention that his prints were on the knob of the safe."

And then all at once Beece began to cry. Wharton heard the faint whimper and switched round again. It was a shameful sort of sight to see the man's lip trembling and the tears running down his reddish-purple cheeks. Then he groped for his handkerchief and blubbered in good earnest, while an uneasy self-consciousness crept about the room, and even Wharton felt the cheap turgidity cutting across the dramatic scene that he had planned.

It took Beece a good half-hour to get his story out, and Wharton could not budge him from the main details. Lewton had rung him up to ask him to come to Homedale at once. The maid had first taken the message, and Beece himself happening to enter the hall, he had taken the receiver and heard it all again. Lewton had wanted to see him urgently, and would give no details. Beece had no idea of what the urgency was, but he got out his car at once. There was a light on at Homedale, and knowing Trench would be out—Lewton had mentioned that—he tapped at the front door and entered. No one was there and he gave a call. There was no answer and he went to the dining-room—

only to see the corpse of Lewton on the floor, where it had been dragged. Horror and terror had seized him, and he had somehow got out to the hall again. Then his foot kicked against the knife, and when he picked it up a still greater horror came over him. Then he saw the drawing-room door was ajar, and somehow he found himself inside the room. A kind of dumb terror was on him, but he saw the safe wide open, and he remembered going to it, and he may have looked inside. Then he knew he was still carrying the knife, and all at once he felt the urge to get rid of it—why, he had no idea, unless it was the continuance of panic—and with a queer, illogical sanity, he had wiped off his prints with his handkerchief and stuck it up the chimney. Then at all costs he knew he must get out of the house, but just as he made for the front door, he thought he heard a car and voices, and with the same panic he switched off the hall light and fled from the house by the back way.

To the score of questions that Wharton put to him, he had no answer, except to fall back upon the unshatterable plea of a blind panic that had taken away clear thought. He knew he ought to have called the police. He knew afterwards it was madness to have run. Even when he had told his wife about it all, the panic had still persisted, and had so communicated itself to her that they were prepared to commit perjury.

Wharton got once more to his feet, and for a moment stood looking down at the furtive face with its grubby stains.

"You can go home now," he said, and there was contempt in the curt dismissal. "And when you get there, stay there till you get other instructions. This afternoon you'll be asked to say all you know about Lewton. Spend your time between now and then in thinking it all out and writing it down."

He watched Beece's assumption of pathetic frailty with a sneer. At the very door he called him to a halt.

"Here, wait a moment. What do you know about this?"

He took from his pocket-book that letter on the underside of which Beece's prints were clearly marked. Beece looked at it, and for a moment was strangely quiet. Then he looked up with an expression of innocent bewilderment.

"I don't know anything about it. It isn't anything to do with me."

"You haven't a niece?"

Beece shook his head. "Not called Ethel, I haven't." He shook his head emphatically. "I've never seen it before in my life."

"Really." Wharton bowed ironically. "That's funny. You see, your finger-prints are on it. Here they are—see?"

Beece floundered into something of the old pathetic surprise. "I might have picked it up when I was in the room. I suppose I *must* have picked it up from what you gentlemen say. Only I didn't know anything about it. I didn't know what I was doing. I was half off my head."

"You'll be damn lucky if you aren't altogether off your head," said Wharton grimly. "A neck like yours won't stand the drop." He nodded. "All right. Off you go—and don't forget this afternoon."

"Well, what did you really make of him?" asked Tempest, when he and Carry got back to the drawing-room again.

"I'd rather hear what you think," countered Wharton.

"Well, of course he was lying. He cleaned out the safe—that's a certainty."

"He was lying like hell," said Carry. "You could see Ananias written all over him."

Wharton nodded. "Well, I venture to disagree; not that he was lying, but about his having robbed the safe. I don't think he did rob it." He caught Carry's incredulous look. "I'll tell you why. What did the murderer kill Lewton for if it wasn't to get what was in the safe? And Beece wasn't the murderer—we know that. When I put my hand on Lewton I knew enough to know he'd been dead a few minutes. Besides, even supposing Lewton wasn't dead when the supposed Trench rang up and said he was, even then Beece hadn't time to do more than he says he did. It's a dead certainty that Beece really found Lewton dead—and that he was scared stiff."

"But what about Beece's prints on the safe?" put in Tempest.

"I'm coming to that," said Wharton. "That's all part of the something Beece is still holding back from us. I say that his first thought when he saw Lewton dead was to rush to this room to see if the safe was still—so to speak—safe. I say the murderer had got there first and the safe was empty."

"Then what about the letter, sir?"

"There I'm stumped," admitted Wharton. "I can't fit the letter in. Beece handled it and yet didn't take it."

"Which means it's utterly unimport," suggested Tempest.

"Damned if I know," said Wharton. "Somebody described it as a middle cut of salmon." He shrugged his shoulders. "Still, perhaps Beece doesn't like salmon. That's one of the things you might ask him when you put him on the toasting-fork this afternoon, inspector."

Tempest tossed his head and a click of the tongue accompanied it.

"Seems to me we're little further forward."

"We're a lot forward," said Wharton cynically. "Every single person who's come to our notice at all has the most beautiful, twenty-four carat, diamond studded alibi. They're the only people Lewton ever had anything to do with, and all we've got to do, therefore, is to find someone nobody's ever heard of."

Carry nodded darkly. "You mind if I ask a question, sir?"

"Why not?"

"Well, about this Beece, sir. How'd you get on to him first. If you remember, you told us last night he was the one who did the burglary—or you as good as told us."

"Oh, that," said Wharton offhandedly. "You remember when I rang him up and his wife answered. Well, as soon as she knew it was the police, she shot her hand over the phone while she spoke to her husband—only, she didn't shoot it quick enough. I heard her say, '*They know* . . .' Informative couple of words, don't you think? Then she did the same again later, and this time I got, '*What shall I say?*' And she was talking to a man supposed to be in his bedroom with a chill!"

Carry did a Whartonian grunt. The expected miracle of deduction had turned out to be a putting together of two and two.

But he dissembled with a nod. "You certainly had him there, sir. But there's something else I wanted to ask you. What would you say, sir, if I was to suggest doing a little private study of my own into the movements and so on of that actor? I'm a long way from satisfied where he's concerned."

"I'd say good luck and get on with it," Wharton told him. "All I ask is that you pool information. The credit you can keep."

"Thank you, sir." Carry was obviously pleased. "I've got an idea or two I'd like to try out."

"Splendid!" said Wharton, and got out his notebook. "When you're testing them out, just add these two or three posers, will you? Who was the lady in the car? Was she Ethel? Who was the lad in the sports car? Was he Albert? Why was the knife taken out of Lewton's back? Why did Trench expect to get more than five hundred? Why was there so much telephoning last night?"

He reeled the list off so quickly that Carry could only gape. And when the inspector did get a word in, Wharton cut him off before the word became two.

"And for a final poser"—he put the notebook ostentatiously away—"just try your wits out on this. *Was it Lewton who phoned the doctor at seven-ten, or was it not?*"

Carry stared—and thought. Tempest stare too, and he spoke first.

"You mean to say you think someone used Lewton's voice the same as they did Trench's?"

"Why not?" asked Wharton complacently. "It had certain well-defined characteristics that lent themselves to imitation—especially over the phone."

"My God!" said Carry, still staring. "Then the same one might have called Beece, too, at five minutes past." The full implication caught him staggeringly. "Lewton might have been killed long before seven! *He might have been killed when that actor was in the house!*"

Tempest had been staring too, and now he carried on. "Yes, and if Howard Trench had anything to do with the murder, he may be lying like hell. Who knows if Lewton really let him out? Why shouldn't he have killed Lewton before he left the house?"

Wharton shook his head. "Steady on. Don't let's lose our sense of proportion. Shinniford can prove on medical evidence—and so can I—that Lewton wasn't killed till after five-past seven. The actor was out of the house at three minutes past, and there was telephoning done *after* that. Howard Trench has a hundred-per-cent alibi. You mayn't like it—but it's a fact."

Tempest let out a deep breath. "Good Lord Wharton! Why, we haven't begun this case yet."

Carry gave a click of the tongue. "Seems to me we're up against it proper. And what do you suggest as the first thing to do, sir?"

"Do?" said Wharton, with a twinkle. "That's easy."

Carry fell for it, as the General knew he would. "Well, what is it then, sir?"

"Go and have lunch," said Wharton. "If you don't feel you've earned some, then I do."

CHAPTER VI
THE MURDERER RETURNS

AFTER LUNCH Wharton had a few words with Carry about the line of action he wished to have taken with Beece, and then rang up Hule. To his exceeding gratification, the doctor was out, and Mrs. Hule expressed herself as delighted at the prospect of seeing him.

If there was one thing in which Wharton had supreme art, it was in his handling of women. Perhaps there was a forlornness in his fatherly face and the hang of the weeping-willow moustache that awoke the maternal in them. He was capable, too, of the finer sympathies. His hawk eye could detect—with the profitable facility of a fortune-teller—the likely trend of a conversation, the likes and the grievances, and the little hidden, unspoken things that lay behind. He could flatter—and know just what to flatter; he could hint—and know the response that was waiting to come.

With the doctor's wife he chose to be something of a man-of-the-world. Mrs. Hule despised Seaborough and its holiday crowds, and its amusing attempts at culture. She had, in fact, a cheap, embittered cynicism, which Wharton found only too easy to fan. For a quarter of an hour he sat in the stodgy drawing-room, nodding gravely, pursing his lips, shrugging his shoulders and going through his repertoire of tricks—and the biggest feat of all was to bring the talk deftly round to the subject of the dead man.

"You think he was drunk, then," said Wharton, with some show of disgust.

"Well, he wasn't himself," she said. "My husband told you, I think, about the way he used to talk over the phone. Quite a common man, you know. Only, last night, I don't know how it was, but I caught something different." She wrinkled up her face affectedly. "You know; something that made me wonder if he was drunk. I don't know why I thought of that, but I did."

Wharton nodded with infinite comprehension. "He attempted some familiarity, perhaps?"

She laughed. "Oh, no! That's just what he didn't do. You see, he used to know when my husband was out, and when I answered the phone he would try one of his jokes." She pouted her lips contemptuously. "Something quite common—but amusing in its way."

"And last night?"

"Well, last night I picked up the receiver in the ordinary way, and I spotted the voice at once." The little smile she gave showed the very one she had given that night. "I said, as I always did to anybody, that the doctor was out, and what was it he wanted? Then he just said a kind of Oh!' like that—"

"A sort of disappointed, drawling oh."

"That's right. And then he went on with his message—only he didn't try to make any of his usual jokes. He was all serious. He was frightened, really he was. His voice was different somehow. That's why I thought he was drunk."

Wharton's ponderous nod expressed a quantity of things, and then he rose from the spindle-legged chair. "Now, Mrs.

Hule, I mustn't keep you any longer. I'm sure there are heaps of things you have to do."

She pouted. "Sometimes I wish I had. You wouldn't believe how boring it gets sometimes."

"Ah, well!" said Wharton. "Doctors' wives, I always say, ought to be numbered among our national heroines." He shook his head. "Very lonely it must be for you sometimes."

A curious hardness came over her face. "It isn't that. If you always knew it was necessary . . ."

She let the words trail away, and Wharton's eyes were suddenly opened. Now he picked up the hidden trend of other hints and obscurities. *Mrs. Hule was a jealous woman.* And the fact registered itself somewhere deep in his mind, and with a curious insistence, as likely to be of use.

The good-afternoons were said, and Wharton strolled back thoughtfully along the pavement of West Cliff Road. The thoughts ran on and returned. They made strange juxtapositions in his mind, then separated again like butterflies that hover and float above a summer border. Sometimes the thoughts had startling colours, that caught the mind and held. Had there been more than casual banter between the doctor's wife and that ancient rip—Lewton? A preposterous idea—and yet . . . The doctor, too, was something of a high-stepper. His manner had been a shade too easy. He had spoken too tolerantly of other men's frailties. He was of the roving age and he had a roving eye. Doubtless he could summon at will a professional reticence, and doubtless, too, he was quite capable of unprofessional relaxations. And the fact remained that he had given his wife cause for jealousy.

Perhaps the cold gust that blew that moment from the sea was the main factor in bringing Wharton back to realities. However interesting it might be to observe discreetly the rifts in another man's household; however much the contact with a tolerably pretty woman might linger in, and colour, the mind, yet the fact remained that the Hule *ménage* had nothing to do with the solving of the problem of who killed Frederick Lewton. And yet—Wharton's restless mind ran on ahead again—it was not uninteresting to think of one more eternal triangle. Mrs. Hule, perhaps, having out of spite and pique some mad intrigue with old Lewton, and disguising it skilfully by pretence of jokes exchanged over the telephone. Hule, there might be, with his own intrigues and maybe jealousy, letting the mice play, and stretching out a paw at the precise, ordered moment.

Wharton smiled ironically, and the irony was for himself. Better dismiss from the mind all thoughts of the Hules, and keep to the problem in hand. And as he forced his thoughts to that new grappling, something that had been dormant suddenly stirred, so that his pace instinctively quickened and his lips began to shape words. He was frowning as he dodged his way among the navvies at the fork, and when he entered the gate of Homedale he came down the path with a sprint of which he was unaware. Polegate opened the door, and Tempest was there too.

"Carry back yet?" Wharton asked.

"Not yet," Tempest told him.

"Then we won't wait," said Wharton. "I've got something on my mind, and I've got to try it out. Sit down and listen to this, and then tell me if I'm right."

He spoke with a slow precision, sorting the thoughts and giving them careful words. There was a desperate earnestness about him that was new to the sergeant, and which Tempest himself had rarely observed.

"First of all, there's something you must take my word for. I've just seen Mrs. Hule about that telephone message she took last night, and I'm sure—not half-sure, mind you, but dead, plumb sure—that it was *not* Lewton himself who called up the doctor."

Tempest nodded. "You foreshadowed that just before lunch, didn't you?—when you were talking to Carry."

"That's right," said Wharton. "Only then it was a theory, now it's fact. Whoever used Lewton's voice didn't know of the peculiar relationships which existed between Mrs. Hule and Lewton over the phone—and that's where he tripped. Also he had to strain his voice away from what I might call the normal Lewton, to get into it the fright he was trying to convey. Still"—and Wharton waved his hand with a gesture of utter dismissal—"let's get on from there. Just note down the points as I make them. And the first point is this. Lewton wasn't frightened at all—*for the simple reason that he was dead*"

There was silence for a moment, then, "That's right," said Tempest. "Whoever killed him, did so at once, as soon as he entered the house."

"That's it. And he entered the house as soon as the coast was clear; in other words, as soon as Howard Trench left it."

"Three minutes past seven," said Polegate, and noted it in his book.

"But that's all nothing," went on Wharton with another gesture. "It's the logical outcome that rather frightens me. If you try to follow me when I've put the case to you, I think you'll see something terrible beginning to emerge. Murder's bad enough at all times. To cut the vital thread of a man's life and end its possibilities is a thing that staggers the mind when you think of it in cold earnest. But now you listen to this. You both remember that there was discussed at odd times—or mentioned, perhaps I should say—the question of why there was so much telephoning. Now picture the scene. The murderer has just been admitted by Lewton. They walk from the door there and—" The word was left in the air. Wharton's eyes goggled. His hand reached for the receiver, and the number he called for was Beece's.

There was a dead silence for a couple of minutes, and Wharton's face was a frowning mask. Then it lightened.

"Who's that? . . . Oh, I want to speak to Mr. Beece himself. . . . Never mind who I am. Tell him it's urgent."

Another silence, and Wharton's eyes watched the table-top on which his elbows leaned. They lifted again.

"That you, Mr. Beece? . . . Superintendent Wharton speaking from Homedale. I want you to follow me very carefully, and I want you to rely implicitly on what I say. . . . Right, then. First I tell you frankly that I know the telephone message you got from Lewton last night—the one that brought you up here wasn't quite the kind you made out. . . . No, no, no! Don't misunderstand me. I'm not at all interested at the moment in what it was. All we'll assume is that it was some secret between him and you. . . . Well, it might have had to do with his estate, of which you now happen to be the sole executor! . . . Now then; this is the point. Taking into account what the message was—and I personally don't give a damn what it was—was it nevertheless of such a nature that you were absolutely sure, beyond doubt, that it was Lewton himself who was speaking to you?"

There was a pause of a few seconds. Wharton's eyes stared out unseeing, and he gave a nod or two. His face set stern again.

"Thank you. Now let me repeat something. I'm relying on you in this—just as you can rely on me. If you've deceived me to the slightest possible extent, heaven help you! You're still sure it was Lewton? . . . Right. Good-bye."

Wharton hung up, and his face was, if anything, rather more serious and grave than it had been before.

"You heard that, gentlemen? Now we'll get back to last night. Lewton and the murderer come in. We'll call the murderer X. X, for some secret reason known to both Lewton and Beece, suggests that Beece should be called to share the conference. Lewton agrees and calls up Beece. No sooner does he hang up the receiver—as I hung it up myself—than the knife gets him in the back."

Wharton cringed as if he felt the actual blow. The room was dim, for it was a cloudy afternoon, and the scene was so vivid that his listeners cringed too from the thrust. Wharton's hand pointed to the floor.

"That's where Lewton fell. X got him by the armpits and dragged him to that room there and he worked fast. But first of all he took out the knife with his gloved hand and laid it carefully by. Then he put out the dining-room light and picked up the receiver again, and this time it was the doctor who was called—and in Lewton's voice. And why was the doctor called?"

Polegate frowned in thought. Tempest shook his head.

"I'll tell you," said Wharton, and his voice lowered dramatically. "The doctor was called *merely to establish the precise time of the murder.*"

Tempest's eyes searched the room unseeing. Polegate scowled as his wits worked desperately at some new deduction. Wharton sank back in his chair for a moment, then he leaned forward again with pointing finger.

"You see the tremendous implications? You see the cold, icy deadliness of it? Lewton was supposed to die at twelve minutes past seven. To make assurance still more sure, X took off this receiver again and in the person of Trench reported the finding of his master's body. And now do you see the further implication? If everybody was sure that Lewton died at twelve minutes past seven, X was implicitly satisfied. And why? For the simple reason that *he himself had an unbreakable alibi for that very time.*"

"My God! you're right," said Tempest.

Polegate gave a little cough. "If I might ask just one thing, sir. I expect it's me that's wrong, but why did X take Trench's voice when he knew it'd be found out that Trench had a hundred-per-cent alibi?"

Wharton smiled. "An excellent point—and I was going to make it myself. Only it answers itself. What *has* actually happened? We've wasted time on old Trench. He was a red herring. But that's only one reason that might have been in X's mind."

And there Wharton paused for a moment, and his finger went out again as he made the most dramatic point of all.

"I believe that X had in his mind something of the same thing that brought in Beece. Let me explain. Why was Beece called on the phone when X knew there wasn't going to be any conference? Why was the knife removed from the body? I'll tell you. *X wanted Beece to come to the house and be caught there by the police.* That's why the police were called. They ought to have found Beece here, and maybe the knife in his hand—or the knife with his finger-prints on it."

"He had a grudge against him," suggested Polegate.

Wharton smiled patiently. "That's what it amounted to, even if it takes far more than a grudge to force a man to do murder. X hated Lewton and he killed him. X hated Beece—and he wanted *us* to hang him by the neck. He wanted the second bird killed with *our* stone. Maybe he called up the police in Trench's voice because he hated him too. Maybe he thought old Trench wouldn't be able to provide a perfect alibi."

And then Wharton rose, as if his brain had suddenly gone tired, or as if he were indifferent to comment, or knew his theories too surely beyond it. At the same moment steps were heard outside, and when Polegate opened the door, who should be standing there but Carry—and with him Rennyet.

"This gentleman and I met at the front gate," said Carry.

Rennyet smiled diffidently. "I didn't know if Mr. Ward would be in—"

"A little error," broke in Wharton. "Wharton's the name. Wharton. And what favourable breeze blows you here, sir?"

"Well"—Rennyet hesitated fatuously—"the fact is—to put it crudely—I hoped I might be allowed to sort of look round. I mean, as a very dud kind of author, I was interested; more than interested."

Wharton smiled delightfully. "I understand. Come along into the dining-room, Mr. Rennyet; there's a fire there." He turned back to Tempest. "I wonder if you'd mind going over with Carry those points we've been discussing."

Wharton waved Rennyet to the easy chair opposite his own.

"So you thought you'd like to see the scene of an actual murder?"

"Well, that's what it amounts to," Rennyet told him. "Gross curiosity, you might call it."

This was a far different Rennyet from the man of the early morning, and Wharton was wondering what had produced the astounding difference. Here was no ironical complacence, but rather a confession of inferiority, and a watchful diffidence.

"What is it you'd specially like to see?" Wharton asked him. "We detectives have got to keep on the right side of you authors."

"You're pulling my leg," laughed Rennyet. Then he suddenly looked almost solemn. "It's a queer feeling, you know, but the last time I was in this room I sat in this very chair, and Lewton sat where you are now. I can see him—that crafty face of his; always looking at you as if he was playing some trick."

"Who was it first introduced you to him? I mean, how'd you know he was an authority on Canada?"

There was now a very present wariness on Rennyet's face.

"The fact is, there wasn't a go-between. I was watching the bowls one day and happened to sit alongside him. Later on, when I wanted that information about Canada, I remembered him and looked him up."

Wharton had a sudden idea. He got out his note-book and produced that curious letter on which were Beece's prints.

"Here's something I'll show you as a very special favour," he said. "This was dropped on the scene of the crime, and if you look at the back you'll see the actual finger-prints where the police exposed them."

Rennyet's eyes opened. Then, with a curious smile, he looked at the tips of his own fingers. He shook his head as if to say that there was no resemblance.

"These are actually the prints of the man who did it?"

Wharton shook his head. "That we don't know yet. Still, it's interesting, you'll admit. And what do you make of it—the actual words?"

Rennyet read, and frowned. He read it a second time before he looked up.

"It seems pretty innocuous. Kind of a servant-girl epistle, don't you think? This other stuff's in a different hand."

"You mean the cut-of-salmon allusion. What do you make of that?"

"Hanged if I know," said Rennyet. "It's a different hand—and it's not mine." There he gave a smile that had something of the morning's Rennyet. He looked at the diagonal words again. "What I'd say is that it's some kind of family joke. You know, some allusion that only the receiver or members of the family would understand and appreciate."

Wharton put the letter back carefully. "I shouldn't be surprised if you're right."

"I wouldn't say that," said Rennyet. "Only, if everybody's guessing, my guess might be as near as anyone else's."

"True enough," said Wharton, and fired a question. "You liked old Lewton?"

"Liked him?" He looked puzzled. "Why, he was an outsider. My private opinion was that he was an utter old swine."

Wharton raised his eyebrows. "But I gathered that you had him in mind as a plausible and amiable rogue?"

The quickness of the thrust knocked Rennyet, for a moment, off his perch of self-possession. It took him a second or two to find the lame retort, "Well, you needn't necessarily draw from life—I mean, not to that extent. There's a law of libel, you know."

"So they tell me," said Wharton mildly. "Now is there anything else I can do for you? That's the very spot where we found the body."

"He was actually killed there?"

"We're not quite sure," said Wharton, and as Rennyet was getting up, he rose too. "Sorry I can't spare you more time, but you must come in again and we'll have a yarn." He smiled rather ruefully as he held out his hand. "Good-bye for the present. I'm afraid you'll have a pretty poor idea of the abilities of us policemen."

Rennyet took the hand, and smiled with an ironic droop of the lips. "I don't know. I think you were extraordinarily clever."

"Clever?" said Wharton, ushering him into the hall, and rushing forward to open the door. "How was I clever?"

Rennyet gave a delicious shrug of the shoulders. "Well, the neat way you got a copy of my prints by showing me that letter!"

"My dear Mr. Rennyet!"

But Wharton's protest was wasted on the cold air, for the author, after yet another delightful smile, was already striding towards the front gate.

Wharton stood there watching him. He watched the blue saloon car move off towards the town, and alongside the driver was a figure in chauffeur's uniform—the handy-man, Tom Meek.

"All swank and show," said Wharton savagely to himself, and knew in the same moment that he was exhibiting a childish resentment of the fact that Rennyet had proved to be a cleverer man than George Wharton.

* * *

Wharton closed the door and came moodily towards the three who sat round the hall fire.

"How'd you get on with Beece, Carry?"

"Bad, sir," said Carry. "He didn't know a thing about Lewton. He swore it on the four gospels. All you could get out of him was that yarn about Canada."

"Get his handwriting?"

Carry handed over a sheet of paper. Wharton once more took out the letter. He looked hard, then he pursed his lips.

"I don't know. Have a look at that cut-of-salmon stuff and tell me what you think? There seems a resemblance to me."

The three compared the writing. The consensus of opinion was that there was a resemblance—but not very marked.

"He'd have the sense to know he was a suspected man, and he'd certainly disguise the handwriting he gave you," he said to Carry. Then he looked at Tempest. "I'll make a copy and we'll send the two up to town at once and let the experts see them. Any news for me yet, by the way? I thought I heard the phone go when I was in there with Rennyet."

"It just came," said Tempest. "Westerley's report the letter that Rennyet sent as being urgent and genuine. Your people have also got some publicity stuff about him that they're sending along."

"And Mrs. Trench?"

Tempest looked round before he spoke. "You'll never question her now. They put her under morphia after her husband saw her yesterday, and they don't think she'll last the week."

Wharton grunted. Then he took a turn round the room for a bit.

"Make a note of this, will you? Send down to the various booksellers and see if you can get one or two—of Rennyet's detective stories. And rush this letter first of all down to the station, and tell your man it's got Rennyet's prints on it."

Tempest passed the letter on to Polegate. "Anything else?"

"Yes, you'd better get in touch with the coroner and arrange for a formal inquest. I suppose there's been nothing in about the requests we made for information?"

"Never a thing," said Tempest. "It's early yet, though."

"Then get it repeated," said Wharton. "Add the news that he left a pretty tidy fortune, and leave it at that. Six o'clock to-night you and I and Carry will have a little talk. Keep in your minds those little matters we talked about this afternoon."

He picked up his hat and slipped into the overcoat which Carry held for him.

"You'll pardon me, sir," the inspector said, "but did you get anything out of that Rennyet?"

"Devil a thing," said Wharton.

"What'd he come for, do you think, sir?"

"Sheer curiosity," Wharton told him. "Also, perhaps he thought he might use what he saw for one of his precious books. Maybe there were other things, too." He flashed a look. "What do *you* think he came for?"

Carry took on a look that was mysterious and profound. "Well, you know the old saying, sir?"

Wharton scowled at him. "What old saying?"

Carry's voice hoarsened. "*The murderer always returns to the scene of his crime.*"

CHAPTER VII
THE BETTER HALF

THE CONFERENCE was in full swing. The three sat round the fire, and on the table behind them was a book in a gaily coloured jacket—*Live Man, Dead Man*, by Raymond Rennyet. On the table stood also three glasses and three bottles of beer, which Tempest had brought in his car, not being minded to accept favours at the hands of Trench. The three had the house to themselves, for Trench had expressed the desire to go to the pictures, and there at the moment—duly under surveillance—he doubtless was.

"You'll excuse me mentioning it, sir," Carry was saying, "but if I get you right, all somebody's got to have is a good alibi and he's under suspicion!"

Wharton gave a look of pain. "Why not? Isn't that what we arrived at this afternoon?"

"Pardon the paradox," said Tempest, "but to go to the only logical conclusion, the one whose alibi is the nearest to a hundred-per-cent, according to you, is the man we're looking for."

"Well"—Wharton pursed his lips—"you're not far out. Logic's logic. You can't have it and not have it. Still, let's draw up a table of possibilities. We'll take all the suspects—alibis or no alibis—and sum them up. What's the primary essential the murderer had to have?"

"Who are to be the suspects?" asked Tempest quietly.

"Well, the two Trenches, Beece and Rennyet—to start with. Any other proposals?"

There were none, and the names were written as initials across the top of the sheets. Carry suggested the knowledge of Trench's absence as the essential for X, and it was put down in the side column. Howard Trench and his uncle each got a mark. Beece, after some argument, got one too, but Rennyet was awarded only a half, as in his case there might reasonably have been a doubt.

"What's next?" asked Wharton, who preferred to hear other people's ideas.

"The distance away of the police. How long it would take them to get here," said Carry.

"Good enough," said Wharton. "In my opinion they all knew that except, possibly, Howard Trench. I vote he gets the half mark."

"X had to know who Lewton's doctor was," proposed Tempest. "And he had to know how long it would take him to get up here."

Wharton nodded. "A good point that. All the same, I doubt if we ought to give Rennyet the whole mark. A half, don't you think? Right; down it goes. And what about the ability to imitate the two voices."

There was at once a stir round the fire. Tempest said he had been trying that over in private. He had actually imitated old Trench's voice so well that he had given the station-sergeant a shock. Carry owned up that he had been experimenting too.

"Frankly, I don't think it's difficult," Tempest said. "I don't know Lewton's voice—except from what Hule told us—but I imagine it wouldn't be any harder than Trench's. I propose, therefore, that we either give them all the full mark or wash it out— which amounts to the same thing."

"Why not give Howard Trench the full mark?" suggested Wharton. "He does imitating for a living. As for old Trench, he couldn't imitate anybody but himself. And I don't quite see Beece doing much in that line either."

So Trench and Beece got nothing, though the mention of the latter produced the next suggestion. An essential was that X must have had a good knowledge of Beece.

"I don't quite see that," said Tempest. "Let's suppose X came in and made some proposition to Lewton. Why shouldn't Lewton have said, 'Hold hard a minute. I've got to have my partner here first.' X, therefore, needn't have known Beece at all, or heard of him till Lewton rang him up."

Wharton smiled soothingly. "But didn't we agree this afternoon that X tried to implicate Beece and get him hanged? Didn't X have that all planned out before he entered this house? I admit that if we take it as an essential, we must leave Beece himself out. He could hardly have telephoned to himself and taken the message!"

So it went on and on. There was an argument about X's knowledge of the telephone numbers; that he had had to work at terrific speed and must have memorized them beforehand. But that was so utterly obvious, and telephone directories such common property, that it was washed out as an essential. There was the question, too, as to whether X was a friend of Lewton. That, too, was washed out. Lewton let him in without delay. Moreover, the only suspects under consideration were known to be comparatively friendly with the murdered man. That X had to have a hatred of Lewton and Beece was washed out too, since, as Wharton put it, that came rather under the heading of motive.

"Who had a motive, then?" asked Tempest.

"Old Trench did," said Carry. "That is if you consider five hundred quid and this house and what's in it as motives."

"Then he might have enlisted the help of his nephew, and he must be put down with a mark too," said Wharton. "What's more, we're all convinced there was some hanky-panky going on between Lewton and Beece, and so Beece ought to have a half mark at the least. Rennyet gets nothing."

"There's the question of cleverness and nerve," said Carry. "It wanted a brainy one to do what we think he did."

"A full mark to Rennyet," said Wharton promptly.

"A half to Howard Trench, don't you think?" said Tempest.

"I'd give him a whole one," said Carry. "And by the way, sir, I've already got to work on him. I know the pub where he and his friends gather of a morning, and I've got the right man ready for to-morrow. If I don't get all the inside knowledge about Howard Trench, I'll stand the whole of Seaborough a drink."

"All right," said Wharton. "Give him a whole one and his uncle a half. And what about Beece, Carry?"

"Him! He hasn't the guts to crack a louse. Look at him when you got him cornered this morning, sir."

The marks were allotted, and they came to the matter of the alibis.

"What's your opinion of Beece's?" asked Wharton. "You went into it this afternoon?"

"It's A1 in a court of law," said Carry. "The maid confirmed the taking of the phone message and the time he went out. What's more, she's what I'd call a first-class witness."

Wharton leaned back in his chair. "Well, as far as I can see, they're all in the same boat. Every man jack of 'em's got a hundred-per-cent alibi—and you don't want more than that. We'll have to wash it out."

"Wash it out temporarily," said Carry darkly, his mind once more on his chief obsession.

"As you will," said Wharton. "And now let's see where we've got."

"Funny, isn't it?" said Carry. "It all comes back to what we"—he barely escaped the "I"—"thought from the first. The two Trenches in partnership."

Wharton was shaking his head. Somehow he could not get away from the feeling that the mountain of laborious compilation had produced a miserable mouse in results. And yet what he had expected from that table of marks—unless it was some miracle of revelation—he hardly knew. Tempest was also doing some head-shaking, and it was plain that he also had been sold a pup.

"Well," said Wharton, and emptied the rest of his bottle into his glass, "we have at least the consciousness of duty nobly done. What's more, I vote that since the stars in their courses seem to bear him out, we support Carry in his hunch, and let him go on with his inquiry into the uncle and nephew."

He got to his feet, wiping his moustache with florid sweeps of his ornate handkerchief. Then he carefully replaced his antiquated glasses. Carry watched him with something of alarm.

"And what's the next immediate job, sir?"

Wharton beamed amiably. "What you mean is, what am I going to do, and what's the Chief Constable going to do?"

Carry grinned sheepishly. "Perhaps that's what I do mean, sir—and no disrespect."

"Then, speaking for the Chief Constable of this borough, I rather think he's treating himself out to the theatre to get a front view of your friend, Howard Trench. I'd suggest that you drop in for a minute or two as well, and see your man in action. Speaking for myself, I propose doing what every decent citizen has to do at times. In other words, I propose to spend the rest of the evening in entertaining my wife."

"At the theatre too, sir?"

"Hardly that form of entertainment," said Wharton modestly. "Just with my own company. To talk pure shop, I'd like to get her opinion of a certain letter—two copies of which are reposing already in this pocket."

He got as far as the door and then turned. He beamed with the same amiable benevolence.

"And if you two find the time hang at all, chew upon this, as the bard says. There's one man who combines most of the things we've been discussing this last half-hour—and like fools we've left him out. He's a man who knows everything, can do everything, and has skill and nerve. He also, doubtless, has a sufficiently good alibi."

The voices came together. "Who's that?"

"*Dr. Hule*," said Wharton, and gently closed the door.

Dinner was over. The hotel was practically empty at that time of year, so the Whartons had the drawing-room to themselves, and the General blatantly smoked his pipe. Mrs. Wharton was a motherly woman, and a shrewd. She was a hospital nurse before her marriage, and there had been a time when Wharton had known her definitely a cut above him. But those days were long ago. They had pulled together, and they were together—few couples more closely.

Mrs. Wharton knew perfectly well that something was in the wind, and she sat reading till George should unburden his mind. Then he went out for a minute and came back with that book of Rennyet's.

"I wonder what you'll make of this?"

She had a look at it, and smiled at once with some sureness.

"If it's got Westerley's name on it, it's sure to be good. They do only highbrow stuff—not too highbrow, of course." She had a look inside. "Why, you remember *Two Shots Missed*? You know, the book I told you was so good." She put her finger to the list of works of Raymond Rennyet, and Wharton saw what she was driving at.

"You'd call him a clever chap?"

"Very clever. He writes well, too."

"Capital!" said Wharton, and calmly took the book back.

"But aren't you going to leave it for me to read?"

"Later, perhaps," he told her. "Not that you'll be able to tell me more than you have done already." And while he was speak-

ing he was getting out those two copies of the letter, and he
passed one over with, "Have a look at that."

Assisi,

Feb.

DEAR UNCLE,—Everything is very nice here and I have
seen Albert. H.M.G. has told me to have two days home
but Albert knows. C.R. has been in twice but I had to go
to the pictures but A. was there. He will write next time
if you want him.

Love from your loving niece,

ETHEL.

The letter was read, and begun a second time; then all at
once she looked up with a funny, startled expression that ended
in a laugh.

"Is this something to do with—what you're doing?"

"That's it," said Wharton. "For all we know, it might be what
the man was killed for. But what were you laughing at?"

"Well, you see, I thought it was just an ordinary letter, and I
couldn't make out who this niece was."

Wharton peered at her roguishly over the top of his glasses.
"You mean you thought I'd been leading a double life. Which
reminds me. Before I forget it, you might make a note that a Dr.
Hule and his wife are coming here to dinner with us to-morrow
night. I fixed it over the phone."

"George! you don't mean that you want me to—"

Wharton raised a placatory hand. "Nothing of the sort, my
dear. I don't want you to do any spying or tattling. All I want you
to do is to be yourself. Of course"—with the faintest shrug—"if
you like to tell me afterwards what you make of them, that'd be
only the sort of thing any people would discuss when the guests
have gone. Now about that letter. I've got a perfectly open mind
myself, and there's no catch anywhere. Have a real good look at
it, and say what you think—who wrote it, what it means, and
so on."

"Well, it's common enough paper. I should say it was bought at Woolworth's."

"Are there Woolworths in Italy?"

"Italy?" The address showed her what he meant. "Oh, I think there are. I believe they've got branches all over Europe." Her eyes had still been on that address, and all at once she began shaking her head. "It's a funny sort of heading, don't you think? Putting the name of a biggish place like Assisi and nothing else; no street number or anything?"

"Maybe Uncle knew it already."

She held it out at arm's length. "I don t know. It looks wrong to me. I don't know why it does. It looks bald—and bare."

Wharton nodded. "And what would you make of Ethel?"

"Ethel? Oh, just a silly little flapper or a servant-girl. The style's servant-girlish."

"Funny," said Wharton, and surveyed the ceiling reminiscently, "but I happened this afternoon to ask the opinion of a very clever man—I might say a very clever man indeed—and he said something about a servant-girl too."

"Really?" She was pleased about that, and began to explain. "You see, there's that bit about going home for two days, and going to the pictures—and the expressions she uses."

Wharton nodded again. "And the actual words. What's she driving at, precisely? Take, for instance, the fact that she's in Italy. Why isn't she telling her uncle all about the wonders of the place, and so on?"

Mrs. Wharton sat up and frowned. "If she's in Italy she must be an Italian. How else could she have two days at home? She wouldn't go back all the way to England to stay two days and then come back again!"

Wharton beamed approval. "Good for you, Jane! Still, why shouldn't she be an Italian?"

"What?—and write like this?" She smiled. "You're supposed to speak French like a native—as people say—but you couldn't say the same sentence over in French in the different accents and styles that all sorts of people would say it in—like a society woman, a gendarme, a grocer, a schoolgirl and so on."

"You're right enough there," admitted Wharton. "But *is* it a question of accent or dialect?"

"I think it is. I'd bet a new hat Ethel's a Cockney. I can't say exactly why, but she reads like it."

It was on the tip of his tongue to say he had thought the same thing himself, but he kept it back.

"Do you know, I'm rather inclined to agree. A Cockney from Soho, perhaps. And what do you make of Albert?"

But there was not sufficient of Albert to make anything of. He might have been a cousin or a mutual friend.

"It's that first 'but' that worries me," confessed Wharton. "Ethel is to go home for two days, and then it says—*but* Albert knows. Albert is, in other words, to carry on. Carry on with what? Then there's something of the same sort farther along. Ethel goes to the pictures and Albert carries on in her absence. Also, it rather reads as if Ethel didn't like going to the pictures. Curious, don't you think, for a girl like Ethel?"

Jane Wharton went off at an amazing tangent. "You know, if only it said *The Assisi* instead of *Assisi*, it'd be ever so much easier."

"*The Assisi*," repeated Wharton slowly. He stared. "You mean a hotel—the one in Kensington Avenue, for instance."

She almost clapped her hands. "That'd fit in perfectly. Don't you see it? Suppose she *is* a servant-girl; a maid it'd have to be. She's gone up to London with her mistress, and her mistress thinks she could have two days at home while they're up there. Ethel says that if she does have two days at home, Albert will—" She broke off in the most amazing way, and her face was all at once strangely serious. "I don't think this is a very nice letter, somehow."

Their eyes met, and Wharton nodded slowly. "I've just had the same idea. Of course it mayn't be right. You stay here a minute or two and I'll be back again."

It was a quarter of an hour before he was back, and then he said nothing of what he had been doing—other than ordering what he called a nice cup of tea. A waiter brought in teapot and two cups, and as Wharton stirred the copious sugar well in, he carried on with the conversation where it had been broken off.

"Just tell me what's in your mind, my dear. You think this letter has something to do with blackmail?"

"I'm sure of it."

He grunted. "Hm! As you say, it fits in. It fits in with the middle cut of salmon!"

"The middle cut of salmon!"

He explained. What had been written diagonally across the bottom of that letter showed that the recipient had hopes of making quite a good thing out of it. Times had apparently been hard and small profits had been taken, but here was a regular windfall.

"I hate blackmailers more than murderers," Jane Wharton said viciously. "Who do you think's mixed up with it, George? Not that doctor and his wife who're coming here to-morrow?"

"There's no telling," Wharton told her enigmatically. "And by the way, there was something else scribbled at the foot of that letter." He consulted his note-book. "Just two sets of figures and letters. Here, let me write them down for you."

She said them over aloud. "R.C. One o five, and B.C. thirty-three. The last's like history, isn't it?"

"And R.C. might be Roman Catholic."

"What about gramophone records? There're the letters in front of them, like 'Columbia three three' or 'Imperial one two'?"

"Imperial one two." His eyes narrowed. "I've got a better idea than that. What about telephone numbers?"

He was so sure that his hand went to the bell. The waiter was asked to bring the local directories, and apologized profusely because they were not allowed to be taken away from the call-desk.

"All right," said Mrs. Wharton, full of the adventure, "well go to the mountain if it can't come here."

The girl at the desk was a help, but it was the hunting through for numbers, rather than names, that took all the time. But they found what they wanted.

GIVERS, Colonel, D.S.O., The Manor, Rawley Chase. CHASE 105.

RAPPWAY, Captain, Little Gables, Badgham Chase. CHASE 33.

A minute after that discovery they were back in the drawing-room, poring excitedly over the letter.

"It's as plain as the back of your hand," said Wharton. "If there's a woman in the case, and it's twenty to one there is, she's the H. M. G., which might be Helen Mary Givers. The C. R.'s the Captain Rappway. Now aren't you going to ask me to tell you how clever you are?"

Jane Wharton shook her head. "I don't feel like being pleased—somehow. I think it's disgusting." She leaned forward quickly. "Tell me, George. Who's this horrible man, Albert?"

"I don't know," Wharton told her, "but I'll know by the morning. I got hold of town, but the trouble was there're two Assisis out of the way enough to suit the circumstances. We're making inquiries there now, I reckon—only you've got to be devilish discreet with hotels."

She noted the somewhat restless stirring in the chair. "You're not going out again to-night?"

"No," said Wharton ruminatively, "I don't know that I am. I'll have to look up the map, though, to see the best way to these couple of Chases. Quaint names they have in these parts, don't you think?" He gave a little chuckle. "I wonder what Tempest and Carry make of the show to-night. *Richard the Second*, isn't it? Bloody enough, if my memory's right. By the way, what was your idea of that actor, the one who did Cæsar?"

She thought for a moment or two. "I don't think I'd call him too good. Good enough for Seaborough, perhaps, but—well, he hadn't quite got something he ought to have had, if you understand what I mean. Very good-looking, though—and a very fine voice."

"Hm!" went Wharton. "Perhaps Tempest'll drop in after it's over and tell us all about it. I shouldn't be surprised if he slips out well before the end." Then his eyes opened and he strained to listen.

Mrs. Wharton sat up too. The door was opening and the waiter was talking to somebody. Jane Wharton caught sight of the elongated figure behind him, and a smile of the completest pleasure came over her face. Then Wharton saw the figure, and his eyes popped still wider open.

"Good Lord! If it isn't Mr. Travers!"

CHAPTER VIII
MORE RUSTIC REVELS

LUDOVIC TRAVERS had had an offer for his Bentley, and with the idea of doing his bit towards stimulating trade, had completed the deal and bought a fine new Rolls. Wharton was taken in it to Homedale that morning, and when they got there, only Polegate was on the job. Carry was apparently laying his plans for the undoing of Howard Trench, but inside five minutes Tempest was along. Wharton let him in, and Travers was in the dining-room.

"They told me you'd gone," he said. "And what's that palatial car doing on the front door-step?"

Wharton put a finger to his lips and craned over to whisper. "A Mr. Travers. A friend of mine. Come in and be introduced."

"This is the Chief Constable, Major Tempest," Wharton said. "Mr. Ludovic Travers—a nephew of the Chief Commissioner, by the way—though you needn't hold that against him."

Tempest had expected to find some sort of lounge lizard. What he sensed was a delightful personality and a sureness that spoke of fine breeding.

"Really?" he said. "I used to know Sir George very well. How's he keeping these days?"

"Pretty fair," said Travers, "in spite of the cares of office. Uneasy lies the head, you know."

Tempest smiled. He was already liking the elongated gentleman in the horn rims. "I suppose you're not a detective by any chance?"

"I? Good Lord, no! I'm a public menace." Tempest cocked his head sideways.

"A company director, in other words," explained Travers, "but you needn't hold that against me either."

Wharton took a hand. Travers had a sister not so far away, and usually spent the week-ends at her place. This particular week-end was to be longer than usual, as he had read the papers.

"To put it bluntly," said Wharton, "he's come along to poke his nose in. You can't get rid of him, and so you'll have to put up with him."

"If my few wits weren't fuddled after sitting up yarning with you till the early hours, I'd have thought of something clever to say to that." He took off his horn-rims and began a careful polish. "You're a lover of the theatre, they tell me, major."

Tempest almost blushed. "So Wharton's been talking, has he?"

"What did you think of him?" asked Wharton shamelessly.

"Howard Trench? Well, to tell the truth, I thought he was a damn fine actor. Otherwise the night was wasted."

"Don't say that," protested Wharton. "The tired brain must rest, you know. Now this morning you're all fresh and bright."

"Never mind about me," said Tempest. "What are you proposing to do yourself?"

"Another little trip out Bicklesham way," said Wharton, and with never a blush. "And talking of Rennyet, Mr. Travers brought with him some of that publicity information from the Yard. He's the son of Lord-knows-who; public school and Oxford and the whole boiling. Got plenty of money, I should judge, and does literary work from a sense of his duty to his public. And now for the big laugh. What do you think his name is?"

Tempest looked surprised. "Why, Raymond Rennyet, of course."

Wharton smiled. "The Raymond's a pen name. His real name is—well, I'd rather you guessed. Give you fifty goes and bet you half a crown you don't get it."

"Get it be damned," said Tempest. "What is it?"

"Aloysius Ringold Rennyet," said Wharton solemnly. "No wonder he didn't want to stagger over Parnassus with a handle like that!"

"And the other night," said Travers, "he had the fortitude to celebrate his birthday."

Then Carry came in and was introduced. He hinted darkly that there were things he had found out at the previous night's show, and when pressed for details, took refuge in more vagueness.

"A fellow who can act as he can—well, it'd be child's play to do what I think he did."

"Hope he did, is what you mean," said Wharton, who was that morning in jocular vein. "By the way, what did you two think of that suggestion I left with you—about Hule?"

"He has his points," said Tempest. "The trouble is, we found more against than for."

"Well, what've you got against him?"

"The chief objection is this," said Carry. "When he phoned to his wife—that is, imagining it was him—he'd have known about the little jokes Lewton used to have with her, because he knew them."

"He told us about them," said Tempest.

"And another thing, sir, do you think he'd have had the nerve to imitate anybody else's voice—I mean, to his own wife?—to the one person in the world who'd have recognized him if he made the least slip?"

Wharton rubbed his chin. "They're good objections. Still, Hule and his wife are dining with me and my wife to-night, and we'd like you to drop in, Tempest. Sorry we can't have you, Carry, but it'd look a bit too obvious. Anybody claiming yet to be a relation of Lewton?"

"Never a soul," said Tempest. "Still, I'm seeing the press this morning, and I'll ask them to keep on repeating." He laughed.

"I suppose I'll have to trot out the old favourite—that the police hope very shortly to make an arrest."

"You're not to tell them," said Wharton, "*but it'd be true all the same.*"

Tempest stared at him. "You really think . . ."

"I don't think, I know," said Wharton. "I'm open to bet that before this day's out, you make an arrest."

"George, you're not being a little gentleman," said Travers. "Didn't you learn at mother's knee that it was wrong to bet on certainties?"

"So you're in the know too?" Tempest nodded to Carry. "You hear that? We mustn't let out a word, but before the day's over there'll be an arrest." Then he smiled winningly at Travers. "Who is it going to be? Let us in on it."

"To be absolutely honest," said Travers, "I haven't the faintest notion."

"But you said it was a certainty! How'd you know that?"

"Very easily," said Travers, taking off his glasses. "It had to be a certainty, because I've never known George Wharton bet on anything else."

The Rolls took the last slope into Bicklesham, and Travers kept his eyes averted and trod on the accelerator, as Wharton directed. But there needn't have been any panic, for never a soul was visible in Rennyet's garden. Half a mile on, they turned into the village, with its fine old inn and spacious green. Two miles on, the car still leaving main roads and turning well inland, came another village, and a long two miles after that was Badgham Chase.

"Go steady and watch out for a pub," said Wharton. "Then draw up outside."

As he spoke, Travers caught sight of the Coach and Horses. It was not long after opening time and the private bar was deserted. Wharton, squaring his shoulders, now looked like a commercial traveller of the prosperous sort. Travers, coat unintentionally open and displaying the fur lining, was not unlike a university don who tries a gay and surreptitious life and finds it enjoyable.

"What's yours, George?"

"Irish hot," said Wharton promptly.

"Don't you know it's wrong to start the circulation too violently," said Travers reprovingly. "Two beers, landlord, and a third for yourself."

"Thankee, sir," said the landlord. "You gentlemen strangers here?"

"For the moment," said Travers enigmatically. "Rather muddling, isn't it, these two Chases of yours?"

The landlord smiled. "Not if you take 'em as one, sir, which is what we all do about here. They are one, really."

"Captain Rappway still living here?" asked Wharton.

The landlord looked surprised. "Why, he ain't been here long enough to move yet, sir. How long would it be?" The question had been put to himself, and he provided his own answer. "About last Michaelmas time."

"Quite close, isn't it?"

"There you are, sir." The landlord pointed at what could only be the superbly timbered house that overlooked the narrow strip of village green. A wealthy man's house it looked. It had that trim and expensive air, and there seemed to be extensive gardens with it.

"Let me see," said Wharton, with a prodigious frown. "Didn't my old friend, Brown, live there before Rappway took it?"

"Brown, sir? I don't know any Brown. A Major Millison had it."

Wharton gave a cunning click of the tongue. "Millison, that's the fellow." He glared at Travers. "How'd I come to mix him up with Brown?" Then he took a swig at the glass. "Colonel Givers still at the Manor?"

"Well, he's away at the moment," the landlord said, and followed with a shake of the head. "The old colonel hasn't been looking very well lately."

"He's not so old as that, surely," pooh-poohed Wharton.

"Depends what you mean by old. I'll bet he's an older man than me, and I shan't see sixty-five again."

"Really!" said Wharton, and appeared so shocked that he finished the glass unknowingly.

Travers was enjoying it hugely. He always loved Wharton's antics, and now he caught the landlord's eye for a refilling of bitter.

"Mrs. Givers is a much younger woman," observed Wharton.

"She's his second, you know."

"So I believe," said Wharton. "Let me see now. Who was she before she married him?"

"Why, old Lord Cannister's daughter; him what have that big estate over Heathersham way. The Honourable Mavis is what we call her."

"A bit of a fast-mover?" said Wharton, with an infinity of innuendo in his raised eyebrows.

"Oh, she's all right," said the landlord indifferently. "Bit on the high-and-mighty side."

"Good-looking?"

"Not what you and me might call good-looking. Still, there's no accounting for tastes, sir. She knows how to dress; I will say that for her."

"Nothing like a well-dressed woman," said Wharton, and, "Give me a box of those matches." Behind the landlord's back he gave a nod in the direction of the door.

"Have another bitter," said Travers.

"No, not for me." He wiped his moustache. "We'd better be getting along or we'll be late."

Travers took his seat and let out the clutch. "Once upon a time I wanted to be an engine-driver," he remarked. "My chief ambition nowadays, George, is to lie with half your fluency."

Wharton looked at him. "Well, we got what we wanted, didn't we? And we got it quick." He pointed to the gate just off the road. "I'd draw right in if I were you. And you'd better do the talking. Millison's the name."

"Thanks," said Travers dryly.

But just inside the short drive Wharton clutched his knee. Before the door stood a sports car, Cambridge-blue in colour—a powerful car and not a cheap one. And as the Rolls drew up, out of the door came a man with two cockers at his heels. He looked about thirty-five; lean, tanned, military and damnably superior. Travers leaned out.

"Pardon me, but is Millison in?"

He ran a quick eye over Travers before answering. Then he smiled. "I'm afraid Millison's been gone some time. I believe he's living in Worcestershire. I bought this place from him some months ago"

"I say, I'm most amazingly sorry."

"That's all right," smiled Rappway. "Awful good car you've got here."

"Yours looks a pretty fast chap," countered Travers.

"I don't know," said Rappway diffidently. "I wouldn't like to race you a straight mile for the two. Bit cold this morning, isn't it?"

Travers said it was, apologized once more, and moved the car off. As soon as they were out in the road again he caught Wharton's little grunt.

"Everything working out all right, George?"

"Rather too right," said Wharton. "Don't stop to ask the way. I shouldn't be surprised if that chap is squinting round his drive gate."

But in half a minute they had dipped to a small valley along which straggled the cottages of the Chase villages, and there was no need to ask for the Manor, for it stood plainly ahead—a noble Tudor building, all mellow with years and twisted quaintly with age. A tall yew hedge sheltered it from the road, from which it stood back a bare twenty yards. Wharton touched Travers's knee.

"You come in with me and speak only if I appeal to you. Back me up through thick and thin."

The car turned into the crescent of the drive and drew up before the line of steps that led to the front door. The two got out, but the ancient oak door was already open, and a butler was peering out at them.

"Is Mrs. Givers in?" asked Wharton.

"I'll see, sir. Who might it be, sir?"

"She wouldn't know if you told her," said Wharton quietly. "Tell her it's rather important."

They waited in a charmingly furnished lounge, and almost before they were ready for her, Mrs. Givers came in.

"How do you do?" A quick, appraising look followed on her smile.

She had a remarkable face, Travers thought. Feature by feature it was ugly. The mouth was large, the cheek-bones high, and the eyes set too deeply. Yet it was a fascinating face, full of character and rare elusiveness, and the voice was fresh and curiously modern. Wharton guessed her age as thirty-two or three.

"You'll pardon me," said Wharton, and closed the door behind her. "I'm not too anxious for your people to know either who I am or what I'm here for." He handed her his official card. "As you see, Mrs. Givers, I'm Superintendent Wharton of Scotland Yard. Mr. Travers is one of our consulting experts."

She gave a little smile. "I'm afraid I don't understand."

"You will do in a moment or two, madam," Wharton told her quietly. "But in your own interests, I'd like you to assure us that we can't possibly be overheard." He glanced over at the far door. "Perhaps there might be another room . . . ?"

The poise had gone. Her smile was now a sort of foolish titter. "Well, if you really wish it. It's my husband's study, when he's at home. I'm afraid he's away now."

"If I hadn't known that, we shouldn't be here now," Wharton observed, with the same frightening reticence.

He waved her to a seat, and then all at once his face softened. He was now a father. He knew the temptations of the world and the weakness of the flesh, and the mind that could understand could sympathize and pardon. His elbows were on his knees and he was leaning forward with a kind of wistful pity.

"Mrs. Givers, I believe you're far too fine a woman to deny what I'm going to tell you, or to trick us out with lies. In the same way, I give you my word that we're here solely to help you.

Whatever is said in this room shall go no farther without your express permission."

Her hands fidgeted nervously in her lap.

"You've doubtless read the papers? About the death of a man named Lewton?"

"Well"—she stammered—"well, I did see it. I mean, as one sees the papers, and . . ."

"Thank you, Mrs. Givers. Then you know why we're here. You were one of the last people to see Lewton alive—although it was morning when you saw him and night when he died. Tell us, will you, just what happened when you saw him?"

Lies, protestations, and ultimately tears—those were the things that Wharton had anticipated. But this woman was different. She looked at him for a few hesitating moments before she spoke, and her voice had never a tremor.

"You were quite sincere when you said this. . . . this talk would be confidential?"

Travers leaned forward with his most charming smile. "Pardon me, Mrs. Givers, but Superintendent Wharton gave you his word."

She smiled, just the least bit wanly. "Yes, of course he did. What was it you wanted to know?"

"Just what happened between you and Lewton," said Wharton.

She shook her head. "I'm afraid I can't tell you that."

Wharton looked grieved. "That's a terrible pity. You see, this morning there has been a formal inquest on the body of Lewton. Next week, early, there will be a much more ornate affair. You, for instance, will be summoned to attend and give your evidence under oath and in public. You'll be *forced* to answer whatever questions I care to put to you then. We three can talk everything over now and never a soul will be any the wiser. But a public inquiry; think of it, Mrs. Givers; the papers, the scandal—just the very things, in fact, that we're here to help you avoid."

"Will you answer me one question?"

"Twenty, madam."

"Then what do *you* know about any connection between—between that man and myself? How do I know you're not trying to trap me into some admission?"

Wharton smiled wearily. "Mrs. Givers—please! Haven't I daughters of my own? Do I look as if I was trying to trap you? Can I promise more than I have done already?" He raised his hands and let them fall. "I might as well say that you're trying to trap me. Still, you'd like to know what we know. You're wondering if we know why you wanted your maid to have two days at home, and why she was sent to the cinema when Captain Rappway called at the hotel."

She was staring. "My maid? Who says my maid had anything to do with it?"

Wharton spread his hands. "There you are. You see the folly of keeping things back? Tell me, Mrs. Givers, did Lewton show you a letter when you saw him—or did he keep it in his own hand?"

She moistened her lips before she spoke. "He took it from the safe and pretended to read from it."

"And he asked how much, for silence?"

"Five hundred pounds."

"I see." He frowned. "A bad business. Naturally Captain Rappway thought it worth while to have a go at the safe before you were forced to pay."

"You know that, do you?"

"My dear lady," broke in Travers, "don't you realize that we're on your side? If you won't tell us everything without reservations, how can we possibly get you out of the really dangerous situation in which you actually are?"

Wharton spread his hands again. "We're not interested in morals. What happened between you and a certain gentleman is your own affair. Lewton's the man we're interested in—and the one who murdered him. Even Captain Rappway, for instance."

"But Captain Rappway didn't know till late that night."

"Now we're coming to it," said Wharton, and drew his chair in closer. "Start at the beginning, Mrs. Givers, from where you first heard from Lewton."

"Well, he rang me up here. I'd no idea who the man was till he told me. Then he began to make insinuations and say he had some writing of mine and I was to come and see him. So I . . . I did go and see him."

"What day was this exactly?"

"On Tuesday afternoon he rang me up."

"I see. And no insinuation on my part, Mrs. Givers, but your husband was away then?"

"Yes, he was. He's staying in Devonshire." She flushed slightly. "You understand, don't you, that I didn't admit any of these disgraceful charges by going to see that man. Only, if he'd gone to my husband with tales, there might have been unpleasantness."

Wharton was ready to admit anything provided she got on with her story. Lewton, it appeared, had brought out a sheet of paper from the safe, and a small book. The former was undoubtedly Ethel's letter, and the latter Albert's notes and observations, keyhole and otherwise. Lewton's price for dropping out of the matter was five hundred pounds, and he boasted that he had never let a customer down. There would be no blackmail. Once the first and only sum was paid, the affair would pass from his memory.

Mrs. Givers had said nothing to Captain Rappway till after her return from Seaborough, and that she swore. Her reasons were that the whole business came as a thunderclap, and that she was wholly ignorant of what the hold could be which Lewton had over her. Also she had no idea of alarming Rappway with what might turn out to be only a trifle. That evening, however, he had dined at the Manor with three other guests, and then she had told him. She admitted that but for the fact that he had been out shooting all day, she would have called at his house on her way back from Seaborough.

Wharton looked serious. "You'd be prepared to swear in a court of law that Captain Rappway had never heard of Lewton till after the time he was murdered?"

"I would." She nodded determinedly. "Even if I didn't, he could prove he was miles away at the time."

"You've discussed the matter together," Wharton observed with a casual wave of the hand. "But it's a pity you didn't go to the police as soon as Lewton threatened you. The police would have been your best friends, as—if I may say it—we are now. You'll allow us to see your maid?—in your presence, naturally."

That rather alarmed her till Wharton pointed things out. If she merely gave the maid notice, she would be free to carry out a blackmailing campaign of her own, or at the least to make mischief with Colonel Givers.

"Give me a free hand," said Wharton, "and I'll guarantee you freedom from worry. You have your maid sent in by that door, and you remain in the lounge with the other door open. You'll hear what we say, and when you are wanted you can make a sudden appearance, as it were."

The maid came trippingly in, and she gave a little start and a giggle when she saw the two men.

"Oh, I'm sorry. I thought madam was here."

Wharton stepped in behind her and closed the door. Then he moved his chair in front of it, while she watched him with a frightened puzzlement. Travers, chair before the other door, watched her with unblinking eyes, and she must have thought she had to do with a couple of madmen.

"We're the police," announced Wharton, and her face coloured violently. "Sit down, will you? Your name's Ethel?"

She nodded, eyes still staring.

"You wrote this letter?" He gave it to her. "Only a copy, by the way."

She shook her head before she had scarcely seen it. "I didn't. I don't know anything about it."

She looked the fluffy, flat-witted sort, and Wharton was not disposed to waste much time over sparing feelings.

"Let me see," he said to Travers; "the last case we had of a maid attempting to blackmail her mistress, what was it she got? Five years, was it, or six?"

"One or the other," said Travers. "Albert, of course, will be lucky to get off with ten."

"Yes, there's Albert," said Wharton ruminatively. Then he looked up mildly. "What's your surname?"

"Peeton."

"I see. Then, Miss Ethel Peeton, as you don't seem minded to tell us the truth here, you'd better get your box packed and come along with us."

Now she was scared stiff. "What are you going to do?"

"We're doing nothing," said Wharton offhandedly. "We're just going to take you for a nice ride to Seaborough police-station."

Five and twenty minutes later, Wharton and Travers were saying good-bye to a slightly reassured Mavis Givers. Ethel was leaving at once, and her home address had been taken. But her mistress had no intention of sacrificing herself on the altar of public duty. In spite of all Wharton's assurances of secrecy, she refused to bring a charge. Travers had tried his own cajolements; Wharton had wheedled and threatened, but the lady refused to budge. What was more, she trusted, she said, to Wharton's own promises, and the public could go hang.

But the parting was amiable enough, and inside five minutes the Rolls was drawing up again at Little Gables, where Captain Rappway was about to sit down to lunch. It was half an hour after that that Wharton called up Tempest on the post-office phone.

"Something most urgent to be done. Get the Yard and say they're to move in the matter of Albert, and rush a statement through to Seaborough police-station at once. And have Beece at the police-station by two-thirty. If he asks why, or whether he's under arrest, tell him he'll be told when he gets there."

"Beece!" The astonishment came clearly over the line. "But he had the best alibi of all."

"Oh, you're talking about that other business," said Wharton blandly. "This is something new. . . . What's that? I offered to bet there'd be an arrest? . . . Well, there's time yet, isn't there? And who said anything about murder, in any case?"

"George," said Travers in mild reproof, when the General had hung up again, "is there nothing you can do without a stratagem?"

Wharton's retort was lost to the world, for as he closed the call-box door, his eye fell on a bill which the local bill-sticker was at that moment pasting on the wall against which the kiosk stood. It was the word Bicklesham that drew his attention. Travers, fearing a splash of paste on the body of the Rolls, had a look too.

It was a dramatic performance that the bill announced, for Good Friday afternoon and evening, and again on the Easter Monday. *Everyman* was the play, and at the bottom—a fact to which Wharton's nod drew Travers's attention—appeared the name of Rennyet as honorary secretary and stage manager.

The man had completed the pasting up of a second bill—of a local auction—and was mounting his bicycle when Wharton spoke to him.

"Are you a Chase man?"

The man grinned. "Not me, sir. I'm a Bicklesham man."

"And proud of it too," said Wharton, with a raising of eyebrows. "This is the first time you've had plays in the village hall?"

"No, sir. Last Easter was the first time. Mr. Rennyet, he got it up, the same as he's doing this one."

"Pretty good at it, is he?"

"Well, so they say, sir. I don't know much about it myself."

"Rennyet." Wharton turned to Travers with a slight frown. "Haven't we met him somewhere? Does he do any acting himself, by the way?"

"Oh, yes; he allust take part himself," the man said. "In fact, they reckon that if it wasn't for him there wouldn't be anything of the sort."

Wharton smiled. "Sort of head cook and bottle-washer, eh?"

They watched him mount his bicycle and ride off.

Travers turned amusedly to Wharton. "What on earth is the good of grubbing down into all those petty details, George? Even if he is an actor—of sorts—Rennyet couldn't have been imitating people's voices at Seaborough and having his dinner at Bicklesham at the same time!"

Wharton nodded heavily as he got in the car. "I know. Still, you'll admit it's funny. Everybody we come up against in this case has a hundred-per-cent alibi. Look at Rappway. What a motive he had!—all the-woman-I-love, he-man, protect-you-at-the-cost-of-my-life stuff, and his alibi is the best we've got yet. And even if he hadn't one at all, he's out of the question. He couldn't possibly have had all the inside information the murderer had to have."

Travers slipped into top gear. "What about the Honourable Mrs. G.? A fascinating woman and most unblushing." He smiled to himself. "I could make up the most attractive theory, you know, George? For instance, she must have known Rennyet. In her trouble she must have remembered him as a writer of detective novels. She might have gone to him for advice. Between them they might easily have doctored something up—"

"The most sensible thing you've said for some time," broke in Wharton.

"But I haven't finished!" protested Travers.

"There's no need to," he was told. "It's that word *doctored* I was thinking of. You've shown me a ray of hope, as the poet says. Dr. Hule is the only one whose alibi hasn't been inquired into."

CHAPTER IX
RE-ENTER HULE

AT TWO-THIRTY there was still no message from Scotland Yard, and Wharton left Beece to cool his heels and work himself into a hot sweat for another quarter of an hour. Then Wharton said he would wait no longer. He had enough information and bluff could do the rest.

Tempest, Carry and Travers entered the room at his heels. Wharton took the desk seat and Carry took the door. Beece was already like a jelly. His lips were drooling into his beard and his hands were all a-twitch. Wharton looked at him with a long, cold sneer before he spoke.

"A blackmailer, eh? Made a regular business of it, did you? And put us off with lies." He surveyed his colleagues. "He didn't know anything about Lewton, gentlemen. He was just a friend who came to play cribbage. He didn't open Lewton's safe—oh dear, no!"

The irony was wasted. Beece was beaten, and it was plain to see it. Scaring him further might have kept him from talking, and the blubbered tears were not far off.

"Don't start that snivelling again," Wharton told him. "We're used to that sort of thing. We've got hearts like flint when we're dealing with rats like you. And we've got two excellent witnesses and we expect more at any minute. Still, we'll confine ourselves to what we'll call your middle cut of salmon; the lady who was indiscreet at the Assisi Hotel, and the opportune presence of a maid and a waiter. Perhaps you'd prefer, however, to make your own statement, and if so I'll just read you over the official caution."

"I don't know what statement you want me to make," was Beece's last show of defence.

Wharton sprang up in a rage. "Let's get out of this. Charge him and lock him up. Get an appeal printed in to-night's papers for anybody else he's blackmailed—or used—to come forward. Go down to his precious domestic agency and seal the place up. Search it under a warrant, and his house too."

That was the end of Beece, and Wharton grudgingly sat down again. Then, while they waited for the stenographer to come in, the telephone bell went and Wharton heard a few things about Albert. From what he let fall and from what he invented, Beece knew precisely where the wind lay. But it took over an hour's catechizing to arrive at what Wharton felt something near the truth.

According to Beece, he had met Lewton in a bar-parlour one night just after Lewton's return to Seaborough, and had got into conversation. The two became friendly, and it had been Lewton who had suggested a further use for that servants' employment agency which Beece owned, and which was then in rather a bad way.

All the time Beece was slavering and slobbering and as good as on his knees.

"I didn't want to do it, gentlemen; God's my witness I didn't, only he made me. He got me in such a hole I couldn't get out of it."

"All right," sneered Wharton. "We know all that. Poor erring sheep, eh? Never took a penny, did you?"

But there was a certain amount of complicity which Beece had to admit, and with that as foundation it was easy enough to see the working of the scheme which Lewton was supposed to have propounded. Beece's office, situated as it was in a hotel and superior residential district, was particularly suitable for the founding of a blackmailing organization. Beece ran his eye over all likely persons for whom employment was found, and out of the hundreds, there were constantly one or two whom it seemed safe to approach. A hint was enough; the suggestion, for instance, that Mr. Beece could use and pay handsomely for information of a particular kind.

The scheme, moreover, was a safe one. The one who is blackmailed has always been the obstacle in the way of justice. Beece could choose those who dared not squeal. There was also a kind of blackmail at both ends. Those who desperately need employment may make no bones about the conditions under which they take it. And all the employee had to do was to address a letter to Beece's house; a chatty letter masking information with oddments of news. Beece thereupon sent the letters to Lewton, who handled the thumb-screw side. Lewton's existence was unknown to the informant, and he dealt with principals only.

The Givers-Rappway affair was now clear as daylight. The firm of Lewton and Beece had had a bit of luck in that a waiter of theirs—Ethel's friend Albert—had also been employed at the Assisi. Perhaps that was why Beece had reported the case to his partner as a middle cut of salmon. But clear as the affair was, it helped little towards the discovery of the murderer, unless that murderer had been a previous victim of the blackmailing pair.

"What we shall want from you," said Wharton, "is a list of everybody with whom you've done business. Don't tell me you've forgotten, or burnt all the papers. And now you'll tell us just what happened on Wednesday night."

Beece found that easy enough. For one thing he had only to tell the truth, and to confess the doings of that night was like owning up to some minor peccadillo. The message Lewton had given over the phone was that there was a chance of big business, and that the informer was waiting at Homedale, where Beece was to come at once.

"Man or woman?" asked Wharton.

"I don't know," Beece told him. "He simply mentioned whoever it was as 'the one we can do business with.' I was to go straight up and the front door would be open for me to walk in, and I'd find them in the dining-room."

And that was what Beece had done. But when he had seen Lewton lying dead, he had lost his head to the extent of a minute's panic. Then he had picked up the knife, and while he had it in his hand he had thought of the safe which held enough evidence to put him in jail for the best part of a lifetime. The knife still in his hand, he had rushed into the drawing-room and had found the safe open and everything gone.

"That doesn't look unlike our friend R.," said Wharton. "If so, he left behind him the very letter he wanted, and that may have been what he came back for. Still, go on with your story, Beece."

But there was no more story to go on with—except the letter. Beece now owned he had found it on the floor by the safe, and had laid it on the table while he hid the knife. Then in his panic he had forgotten it, and after he had gone the draught of the opened door must have blown the letter to where Polegate found it.

"Right," said Wharton. "Now we'll meet you to this extent. Your wife know anything about all this blackmailing business of yours?"

Beece's horrified look was the answer.

"All right then," Wharton told him. "You'll be allowed to call her up from here to say that you're helping the police, and may not be home for maybe even a day or so. We'll verify it. What you're going to do is to get out a complete list of all your clients, ever since your business started. When we've got that we'll think things over. If you do as you're told—and if you decide to retire from the domestic agency line—we may keep you out of jail; unless one of your customers decides to lay a charge."

At the door Wharton halted him.

"Just one other thing. Was old Trench in on this?"

"Well, he wasn't—really—"

"But he was." Wharton finished the sentence for him. "He was doing a little private blackmailing of you two on his own, was he?"

According to Beece, it was hardly that. Trench found out what was going on, and Lewton suggested that he ought to be kept on the right side. The placating of Trench was done by keeping him on at Homedale, and the paying of his wife's expenses and Trench's weekly visits. He also had had his wages increased from the original ninety to a hundred a year, and continued to draw the full amount even when his wife was taken ill. He had, moreover, been promised a fine, fat sum in the event of either his master or Beece dying.

Beece was handed over to Polegate, and Carry came back. Evidently he had been doing some private thinking in the interval.

"You really think it was Rappway, sir?"

"Yes," said Wharton, and immediately qualified it. "If we're working on the principle of the best alibi, that is. Rappway was out all that day rough-shooting with people six miles the far side of his house. He didn't leave till a quarter to seven, and he called in his man, who verified that his master arrived at seven o'clock, and then he had to get dressed at once for dinner at the Manor. If that isn't a good alibi, I don't know what is. Also, when you come to work things out, he didn't have the special knowledge that was absolutely necessary."

"Don't forget those prints for town," Travers reminded him.

Lewton's prints were sent off at once. There was just a hope that they might be recorded, though Wharton was inclined to the belief that it was in the colonies that most of his life had been spent.

"Now let's hear that news of yours again," he said to Carry. "I haven't had time to digest it yet."

Carry's news referred to Howard Trench. The man he had planted in the morning rendezvous of Trench and his friends, had picked up a surprising amount of gossip. Himself an old actor, he had known the jargon, and how to draw a conversation round.

The first thing he had learned—or, rather, verified, for he had been aware of it before—was that the touring company itself was not the best of its kind. Howard Trench might be a big noise, but it was in a small band. He was popular enough among his colleagues, but not really liked. He was inclined to give himself airs, and to mention a London engagement as something which he could have for the stretching out of a hand.

As for his private affairs, they were not as private as he imagined. He was separated from his wife, to whom he had to make an allowance. There was also known to be another woman, who often appeared discreetly in towns where the company was on tour. Howard Trench was, in fact, hard up, and he made little secret of it. And far more to the point, Carry could produce a couple of witnesses who would swear that before coming to Seaborough, Howard Trench had spoken of the town as a likely source of income.

"Just a moment," said Wharton. "We don't want to get involved. How did he speak of it? What were the words used?"

"That's the very thing I was coming to, sir," said Carry. "He did it with a sort of wink. You know, sort of 'you-wait-and-see-till-we-get-to-Seaborough' sort of business. You see, he owed money to one or two, and he promised definitely he'd pay everything off by the time they left here."

Tempest shrugged his shoulders. "I still think he was referring to his uncle."

"How should he know his uncle had money, sir? You don't expect people like him to have much."

"Well, you keep on with your inquiries," said Wharton. "Get an idea how much he owed. And don't forget you've got to work fast. Howard Trench will be here for the inquest resumption, but the others won't." He put his glasses back in their case and got to his feet. "I suppose you all realize that we've got some spade work to do now. Every name that Beece produces will have to be inquired into—and it will have to be tactfully done. Even then I doubt whether we shall get anything."

"But surely," smiled Tempest. "I mean, we virtually know now that the man who killed Lewton was one of his victims. If not, why did he try to catch Beece at the same time?"

"And old Trench, too," added Carry.

"That's my very point," said Wharton. "I should say that most of the victims lived well out of Seaborough. After any scandal—or the fear of it—people would get as far away as possible, even if they were living here. What we want is someone who's been living in Seaborough; someone who grubbed down deep enough to find out that Lewton and Beece were in partnership, and someone who knew every detail of Lewton's household. Someone, in fact, who meets every essential we put down on our papers when we had our first conference."

Tempest was shaking his head. "And what if he has an alibi?"

Wharton shrugged his shoulders. "That's the luck of the game. It'll be up to us to break it. If he's cleverer than us, then he wins." He gave a queer look round. "And if I weren't a policeman, I'd say, 'Jolly good luck to him!' He'll have finished off that swine Lewton and saved his own skin. But as I'm not an ordinary member of the public, I'm going to do my damnedest to get him hung by the neck."

Travers was polishing his glasses. "It's refreshing to hear you speak like that, George. But you've got a clever fellow to deal with. I'd almost call him a genius. That should limit your search."

"Don't I know it?" asked Wharton, almost querulously. "Isn't this case thick with clever ones? Even Beece was clever, wasn't he? So are the whole lot of 'em." He nodded impatiently. "Come along now and let's see what we can prise out of old Trench. You go and see how Beece is getting along, Carry, and we'll make a start on the list as soon as the first name's down."

At the door he collided with the station-sergeant, who was bringing in a small postal package for the Chief Constable.

"This just come by the post, sir, and I thought you'd better open it yourself."

Tempest had a look, then handed it round. It was addressed to the Chief Constable, with a "Personal" in the left corner. The postmark was Seaborough, and the address was neatly hand-printed. Wharton sniffed and passed on, thinking it some sort of circular and wondering why Tempest had passed it round. Then he was called back. What should the package be but a small black book, which had been used by Lewton as general notebook. Wharton's eyes bulged as he saw the medley of addresses, comments, synopses of interviews, dates and even receipts and payments. Then he took off his overcoat again.

"We'll see Trench later. What's the time of posting?"

Tempest looked at the stamp. "Two-thirty this afternoon."

Wharton grunted, then gave a wry smile. "Somebody didn't have much faith in us, anyway. If they hadn't been so damn sure we'd never have the sense to find out about the blackmailing, they'd never have sent us this."

"You mean the murderer, of course."

"Most likely," said Wharton. "Certainly the one who emptied Lewton's safe."

"My God!" said Tempest, "it almost makes your flesh creep. The man who murdered Lewton was walking about in Seaborough this afternoon."

Wharton was already at the desk again and adjusting his antiquated spectacles. "Why not?" he remarked mildly. "Murderers have got to walk like everybody else. For all we know we may be talking to him in a few minutes. If you're coming to dinner to-night, you may be drinking his jolly good health!"

He opened the note-book and began peering at the first page. Then all at once there came over his face an expression of comical dismay.

"Do you realize what's happened from what Beece has told us? You remember I rang him up and asked if he was plumb sure it really was Lewton who spoke to him that night over the phone, and how the test would be if Lewton had mentioned something nobody knew but themselves?"

Travers hooked off his glasses and blinked amiably round. "What you mean is that since the murderer knew all about Beece and Lewton, he knew sufficient to be able to call up Beece and mention enough—very guardedly—to convince Beece that it was Lewton."

"That's it," said Wharton. "The murderer knew the secret. Beece never had the slightest suspicion it wasn't Lewton."

"But surely that's going too far," protested Tempest. "You're making the murderer do three lots of impersonations."

"Oh, no," said Wharton. "Only two. And both of them were voices easy enough to imitate—and that on your own confession. As soon as the murderer entered the hall and Lewton turned his back, the knife got him. Then the murderer did all the telephoning. What's more, I see a whole lot of things. The murderer implicated Trench by imitating his voice. He'd already implicated Beece by getting him into the house. The knife lay on the ground at Beece's feet, where he'd be bound to see it and pick it up. By that time the police should have been there and caught him red-handed. Then X knew the police would make inquiries, and see the connection between the three of them and uncover the blackmailing business." He smiled dryly as he tapped the note-book. "And as we were such fools that we didn't do it, he grew impatient and sent us all the facts so that even we couldn't miss 'em."

"I see even more in it than that," said Travers. "He's quietly suggesting to you that now you know that Lewton was what he was, you'll know the murderer himself wasn't such a bad chap after all. He repeats, in other words, the very expressions that you yourself used as a private citizen just now. And to come right down to facts, he's given you information about himself. You've got to find the man who'd be likely to do such a quixotic thing."

"Sounds easy," said Wharton, peering at him over the top of his spectacles. "However, we'll get on with what's in this book.

For all we know, the murderer may have put in his name and address."

Travers laughed. "George, you're delightful when you trot out that heavy irony."

He stopped. Wharton had flicked over the pages of the book and now was staring at something. Once more he looked round startled, and his finger was pointing to something almost invisible on the very last written page—the faintly scribbled *Rennyet*.

"My hat!" said Tempest, eyes goggling, when at last he too had identified the name, "that's a startler, isn't it?"

Wharton licked his lips. "Yes. It's pencilled so faintly that it's a thousand to one I didn't miss it. No date, either. No nothing—just the bare name."

"Same writing?" asked Travers.

"Looks like it," said Wharton. He nodded. "So Lewton was blackmailing Rennyet! That's why he went to the house once or twice, and pretended to us he was coming after local colour." He nodded again. *"Rennyet had a motive!"*

Travers was fumbling at his glasses. "Pardon my suggesting it, but isn't there something wrong somewhere? Wouldn't a man like Rennyet—a writer of high-class detective novels—be well aware that blackmail's out-of-date nowadays, if a man's got the guts to go to the police? Everything's anonymous; the blackmailer hasn't a dog's chance."

Wharton's eyes had lit up and now he smiled. "What you've said only convinces me the other way. Everything you've brought forward only proves that Rennyet wasn't the kind of man to go to the police. *He preferred to settle matters in his own way."* There Wharton tossed the book contemptuously aside. "Get that gone over for prints, will you, John? Not that there'll be any—except Lewton's. And have it compared with the list Beece makes out. And while we're waiting, what about a nice cup of tea?"

Wharton resumed his examination of the notebook, and by seven o'clock he had half a dozen series for dispatch to the Yard. Carry and Tempest interrogated old Trench, who got off lightly. He had just heard from the hospital authorities that his wife was critically ill, and Tempest gave him leave to go to town the next day.

Pressed about his association with Lewton and Beece, Trench swore by every cardinal virtue that he knew nothing. He admitted, however, that some months before, he had been suspicious of some hanky-panky going on, and after consultation with his wife had given in his notice. Thereupon Lewton had pressed him to stay, and had treated him handsomely.

"You know how it was, sir," Trench wheezed. "It paid me to keep my eyes shut. What I didn't see I couldn't be held responsible for. Not that I thought there was anything wrong, sir, if you know what I mean."

"I know what you mean all right," Tempest told him. "I know you're laying everything on Lewton, knowing he can't answer. What sort of people were they you used to let in here sometimes?"

"I never did let anybody in, sir. Mr. Lewton always used to say that I was to stop in the kitchen and he'd let people in. But that wasn't often, sir not once in a blue moon, as the saying is."

Then Trench followed with a peroration about having fought for his king and country, and having had his troubles, and being an old man with few years to live. Tempest ordered him back to his kitchen and said he'd have more troubles still—if he lived to get out of jail.

"Plausible old liar!" said Carry. "I'll bet he was up to the ears in it in his small way—he and that precious nephew of his."

Tempest hurried off to change for Wharton's dinner.

When that meal was over, Jane Wharton and Mrs. Hule went off to the theatre again—Wharton having planned that out—and the men gathered in a private sitting-room. There was a lot of general gossip before Travers took up the cue which Wharton had given him, and brought the subject round to blackmail.

"Between ourselves," said Hule, lapsing into the unprofessional, "I could tell a thing or two if I liked."

"I reckon you could," said Wharton. "I might do a little in that line myself. But tell me. What would you do if somebody tried to blackmail you?"

"Depends on how much he knew," said Hule.

"Well, suppose he knew a lot," said Travers. "Enough to make things devilish awkward."

Hule laughed. "I'd attend him professionally. Then I'd send a wreath."

Wharton tried a chuckle. "But you wouldn't pay?"

"Pay? My dear chap, only a lunatic would pay a blackmailer nowadays."

That part of Wharton's scheme had missed fire rather badly, but the General was of the resilient kind. He gave one of his prodigious frowns.

"Pardon me talking shop, but I'd better get it off my chest before I forget it. Also, you'd like to know before you're warned officially. Tuesday we're carrying on with the inquest, and it may be a long affair. You and Mrs. Hule will be two of the star witnesses."

Tempest laughed hollowly. "You'd better look through the family album, Hule, and get some pictures ready for the press."

"A little publicity wouldn't do me any harm," said Hule complacently.

"One thing you'll have to be pretty sure of," said Wharton, "and that's the precise spot you were when that telephone message came."

Hule looked up quickly. "Why? They don't want me to give them an alibi, do they?"

"Heavens, no!" said Wharton. "I'm just giving you the tip, that's all. Your wife will say you were out. The coroner will ask you if you were out, and it's ten to one he'll ask where."

"I think it would be frightfully good publicity if you had the answer all pat," said Travers. "Think of an epigram or something to tag on the end of it." He fumbled at his glasses. "But since you're among friends, why not let us in on where you were."

Hule laughed. Travers's innuendo had been impossible to miss. "Nothing of that sort, my lad. Never confuse business with relaxation." His face straightened. "As a matter of fact I was with an old chap who'd broken his thigh. I don't know if you've run across him, Tempest. That old fisherman with the monkey whiskers, who lives off the East Harbour. Densome his name is. Old Sam they usually call him."

"I think I know him," said Tempest, and the conversation veered again.

Then when the clock said only nine-thirty, Hule got up and said he must go. He was sorry to break up the party, but he had a call or two to make. Wharton saw him off and came back with his tail well down.

"So much for that," he grunted. "Wasn't worth putting these damn clothes on for. All the same, John, you might make a note to look up your friend, Sam."

Travers poured out some more drinks. "If I might say so," he observed, "I always did think the major's objection an insuperable one with regard to Hule. He wouldn't have made the error of missing out those merry little quips when he rang up his wife in Lewton's voice." He noticed the frown on Wharton's face and tried a little sympathy. "The trouble with your game, George, is that you've got to suspect everybody and everything. Still, something's bound to happen."

"If it doesn't happen soon, they'll be putting me in a padded cell," said Wharton, and looked as if he meant it.

Then Travers related the strange history of the despondent curate, and Tempest followed it up with another, and when Mrs. Wharton came in, just before eleven, the party was far from gloomy.

"Well, what did you make of her?" Wharton asked.

Mrs. Wharton shuddered. "What a woman! If I'd had to spend another hour with her I'd have gone mad. Affected, obvious, insipid—"

"All right," said Wharton, raising a hand. "Forget all about the Hules, my dear, and get the night's bill ready for John here. I don't mind footing the bill for hospitality, but when it comes to hard work, then the Corporation pays."

Then a waiter came in and said Mr. Wharton was wanted on the phone.

Wharton registered surprise, but when he came back in five minutes' time, he was strangely communicative.

"I had a brain-wave," he said, "and got Carry to put a man outside on Hule's tail."

"But why?" asked Tempest, considerably surprised.

Wharton shrugged his shoulders. "Well, he knew his wife would be safe at the theatre, didn't he? And he did make an excuse to go early, didn't he?"

"And what happened?"

"Nothing particular," said Wharton, with an elaborate shrug. "Just a visit to your old friend, Sam." He once more became aware of his wife. "If I were you, my dear, I wouldn't wait. I'll be up as soon as I can."

The good nights were said, and Mrs. Wharton departed.

Travers turned to Wharton with a dry smile. "Well, what's the rest of the news, George?"

"Oh, that," said Wharton. "Well, why did Hule bolt off to see Sam if it wasn't to fix an alibi? Put that down in your note-book as marked urgent. What's more, he wasn't there two minutes before he was off again to a little villa at the top of the same road, and he stayed there till just in time to get home to meet his wife."

"And who lives at the little villa?" asked Travers, knowing the question was expected of him.

Wharton lowered his voice. "A little lady who gives out that she's a widow!"

CHAPTER X
ELIMINATIONS

LUDOVIC TRAVERS departed early the following morning for his sister's place. Wharton was up and away early too, for he looked like having a full day. By the middle of the morning he had mapped out the main course of the inquest, and then the telephone bell went. It was Carry, ringing from the station. A message had come from town that Lewton's prints were those of a man who had been convicted of swindling—a confidence trick job—and sentenced under the name of Frederick Roberts to three years, expiring in 1921. In 1917 he had been deported from South Africa as an undesirable, under the name of Robert Baxter.

Tempest came to Homedale and let himself in. He watched Wharton hang up.

"You were right about Lewton, then. The only reason he talked about Canada was because he'd been somewhere else."

"Yes," said Wharton, "but how's it going to help?"

Tempest smiled. "Never mind about Lewton for a moment. Just listen to this. I sent a reliable man round to Sam Densome's house this morning, on the plea of possibly having to warn someone in the house to attend the inquest—you know, to confirm Hule's whereabouts. The woman—a sister of Sam's said she knew the doctor was there at ten-past seven, so my man asked her why she was so sure. What do you think she said? That the doctor knew it, *and only last night he'd happened to remind her.*"

Wharton nodded. "Well, I'll strike while the iron's hot. You stay here, and when he comes let me do the talking."

He got the Hules on the phone. The doctor was just off on his round, and would certainly come to Homedale at once.

Inside ten minutes he was in the dining-room, with a "Well, what's it all about?"

"Sit down a minute," said Wharton. "I want to talk to you like a father. Do you know, if it hadn't been for a great stroke of luck, you might have landed yourself in a nice muddle? Just by accident we go warning witnesses to attend the inquest, and one of them informs us that you've been seeing her and reminding her that you were in her house at a certain time. Suppose she had said that in a coroner's court instead of to friends of yours!"

That was a facer for Hule. Wharton could read the quick workings of his mind; the hunting for a plausible explanation, and the relaxation when he had found it. But it was never given.

"Get this into your head," said Wharton, with not too much seriousness. "You're among friends. We want to know where you really were at ten-past seven, and we give you our word that if you swear it's the truth, then you'll hear no more about it. This is a private matter, just between ourselves."

Hule had a good look at both of them, and decided to let a certain amount out. There was a patient of his about whom he had already had words with his wife—something had slipped out over the telephone—quite near Sam Densome's, and as a matter of fact Hule had actually called to see Sam as a kind of blind, just before going on to the fair patient.

"That's all right," said Wharton in his best man-of-the-world manner. "You were attending to the lady."

"Well, yes," said Hule. "Absolutely, honest-to-God. That's where I was, and between ourselves, I'd rather my wife didn't know it."

"We'll fix it," Wharton told him. "There's no need for the coroner to ask where you actually were. Only, you do see, don't you . . ." and so on, till when Hule left the house it was with a feeling of gratitude and a warmth at the heart that there should be in the world such fine, understanding he-men of the type of George Wharton.

Wharton sat down again, and prepared for another hour with Lewton's note-book. He was looking rather pleased.

"Between ourselves," he said to Tempest, "I'm inclined to put Hule as out of it. I think he's telling the truth, and what's more, his name isn't in this book. Lewton wasn't blackmailing him as far as we know, so he hadn't a motive."

He was flicking over the pages, to find where he had left off, when his eye caught something.

"Just have a look at this, will you? I noticed it last night, and as it was crossed out I left it for later."

Those jottings which had been scored through occupied about half a page. As Wharton pointed out, there were other items in the book which had been scored through, but none with such thoroughness. What was more, careful examination gave the idea that there had been two scorings out, one with a hard pencil and one with a softer.

"What are things crossed out for at all?" asked Tempest. "To show they were under consideration and then dropped?"

"That's about it," said Wharton. "Perhaps Lewton decided things weren't going to work, or would be too dangerous. But have a look just at that corner. Can't you make out what looks like . . . *all* . . . ?"

Tempest said he thought it was that. Then Wharton showed him the back, where the pencil had left an indentation. Now the whole word could be guessed at—and it looked like *Mallow*.

"Do you know, I've half a mind to let one of your people have a go at it," Wharton said. "I'd like to know why it was so important that Lewton should cross out something so carefully from his own private note-book."

The house was locked behind them, as Trench was away, and they went down in Tempest's car. Wharton got a man to work, and what with delicate manipulations against the light, and impressions of the back, they got what looked like *Pigh* . . .

Carry happened to come in and the word was referred to him. He squinted and scowled at the four letters, and then his face took on a look of wonderment.

"I know what it is," he said. *"It's Pightle.* The Pightle, it means. You know, sir, that little street leading up to East Cliff, just behind the memorial."

"A local address, eh?" said Wharton. "Then what about this word that looks like *Mallow*?"

"Mallow?" He stared. "Mallow, The Pightle? Well, if that isn't a perishing marvel! You remember, sir?"

Tempest did remember, and he was looking uncommonly serious too. He nodded heavily. "Do you know, Carry, I always thought there was something fishy about that." He looked up at Wharton. "We'll get you the whole story in a minute—what there is of it. But you remember Meek, who works for Rennyet? Used to be sergeant here?"

"Didn't I see him on Thursday morning—and his wife too?"

"That's what's funny," said Tempest. "If it's who we think it was, she was Meek's sister-in-law. He lived up at The Pightle, and that's where she committed suicide. We never found out why, except that she got dismissed from her situation. She was a nursery-governess, by the way, and we saw her employer, and the reason she gave was that she didn't need her any more. But the really strange thing is that Meek worried himself nearly to death over the job, and never found out why she'd done it. Now here we run up against it as a sort of million to one chance!"

"Let me get this clear," said Wharton. "Stop me if I'm wrong. Mrs. Meek's sister was a nursery-governess. Her mistress sent her home as she didn't need her any more. But the sister soon afterwards committed suicide, and nobody knew why. Meek made himself ill over trying to find out, and that's why he was allowed to retire."

"That's right," said Tempest. "You see, she was the last person in the world to commit suicide. She was a smart-looking girl; always jolly, and straight as they make 'em."

"She certainly was," said Carry. "She was as nice a girl as ever I met, sir. I know when it happened I felt just as if it was one of my own."

"What was the name of her employer?"

"She's dead now," said Carry. "Died about a year ago."

"I see." He nodded. "So we can't go to her for information. What about her husband?"

"She was a youngish widow," said Tempest. "I saw her myself, and I thought she was decent enough. All the same, there was something fishy going on. We knew it, but we couldn't prove it."

Wharton nodded again. "And without hurting anybody's feelings, might I suggest that if Lewton was blackmailing her, she must have side-slipped somewhere—Meek's sister-in-law, I mean."

"You never know," said Tempest. "It certainly seems plain enough now. Also she did commit suicide. And Lewton crossed her off his book as being of no more use."

"The bastard!" broke out Carry. "Excuse me, sir, but I couldn't help it. I wouldn't have minded doing him in myself if I'd known that."

"Speaking as a private citizen, of course," Wharton added quietly. Then he picked up the book and put it in his pocket. "Well, once more this morning I'm going straight to the point.

Rennyet's name's in this book, and—in a way—so is Meek's. You and I will pay a little visit to Bicklesham straightaway, and there'll be some plain speaking."

Rennyet's house appeared to be deserted when they drew up, but it was only because everybody was indoors. Tom Meek, who answered the ring of the front bell, had a footman's apron on, and had evidently been working indoors. Rennyet himself was at work in his study, where there was a cheerful log fire. He got up with a queer, amused look on his face when the two were shown in.

"We're sorry to disturb you," said Wharton, "and we wouldn't have done so if it hadn't been urgent."

"I'm not so busy as all that," said Rennyet, and pulled up a couple of chairs. "May I get you some coffee? I always have some in the middle of the morning."

"Thanks—but not at the moment," Wharton told him. "Also, by the time this conversation's over, you mayn't feel like offering us anything—unless it's the order of the boot."

"I hope not." Rennyet smiled charmingly. There was no semblance of perturbation about him. His whole bearing was that of a man who walks and sleeps secure.

"I'll come straight to the point," said Wharton, and under a promise of the strictest secrecy told about Lewton's chief source of income. Then he took out the note-book with, "What we want you to explain is why your name appears here."

"My name?" He gave a little puzzled smile. "I don't understand. You mean to tell me that my name's down in that book as one of the people that swine Lewton blackmailed!"

"I don't say that. I simply say your name's written in the book."

Rennyet pulled himself up. "It's preposterous. Utterly ridiculous. I've done some queer things in my time, as you doubtless both have, but there's no man living who's got enough on me to attempt blackmail. If anyone tried it I'd go to the police inside five minutes."

Wharton shrugged his shoulders. "We believe what you say. Still, how do you explain it?"

"I can't explain it," Rennyet said. "All I can suggest is that he jotted my name down to remind him of an appointment; that I was coming in. Unless"—and there he hesitated curiously—"he put my name down as a likely person for victimization."

While he was speaking he was making for the desk by the south window, and he took from a drawer two piles of manuscript, each of which represented six or seven chapters.

"I don't mind telling you that if anybody else but you, gentlemen, had insinuated what you've just told me, they'd have been told to go to hell, and been kicked out of this house inside two minutes." A wry smile. "And that's not taking into account my privileges under the laws of evidence. However, to show my absolute good faith, if you care to look through this manuscript, you'll verify what I told you. Here's a detective novel I began, and for which I wanted the local colour I mentioned. Here's the straight novel I began afterwards, and you'll recognize Lewton in it—or I hope you will."

Wharton gave the most casual of glances.

"Take it home with you," said Rennyet. "Study it, and see for yourself that it must have been written in the way I told you."

"We'll take your word," said Wharton. "You'll swear that Lewton never tried to blackmail you?"

"I'll swear it on anything you like to name," said Rennyet, and his tone had a fierce earnestness. "If Lewton ever tried to blackmail me, or if what I told you about my reasons for seeing him isn't true, may I die in the most horrible agony."

"Right," said Wharton. "We've settled that, and in a man's way. Now may I speak to your man, and I'd prefer it to be in your company."

"By all means." He pushed the bell. "Don't tell me his name's in the book?"

"Something rather more serious than that," said Wharton, and caught Rennyet's eyes fixed on his with a strained intentness.

"Come in a minute, Tom, will you?" said Rennyet quietly. "The superintendent wishes to ask you some questions."

"I didn't say so," Wharton added bluntly. "At least, not at the moment." Then he looked round at Tempest. "Perhaps the Chief Constable will tell you about it. It'd come better from him."

Tempest went back to Meek's illness and what everybody thought had brought it on. He spoke very kindly of the dead woman, and the grief he had to recall. Then with a gentle tact he came to what had been discovered in the note-book. Wharton, whose eyes had never left Meek's face, saw the ex-sergeant suddenly go a greyish-white, and he sprang up to catch him before he should slither in the chair. But Meek pulled himself together and shook Wharton's hand fiercely away.

"You mean to insinuate that she'd done something that swine Lewton could blackmail her for?" His eyes were staring and the veins stood high on his forehead.

Tempest came over. "Steady now, Meek. Take it easy. You ought to know me better than that. I'm merely telling you the facts."

Meek glared again. "Blast the facts!" Then his shoulders sagged a bit and he began to shake his head like a man bemused.

Rennyet leaned over him and patted his shoulder. "Take it easy, Tom, as Major Tempest advised you." He looked round at them, none too pleased. "Don't you think you've rather overdone things? It's not too wise when a man's been ill to rake up what he'd like to forget."

"Don't blame us," said Wharton, assuming a dignity of his own. "No one could have spoken more kindly than Major Tempest did. For my own part I'll say that I'm deeply sorry to open old wounds, but all the same, Meek and his wife had a right to know what we've found out. How're you now, Meek? Feeling better?"

"Yes, thank you, sir. . . . Only it was a bit of a shock."

"It was," said Wharton. "My advice is to forget it, and to continue to think as we thought before. But before we go, it's my duty to speak to you both for your own good. The mention of what I've told you, in this note-book, will be kept out of the coroner's court only if I'm implicitly satisfied on one thing. As sensible men, you'll understand that what's written in this book might place either of you under suspicion as having had a possible motive for committing murder. Satisfy me here and now as to your alibis, and this house'll see me no more. I'll eliminate you once and for all."

Rennyet was already at the bell. "Some people might have been indignant," he said, "but, as you say, we're sensible men. But you remember, of course, that you've already been given a perfectly good alibi?"

"I know it," said Wharton doggedly, "but I'll hear it again officially—once and for all."

Mrs. Meek came in, and all at once Wharton caught Meek's eye and the motion of his hand that signalled she was not to be told. Wharton signalled back, and Rennyet was already talking.

"Oh, Helen, just as a matter of form, Major Tempest has to know the exact whereabouts of your husband and myself on the evening of Wednesday last. It's important because of the inquest? Say from a quarter to seven and on."

She was just the least flustered. "Well, there wasn't anything different from what there always is." She turned to Tempest. "Mr. Rennyet, though I say it, sir, is a stickler for punctuality, and all his meals have to be regular."

Rennyet smiled. "Major Tempest doesn't want to hear my habits, Helen. Tell him just what happened."

"But nothing happened, sir. You was in just before seven and Tom put the dinner on. Then when he brought the joint in, you kept him for a bit, talking to him, and I was five minutes over the time I usually clear away."

"And did I go out again that night?"

"Not that I know of, sir. Tom brought in your coffee—" She broke off into a smile. "Of course you didn't go out, sir."

"There you are," said Rennyet, with the cheery ease of a showman. "The house is full of clocks, and if one had been wrong the others wouldn't. Besides"—it seemed a sudden idea and he turned to his housekeeper again—"I suppose you heard the church clock, Helen?"

"Once we did. Eight o'clock it would be, Tom?"

"That's right," said Meek, with a wan, apologetic smile. "I didn't want to put my oar in, gentlemen, only she made me."

Helen Meek left and Wharton got to his feet.

"Well, we'll keep you no longer. I'm satisfied, and I think Major Tempest is. Good-bye, Meek. I'm very sorry about this news we brought, and I can't say more than that. Good-bye, Mr. Rennyet. I hope we'll see you at the inquest. It's going to be interesting from an author's point of view."

Tempest held out his hand. "Good-bye, Meek. If you care to drop in and ask for me, I'll give you all the information we have. Good-bye, Mr. Rennyet. Let us know if you're coming to the inquest and we'll reserve you a seat. And let me tell you they're going to be fought for before it's all over."

The car was coasting well down the slope before Wharton spoke his mind, and then with an unexpected cheerfulness.

"Well, it's a great morning's work. We've agreed to let out Hule, and unless we refuse to face the truth, we've got to let out those we've just seen."

"I quite agree," said Tempest. "It's no use smashing your skull against the brick wall of a hundred-per-cent alibi. Besides, I knew all the time that Tom Meek wouldn't be mixed up in anything shady—though I hadn't the pluck to say so. Rennyet I don't somehow like. He's a smooth devil. He carries too high a polish; don't you think so?"

"Why think?" said Wharton. "Give a man an alibi and he can have a face like Charlie Peace." He grunted. "Wonder if Carry's found out anything about his friend, Howard Trench?"

But Carry had very little news. His man had spent the morning with two of the touring company, and all he had been able to elicit was that Howard Trench had spoken of "the old man" as his certain source of money to put him financially clear.

"That'd be his uncle," said Wharton. "He couldn't possibly have been referring to Lewton. If the sort of scheme you have in mind was the one actually worked by him and his uncle, it'd have taken the devil of a lot of preparation." He pursed his lips. "Perhaps I'd better see him myself."

It was well past lunch-time, but he went off at once. There would be a matinée that afternoon, and Howard Trench would be a busy man. He had just finished his meal when Wharton was shown in, and there was nothing on his face that remotely approached alarm.

Wharton came once more to the point. At the inquest the coroner might ask awkward questions on the spur of the moment. For instance, was Mr. Trench aware that there was already gossip in the town that the death of Lewton had done neither himself nor his uncle any harm?

"Mind you," said Wharton, with an expression that spoke reluctance to discuss the subject and no small disgust, "we get these things reported and we have to take them into account. But you wouldn't like your private business to be discussed in court?"

Trench's face showed considerable annoyance. "Is it an unusual thing for a man to be short of money? Have you always paid your way?"

"Not by a long chalk," said Wharton. "But you don't see that I'm trying to help you. You know what people are. You don't want to have your name bandied about, and people saying that even before you got to Seaborough you were telling your friends that you'd be all right when you were there."

Trench gave him a look. "So that's what they're saying, are they?" He nodded. "Well, what about this?"

He handed over a letter from his breast pocket. Wharton ran a quick eye over it.

"You see?" went on Trench. "I don't mind admitting to you that I was pressed for money, and last week I wrote to my uncle. You see what he says—that of course he'll let me have what I want. As a matter of fact he was to have given me the money last Wednesday night."

Wharton gave the letter back. "Damnable how people will talk. Still, you needn't worry. No matter what gossip reaches us, you'll be protected. All you'll have to do at the inquest is to give a straightforward account of what happened that night."

Wharton had the trick of finding lions and leaving lambs, and Howard Trench was no exception. But however relieved in mind the actor was, Wharton himself was feeling the earth removed from under his feet. Piece by piece the solid ground was going. Sheer hard sense told him that Howard Trench had nothing whatever to do with the killing of Lewton, and behind him and his uncle stood the bulwark of a hundred-per-cent alibi.

Perhaps it was because of those general disquietudes that Wharton turned his steps towards Beece's house. Beece had compiled his list, and had thrown himself on the mercy of the law. The discrepancies between that list and Lewton's notebook had not yet been looked for, but there was just one point that was asking to be cleared up.

Beece took Wharton to a private room upstairs, and he was scared with new apprehensions.

"You needn't get in a panic," Wharton told him. "We're in charge of you now, and we'll look after you. And now about that list you made up. There's one name left out—a Miss Barbara Mallow."

There was a quick response that died away as quickly. Beece shook his head. "I don't remember that name, sir."

"Think again," said Wharton. "She lived at The Pightle, with her sister—a Mrs. Meek. Their parents were dead and that was her recognized home. We've found her name in Lewton's book. Does that recall anything to you? It doesn't? Well, she also committed suicide on account of what you and Lewton did to her. Now do you remember?"

Beece remembered nothing. Lewton, he said, often began and finished business on his own. He would note down schemes and then abandon them. He—Beece—had been the under-dog. For years he had been trying to get clear of Lewton. . . .

Wharton gave him a look. "Shut up!—or I'll close your mouth with this fist of mine. Answer me this, and God help you if you tell me a lie! Did you and Lewton ever blackmail a woman—a nursery-governess—of the name of Mallow?"

Beece cringed and swore—and Wharton sensed that for once he was telling the truth. And yet there was still a vague something, so that Wharton turned abruptly on his heel and made his own way down the stairs and out of Beece's house.

That afternoon Wharton's mind was made up. It was, in any case, necessary that he should return to town, and to town he would go. Though his heart was not in it, and cool reason spoke plainly of futility, his last plan was to inquire himself into some of the likeliest cases compiled from the accounts of the blackmailing pair.

"On Monday afternoon I'll be back," he told Tempest and Carry. "If anything happens meanwhile, let me know. And you let out to the press that the inquest's going to be the sensation of the century. We're putting all our cards on the table, and all we shall ask from them from day to day will be appeals to the public to come forward with anything that's likely to help. We'll have the whole of Seaborough and half the county on our unpaid staff."

"What about Beece?" asked Tempest. "We can let him loose for Lewton's funeral?"

"Why not?" said Wharton. "It might do him good."

So Wharton and his wife returned to town, and that evening Wharton went along to the Yard to report to his superiors and talk the case over. It was about nine o'clock, in the middle of an informal conference, that Wharton was called on the phone. Tempest wanted him urgently.

"Bad news for you," he said. "Beece has slipped us."

"What, bolted?"

"No," said Tempest, "he's taken spirits of salts, and we've just carted him off to the hospital. They say he hasn't an earthly. We've got a man sitting by his bed."

Wharton was staggered. "But why'd he do it? He hadn't the guts of a good-sized louse. Besides, we promised to let him off as lightly as we could."

"I know," said Tempest, "only I rather fancy Carry put his foot in it. He went to see him as soon as you'd gone, to tell him about being allowed to go to Lewton's funeral on Monday morning, and I gather that Beece had the wind up. And then what did that damn fool Carry go and do but hint that Beece'd be arrested as soon as the inquest was over."

"What are the doctors doing?"

"They're working on him now," said Tempest.

"Well, you have a man with his ear wide open," Wharton told him. "Have two if necessary. If anything develops, let me know—otherwise I'll be down first thing Monday."

But nothing did develop. While Tempest was talking, Beece had lapsed into a merciful unconsciousness. In the early hours of the morning he slipped away for good, and whatever lies and treacheries his shifty brain had held became part of the nothingness that was now himself.

PART II

CHAPTER XI
AFTER THE FIREWORKS

THE SCENE of the inquest was the old board room at the Town Hall, and Tempest's publicity had been effective, for on the Tuesday morning the queue stretched round Windygate Street as far as the market, so that more people were shut out than got in. What, then, with a six hundred audience, busy ushers, packed press quarters and the general expectancy, Wharton had no quarrel with the setting of his drama when he took a look from his peephole behind the stage.

Three days that inquest took, and for the audience they were days of amazing thrills. Wharton let the tragedy unroll in its sequence of the Wednesday night. Howard Trench paid his visit to Homedale and left again. Juker took him over from the fork, and the tobacconist saw him enter the theatre. Next came Beece's maid, who told about the telephone call. She identified Lewton's voice, and was certain that her dead master had done the same, for she had heard him say—apparently to his wife—that Lewton wanted him to go along for something urgent.

"We will leave that for some considerable time, gentlemen," the coroner told the jury, "but I would suggest that you keep in mind this telephone message and the time of departure of the late Mr. Beece."

Then Mrs. Hule was called and described the message she received. There was some argument about the badinage that had always passed between her and Lewton, and why she had assumed Lewton had been drunk. Then, by means of a deft insinuation, the coroner sprang the first mine by the suggestion that the voice had not been Lewton's at all.

The sensation had not died away in court when Hule stepped down from the stand. His evidence had merely been the receiving of the message from his wife, and the setting off for Homedale. Then the station-sergeant related, in the dramatic words Wharton had put in his mouth, the story of the telephone bell that had burst so shrilly into the quiet room and the evening's routine. His voice croaked as he described the voice at the other end of the wire, and no sooner did he step down than old Trench was on the stand.

That was the sensation that ended the first day. No person in that audience could fail to see in Trench the man who had wheezed and croaked the news of his master's death. The sergeant had been the prologue, and now the lights played full on the man he had foreshadowed. A stir went round the huge room when Trench's first word oozed from his throat. He was Robert Trench, he said, and servant to the deceased. He had been absent when his master was killed.

"And it was you who found his body and telephoned the police?"

"No, sir," said Trench, and once more the words were Wharton's, "it wasn't my voice that called the police. I was a mile away and more, sir, when that telephone message was sent."

Then Carry proved that the message had really come from Homedale, and with that business-like ending the court stood adjourned.

That evening the papers reaped a superb harvest. By ten o'clock, bitter though the night was, there were twenty people in the queue, and by dawn the next morning hawkers and entertainers were doing a good trade. But that day's proceedings were varied rather than sensational. Old Trench's alibi was established by means of the collector and Juker. The police arrived and described the finding of the body. Shinniford gave medical evidence, and a thrill went round when the knife was displayed. Then came the discovery of the open safe. Certain prints had been found on it, and they tallied with those on the mantelpiece. Later on, a note-book which the police had every reason to believe had been taken from the safe, had reached the Chief Constable anonymously. It was with the contents of that book that the police proposed to deal the following day.

But there had been some argument about the proceedings of that final day. Beece had gone, Tempest said, so why rake things up and harrow unnecessarily the feelings of his widow and children?

"His children are grown men and women," said Wharton. "Besides, they'll share his money when the widow dies, and it's just as well they should know where it came from. We're out to tell the truth, not conceal it."

So the movements of Beece were traced that night by Juker's evidence and that of the woman who had seen the light. Then extracts from Beece's own statement were submitted. On those admissions Beece stood clear as a blackmailer, and Lewton had been his partner.

"And have you any other evidence to substantiate the contents of that note-book?" Tempest was asked.

"We have," he said. "One name is mentioned both by the note-book and the list compiled by Beece. That person is prepared to swear that from time to time he parted with sums amounting to over three thousand pounds."

Thereafter the jury brought in the only possible verdict of murder against some person or persons unknown, and the inquest was over. As Wharton said, all that remained was to await results. Someone who had seen something was bound to come forward. The murderer had entered Homedale and he had left it. He had been admitted by Lewton and had made a furtive escape. Some strange occurrence or suspicion might now come back to someone's mind, and by that clue the murderer might be traced. In the meanwhile those lists of the blackmailed could be worked on. Maybe some victim had come to Seaborough, and there had planned a patient revenge. All Lewton's haunts should be visited—the bowling-greens and hotel bars where he had acquaintances, and even the cinemas which could have made a convenient rendezvous.

And that very first night, Wharton did something else. He had never appeared publicly in the case and his features were unknown. For hours, therefore, he paid quick visits to barrooms; took rides in corporation buses and had a shave in a busy shop. He heard the gossip of others and sifted it dexterously, and what he heard he knew that others would hear wherever the papers were read. Some said Howard Trench was keeping a lot back. Some fancied his uncle, and most chose Beece, but out of the night's listening and that of the nights that followed it, there was never a helpful thing that emerged.

The week went and another went after it. Not a soul came forward with news of that night. Lewton's murderer had entered unseen and left unseen. Of those victims who had admitted in confidence that they had paid money to Lewton, not one had been near Seaborough that night. Scraps of gossip and scandal were tirelessly traced down, and found to be nothing else.

March had almost run its course when something did happen. Old Trench announced that he was leaving Seaborough, and he refused to say where he was going. Wharton, who had gone back to town, came down specially and wormed the information out of him. Trench had received a threatening letter.

Don't think you are going to get away with your share of the money your two dead partners got. Unless you give a thousand pounds to the local hospital and clear out of the town before the month is out, the three of you will be together again. Enough said!

Wharton took it along to the station and compared it with the printing on the paper that had covered the note-book. But this was cruder printing, and cheap paper, and he and Tempest decided that some local sensation-monger had been taking a hand. After all, the facts were known, and it didn't need much perspicacity to make Trench a third sharer of the proceeds of the blackmailing business.

"If you take my advice, you'll clear out all the same," Wharton told him. "Only, we'd just like to know where you are. You wouldn't believe what a fatherly interest I take in you, Trench."

Even that remark showed Wharton was getting rattled. The days were going and the case was fizzling out. Other things had happened to take the public eye, and only an occasional paragraph reminded the world that Frederick Lewton had ever existed. Wharton's grand display of fireworks had ended as fireworks do, with merely a faint sniff of stale powder and an occasional empty squib.

Then March went out and April came in. Easter would soon be coming, and, as Wharton remarked to his wife, the murderer of Lewton would eat his hot-cross buns in peace. At Scotland Yard and down at Seaborough, the routine inquiries might still be going on. Something might turn up, and something might not, and it was that latter alternative that was present most cynically in Wharton's mind. In his heart of hearts he knew the case was over—and the knowledge fretted and gnawed like a deep, rheumatic pain. There were times when he would have given two fingers to know the killer of Frederick Lewton, and one evening in early April he ventured to go as far as three. That was when Ludovic Travers dropped in most unexpectedly for a chat. Moreover, he was returning Wharton's own voluminous notes on the case, for which he had asked some days previously.

Jane Wharton had tremendous faith in Ludovic Travers. He was enormously different from the range of her usual experience, and though he had never achieved off his own bat anything intrinsically spectacular, yet his queer points of view, and the paradoxical twists of his mind, had often arrived in startling ways at things which more than once had made Wharton himself retrace his steps. Wharton, for all his frequent pulling of Travers's leg, had learned the value of his acute discernment, and now there was some anxiety mixed with the irony as he laid the pile of notes aside.

"Well, I suppose you've got it all cut and dried?"

Travers smiled diffidently. "The only thing I've got cut and dried is that I'm the world's worst sleuth. But what about yourself? What are your private ideas?"

"What they always were," said Wharton. "I know—I'm dead certain, if you prefer it that way—that the man we want is one we've had in mind. The facts are clear as day. He's a man I've shaken hands with. He knew the house and all about everybody in it. He'd made a study of it. You're not going to tell me a man like that could have escaped all the inquiries we've been making?"

"I suppose you haven't been trying to break one of the alibis?" Jane Wharton asked.

"Oh, but I have," Travers admitted. "I've put myself in the place of Howard Trench, and his uncle, and Beece, and Hule, and Rappway, and Rennyet, and the whole lot of them. I've even tried to make a wholly new alibi of my own, starting with the intention of killing Lewton and getting away with it."

Jane Wharton put away her sewing. "Well, and how did you do it?"

"I didn't," said Travers ruefully. "Still, I got a whole collection of beautiful ideas. But tell me, George, you still think that anonymous letter old Trench got was sent by some outsider who was trying to be clever?"

"Don't you?" countered Wharton curtly.

"I don't know. After all, X killed Lewton for the sole reason that he was a blackmailer. He tried to dispose of Beece also, and if Beece hadn't thereby got himself into such a mess that he took the short way out of it, there's no reason to suppose that X wouldn't have polished off Beece too. Surely, therefore, it's logical to suppose that X warned old Trench off the premises? He only gave him a chance to get clear with a fine of a thousand because he thought he wasn't in the game as deeply as the other two."

Wharton smiled wryly. "I've one answer to all speculation about this case. *Bust one of those alibis*—that's all."

"Come, come, George," expostulated his wife, "you're not being reasonable. If you didn't discuss things you'd never arrive at anything."

"Well, we'll have just one more peep at the alibis," said Travers. "There's only one with which I'm implicitly satisfied, and that's Beece's. About Howard Trench and his uncle, I'm still like Carry—intrigued about the dropped ticket and the consulting of the tobacconist's clock instead of the one at the memorial."

"Very well, then," said Wharton. "*Bust the alibi.* Bust the evidence of Juker, the tobacconist and the ticket-collector. Nobody could make a mistake about old Trench, with his type of face and voice. The same with Howard Trench. Not a single man in his company could have impersonated him, nor could he have impersonated his uncle."

"Take Hule, then. You've only the word of his girl-friend that he was there while Lewton was being killed."

Wharton raised his eyebrows. "Well, that'd be good enough in a court of law, wouldn't it?"

Travers smiled. "All right, George. Then I'll approach the question another way. Let's divide all the alibis into groups. For convenience we'll speak of the Trench, the Hule, the Beece, the Rappway and the Rennyet groups; five groups in all." For the first time Travers hooked off his glasses and began a careful polish. "Is there any one of those groups that is markedly different from all the others?"

Wharton thought for a moment, then, "You're serious about all this?"

Travers smiled still more diffidently. "Well yes, I suppose I am. I mean, I hope you won't be disappointed."

"I'll get a sheet of paper," said Wharton, "and work them out."

Mrs. Wharton asked for one too, but five minutes, united effort produced nothing. Both gave it up.

"I'm afraid I'm wrong, then," said Travers. "Still, on whose evidence did Beece's alibi depend?" "His maid, his wife, and Juker."

"That's right," said Travers. "The Trenches' we've already had. And Rappway's?"

"On the people with whom he was shooting, his man, and the servants at the Manor."

"And Rennyet's?"

"On his two servants."

"Exactly," said Travers. "We've already mentioned Hule's alibi, and we take into account the fatal slip he'd have made in not ogling his wife when he rang her up as Lewton. What I claim, therefore, is that the Rennyet alibis stand apart as being self-contained. No verification is to be obtained outside the walls of the house."

"Oh, yes, there is," said Wharton, and put his finger to a line he had written on his sheet of paper. "There's the evidence of Bicklesham church clock. Mrs. Meek heard it strike eight. That very morning after she told me so, I came out of Rennyet's house and heard Bicklesham clock strike twelve. The wind was in the north-east, as it was the night Lewton was killed. Even admitting that Mrs. Meek was slightly deaf, she couldn't have missed hearing it. What I mean is that if she thought she heard it, then she did hear it."

Travers looked surprised. "You're wandering far from the point, George. You're assuming that something absurdly out-of-date, like altering clocks, was done. I'm merely thinking in terms of three people, all in one house. Could there, for instance, have been collusion?"

"Meek didn't strike me as that sort," said Wharton. "But when you come to his wife, then I'm dead sure she'd never have lent herself to anything like that."

"I expect you're right," said Travers, and then with a queer, pleading sort of look, "Then, suppose you decided that all the alibis might be gone over just once more officially, you wouldn't be of the mind that the Rennyet one was the likeliest at which to begin?"

Wharton looked at him. "Now what is it you're driving at? You've got something on your mind."

Travers assumed a look of pain. "Of course I have. First you ask me what I think, and then you tell me I'm thinking. But you haven't answered the question."

"You mean about beginning a new inquiry at Rennyet?" Wharton shrugged his shoulders. "I don't know that I would. As far as a jury's concerned, his alibi is a hundred-per-cent—like all the others."

Travers's hand went to his glasses, and fell again. "But supposing one discovered something fishy about—well, about some of the evidence he's given."

"Find me anything fishy about *anybody's* evidence," said Wharton, "and I'll be down at Seaborough inside three hours."

Travers's glasses were now off and he was rubbing them abstractedly with the silk handkerchief.

"Perhaps I shouldn't have said 'fishy.' 'Funny' was the proper expression. You see"—he blinked affectionately at Jane Wharton—"I happened to be in the Strand yesterday, and thinking of this unusual case, when I looked up, and behold! I was outside Somerset House." He replaced the glasses by way of pause. "Then I thought I'd go in. There was a delightfully courteous young man who looked after me, and when I asked him for a copy of my birth certificate, he made no bones about it at all, even though I didn't know the exact name of the place where I was born, or the day."

"But you do know your birthday!" Jane Wharton told him, with a puzzled little frown.

"Let Mr. Travers go on," said Wharton impatiently.

Travers smiled. "Well, you see, I was under false pretences. But naturally he asked for my name, and I told him—*Aloysius Ringold Rennyet.*"

"My God!" said Wharton, staring. "And you're the one who told me the other day that you'd like to become a good liar!"

"You're not accusing me of lying, George," protested Travers. "After all, there's lying and lying. But the fact I'd bring to your notice is that I discovered in my capacity of Aloysius Ringold Rennyet *that my birthday was the eleventh of August.* What do you make of that?"

"The eleventh of August? And he celebrated it the night Lewton was killed?" Wharton's forehead was suddenly creased in thought, and then the creases went, and he actually laughed. He went further. He leaned over and dug Travers in the ribs. "His birthday, eh? Haven't you ever treated yourself to a birthday? Haven't you ever made it an excuse for something?" He chuckled again. "Rennyet wanted an excuse for that glass of special port, and for giving one to his two servants, towards whom his heart had suddenly warmed. So he called them in to drink his health, and made a birthday an excuse."

Travers smiled charmingly. "George, you're always too clever for me—not that I didn't think of the same objection myself. Only—to be perfectly frank—I thought it a footling objection. I believe Rennyet had something definite to celebrate. He did make the excuse of a birthday, but he celebrated all the same."

"Oh, and what did he celebrate?" asked Wharton.

"Well, he might have celebrated his night's work," said Travers. "He might have been bubbling over with joy at the fact that he'd disposed of Lewton, and had a hundred-per-cent alibi."

Wharton gave another chuckle. "Ingenious as ever. Still, there's the same chorus to the song. *Bust the alibi.*"

Travers pretended to take him at his word. "Do you know, that's what I'd like to have a shot at."

"What's your special theory, Mr. Travers—if I may ask?" Mrs. Wharton said.

"I don't know that I have any," Travers told her. "I have a hunch that Rennyet was blackmailed by Lewton, and that he

knew something about Meek's sister-in-law. I believe he mould-
ed the two Meeks so that they accepted unquestioningly a certain combination of circumstances. I believe he counted on
the support of Meek if anything happened to be found out. It's
vague, I grant you, but taken in connection with that birthday
business, it's good enough to risk a couple of tenners on."

Wharton cocked his head sideways. "A couple of tenners?"

"Yes," said Travers, and got to his feet. "If you had no objections—and that's what I really came to see you about to-night—I
thought I'd put in a fortnight at that excellent Bicklesham inn
and cultivate the acquaintance of a fellow-author."

Wharton's eyes narrowed. "He doesn't know you. It might
work—I mean, you might get into the house all right, though I'm
damned if I see what you can find out."

"You never know," said Travers cheerfully. "Now had I
Jubal's lyre, of course—"

"'Liar' is right," said Wharton. "Still, let me know when you
get there. I'll probably have to come down and bail you out."

But that very same night, hardly before the toot of Travers's
horn had died away, Wharton himself was to have a sudden new
hope. The telephone bell went—the Yard repeating a message
just received from Seaborough.

Carry, it appeared, had never given up his Trench theories,
and had made in that connection a further overhaul of Juker.
What had arisen had been what he considered—if not a dramatic discovery—at least something worthy of Wharton's serious
consideration.

That night when Howard Trench had asked Juker if he knew
a short cut to the town, Juker was holding his watch in his hand,
and in spite of his professed hurry Howard Trench had asked if
he might see the famous watch, which had just been consulted,
and about which Juker had talked on the previous night. Juker
gave him the watch *and Howard Trench held it in his hand for
a minute or so.*

Wharton talked it over at once with his wife. "It's hard to
strike a balance between the natural and the unnatural," he told
her. "There was every reason why he should have wanted to see

the famous watch, and yet somehow there wasn't. He was in a hurry, as Carry says. Also, if he did hold the watch and move the hands, I doubt if he could have swindled old Juker."

"Yes, and you asked Juker what the time was later in the evening, and the watch was then right."

"I know," said Wharton. "Still, it's a new aspect of the alibi—or a new chance of a flaw, and that's something in these lean times."

"Well, you can say what you like," his wife told him, "but I still think Dr. Hule had something to do with it—him and his wife between them."

"Very well, my dear," said Wharton blandly. "The same remark applies to you that I made to Mr. Travers. All you have to do is to *bust his alibi*."

CHAPTER XII
RECONNAISSANCE

TRAVERS HAD no delusions whatever about that trip to Bicklesham. He needed a holiday—at least, so he assured himself—and he proposed to take one. As for Rennyet, there was everything to gain and nothing to lose. Rennyet was entrenched behind his alibi. It might be a genuine alibi; indeed, it could hardly be anything else, and yet about that same impregnable alibi Travers had a thought that was paradoxically preposterous, and—to one of his curious make-up—provokingly alluring. That alibi had been weakest at the first moment of its existence. As time went on and it remained unassailed, it gathered strength from the very security which the passage of time gave to it. On the morning after Lewton's murder there might have been questions asked and answers demanded. Now those questions could not be asked, for the simple reason that it was unreasonable to expect the events about which the questions centred to have been remembered; or if they had been remembered, then some vagueness, confusion or even errors could be explained away by the same passing of time.

But Travers was a tenacious soul. He expected no immediate results—if results at all. He was prepared for a fortnight's siege, and was only too aware that hurry or over-keenness might awake suspicion in a mind that was ready to be suspicious. But, strange to say, even before he set foot in Bicklesham at all, he was to have such a stroke of luck as his wildest optimisms could never have contemplated.

It arose out of a visit to Rappway, for Travers was leaving no unguarded loophole in his precautions. His car passed the Manor and drew in at the drive of Little Gables, and Captain Rappway was luckily at home. He cast no friendly eye upon the visitor, and was distinctly uneasy when Travers asked for a few moments of his private time.

"What I'm telling you is in the strictest confidence," he said, "but I'm staying for a fortnight or so at the inn at Bicklesham; at least, I hope they'll be able to put me up. My business there is highly confidential, and I don't want you or Mrs. Givers to mention that you've seen me before."

"We're hardly likely to do that," said Rappway.

"Sorry," said Travers, "but I'm putting it rather crudely. What I mean is that my name might be mentioned by people I happen to call on, and I don't want you even to let out that I've ever been in this part of the world before—that you've seen my car, for instance. Also"—and there he gave his most delightful smile—"I don't want to alarm you or anybody else who might have reason to be alarmed. I'm not down here on business which concerns you in the least. Further, I can assure you that you'll never hear another word about certain matters which we both have in mind at this moment."

"Thanks," said Rappway curtly. "That's very good of you." But behind the curtness was a something that was striving for utterance, or else was a self-consciousness that felt itself shamefully apparent.

Travers, for all his tact, knew what Rappway was thinking, and while he made allowance and himself somewhat shamefacedly let a sympathy be seen, he forgot, as he always did, the rare, appealing charm of his own personality. That was why Rappway's confession was to surprise him.

"You've been very decent over all this," Rappway said, and still hesitated slightly. Then he took the sudden plunge. "Look here. I wonder if I might tell you about something that's been worrying me a good deal—and Mrs. Givers too. Frightfully confidential, of course."

"By all means tell me," said Travers, and tried to look as if he knew the skeletons in the cupboards of every European palace.

"Well," said Rappway, "it's about a man at Bicklesham. You wouldn't know him. His name's Rennyet. He writes books, and all that. Quite well connected, but too top-heavy for my liking. Very brainy, you know."

Travers nodded sympathetically. Rappway evidently was suspicious of brains.

"I know him pretty well," went on Rappway. "He's been here once or twice, and he always insists on telling everybody how he writes his blasted books. He did the same, I believe, at the Manor once."

Travers was more than interested, though behind all the talk he knew that Rappway was summoning a courage for some more personal information. He lent a hand himself.

"You mean you think this man Rennyet is implicated in certain matters in which I'm interested?"

"Not quite that," said Rappway. He plucked at the minute, stubbly ends of his black, tooth-brush moustache. "I say, I wonder if you'd let Mrs. Givers tell you herself." His face lit up with the bare suggestion. "Tell you what, I'll try to get her over here."

Ten minutes later Mrs. Givers entered the room into which Travers had been parked. She greeted him with that effusiveness which speaks of past indebtedness and foreshadows more. Rappway hovered round restlessly, and there was a considerable deal of idle prattling before the lady approached the main point.

"About the matter which Captain Rappway thought we'd— that is, I had better speak to you," she said. "It was this Mr. Rennyet. I think he knows."

Travers was startled. "Knows? You mean about that attempt at blackmailing?"

She nodded. "I'm not sure, but I'll tell you just what happened. He called a few days ago to see my husband about some plants he had been promised for his garden, and Harry—that's my husband—brought him in." She swivelled round there to get Travers full face, and for all the little shrugs and smiles and assumptions of indifference, there was no mistaking the underlying uneasiness of her manner.

"Then he began talking about that murder, and I'm sure he dragged it in. He simply made us talk about it. I could feel it."

"You thought he was talking for your special benefit? Talking at you, as it were."

She nodded. "That's right. And when my husband left the room for something, he turned to me with the most extraordinary look, and he said, 'I think everybody ought to be very pleased that Lewton was killed, don't you?' So I said I didn't care two straws either way, and then he gave me another perfectly amazing look and he said, '*Are you quite sure about that?*' That's how he said it."

Travers made a face. "It certainly looks as if he had some knowledge—though I can assure you it's beyond the bounds of possibility that he got it from the police."

"You see my difficulty," she said. "All this absurd talk about Captain Rappway and myself—well, we thought it was all over. And of course we thought now that nobody in the world would ever know a thing about it."

"I shouldn't worry if I were you," Travers told her. "I can't tell you the exact methods I shall employ, but I can guarantee that you'll hear no more about it. I wonder." He smiled reflectively, then turned the smile dazzlingly on Rappway. "Could you possibly give me an introduction to Rennyet, so that I could make his acquaintance without exciting suspicion?"

Rappway set about its concoction at once, and a most inveigling letter was manufactured. Travers, a friend of Rappway, was an author, and as he was staying at Bicklesham, Rappway thought he and Rennyet might have something in common.

"But you're not an author really?" smiled Mavis Givers.

"My dear lady, if I could be of service to you, I'd even be an author," Travers told her. He held out his hand. "Good-bye. Perhaps if Captain Rappway is good enough to ask Rennyet and myself over some time, I may see you again."

But that news about Rennyet was of such staggering importance that Travers paused at Bicklesham merely to fix up about rooms, and then went on, meal-less, to Seaborough. It took him another half-hour before he could get Wharton himself on the phone.

"You see the point, George," he said. "If Rennyet knew about the two love-birds, then he got the information from the notes in Lewton's book—which means he must have had it in his hand. He may be the one who sent it to Tempest."

"I don't like women's chatter," came Wharton's voice dubiously from the other end. "When a woman's got a guilty conscience, she imagines all sorts of things. Rennyet's may have been the most harmless of remarks."

"Well, I'm sure there's something in it," insisted Travers.

There was a grunt, then, "As you like. Carry on with what you're doing and I'll be along in a day or two. You'll get news of me through where you are now."

Travers drove back to Bicklesham in a mood of tremendous optimism. There had come into his mind an idea that would need exhaustive examination—no less a theory, in fact, than that Rennyet, instead of being blackmailed by Lewton, might actually have been a third partner to the other unholy two. He might have been a kind of sleeping partner, or expert called in for cases that looked like being middle cuts of salmon. He would have a suavity and a certainty of touch which Lewton and his still cruder partner lacked. That would explain the knowledge of the contents of the book, and—if it really had been Rennyet who called at Homedale that night—it would explain why Lewton let him in without question and at once called up Beece. And then Travers, in the midst of theories and optimisms, remembered George Wharton. Theories, however apt and plausible, were

nothing. The case could be solved by one simple formula alone—
the busting of an alibi.

But in spite of Wharton's formula, Travers was so satisfied
with the foundation on which he had to build, that he sent a
telegram to his man, Palmer, to come to Bicklesham forthwith,
instead of taking the holiday on which he had been none too
keen. Palmer, an old servant of the family, had that unobtru-
sive competence, that sureness of bearing, that patrician dignity
of silver hair and episcopal profile which would admit him to
the confidences of better men than Meek. Palmer had a stock
of reminiscences that would interest Meek's wife, and an old-
world manner that would fascinate. Palmer, in fact, might learn
a lot. To suspect him of ulterior motives was absurd. As well
suspect the pontifical hand stretched forth in blessing as being
about to pick your pocket.

It was six o'clock that night when Palmer arrived, and
Travers forthwith had an hour with him. Palmer knew all about
the Seaborough murder. Thanks to Wharton's spectacular inquest, there was little of which any discerning mind could possibly be unaware.

"The great thing, I take it, sir, is tact," was Palmer's final
comment.

"That's right," said Travers. "On no account are you to drag
anything in. Let the conversation make itself. Sooner or later
you're bound to talk about the murder, and even then I shouldn't
show any curiosity. Let them do the talking."

It was the following afternoon at about three-thirty that the
call was made. The Rolls was spotless, and Palmer, like an elderly patriarch, sat by his master's side. Meek, who opened the
door and saw him standing almost disdainfully by the superb
car, must have thought the call a ducal one at least. Travers,
who had been interested in the moving aside of a curtain and
Rennyet's quick peep, presented his card and was asked inside.

Rennyet ran his eye over Rappway's note, and Travers surveyed the room. It was the study, where Wharton had done
his interviewing, and the furniture showed sound taste and a
knowledge of the finer arts. The grandfather clock was a gem,

and so was the corner cabinet. Family pieces, no doubt—and then Travers's eye returned to his host again, and there was Rennyet beaming at him.

"This is a tremendous honour," he began. "I say, let me take your coat. You'll have some tea. We always have tea about this time."

He was all enthusiasm and movement, what with ringing the bell, helping Travers off with his overcoat, giving it to Meek, ordering tea and getting Travers safely in the chair again. Then he had a look through the window.

"What about your man? Would you mind if Meek took him to the kitchen? It's frightfully nippy out there."

"That's very good of you," said Travers, and there was Rennyet pushing the bell again and making arrangements. Then at last he sat down, and again he beamed.

"Do you know," he said, "I've wanted for years to have the luck to meet you, Mr. Travers. And you're really the man who wrote *The Economics of a Spendthrift*?"

Travers modestly admitted it.

"A great book," said Rennyet. "Do you know, I have it at my bedside with The *Wallet of Kai-Lung*, and Rabelais, and *Pilgrim's Progress* and all the rest of them?"

"I'm afraid my glow-worm shines rather small in that galaxy," said Travers. "But you're a much more important person yourself. Only the other day I read a book of yours, and enjoyed it immensely. That's why I was so amazingly delighted when Rappway mentioned your name."

"Really?" Rennyet looked tremendously pleased at that.

Then the tea came in, and they gossiped away between bites.

"You're staying down here long?" Rennyet asked.

"To tell the truth, I can't say," Travers told him. "There's certain information I'm collecting, and as soon as I have it, I may have to go back to town. You know, perhaps, what that kind of collecting is?"

"You're not writing another book?"

"Well—" began Travers diffidently, but Rennyet cut in:

"I say, that's tremendously exciting. It's quite an event, you know—a new book by Ludovic Travers."

"Nonsense!" Travers told him. "People would much rather have your kind of thing; I certainly would myself." Suddenly he gave a whimsical smile. "Do you know, I'd love to write a detective novel."

Rennyet seemed taken aback. "But why? I mean, you do the other thing so uniquely. Anybody can write my kind of stuff."

"And everybody does," suggested Travers.

"You're dead right," said Rennyet. "Surely you'd rather have the honour of being the only writer of distinction who hasn't tried his hand at it, than just be one of the gang?"

"It's cussedness with me," confessed Travers. "I want to write one just because I know I can't. I'd rather write one under an assumed name, so that I shall really be told just what it's worth—that is, if any critic thinks it worth reading."

"I think I could fix that for you," said Rennyet, and mentioned one notorious thruster.

So personal did he get that Travers found it none too easy to steer the conversation round to mere murder, and when he did, Rennyet made the running, and all his hearer had to do was to sit back and chuckle.

"We've had a murder here, you know," said Rennyet.

"Murder here?" repeated Travers blankly.

"Yes, the Seaborough murder."

Travers looked more dumb than ever, and then allowed some semblance of understanding to appear.

"Yes, there was something in the papers, now I come to think of it."

Rennyet laughed. "Something in the papers! My dear fellow, they had nothing else." He touched his chest with his finger. "I had the honour of being a suspect!"

Travers began a smile, and allowed it to become a look of horror. "You're not serious?"

"Perhaps I'm not," said Rennyet. "All the same, absolutely in confidence, I happened to know the man who was murdered. Lewton his name was. I see you remember him now. Well"—he drew his chair in to make the story more intimate and friendly "I had the police come here to inquire if I knew anything about Lewton. You see, they couldn't find out anything about his past—so I gathered—and they wondered if he'd let anything drop to me."

"This is frightfully exciting!" Travers smiled expectantly, and drew his own chair a shade nearer the fire.

"Yes," went on Rennyet. "But you listen to this. The Seaborough police had one of the big noises of Scotland Yard down here, and he paid me a visit the morning after the murder. He called himself Ward when his name was really Wharton. Why'd he do that if he didn't think I had something to do with it?"

Travers smiled. "I don't know—unless he knew you as a writer of detective novels and thought he'd better go carefully. I suppose one can find out by consulting books of reference and that sort of thing who the chief people at Scotland Yard are?"

"I suppose you can," said Rennyet. "All the same, it was very funny, don't you think? Most amusing, too, from my point of view. Mind you, I'll give him this credit. You'd never have taken him for a policeman."

"Really?"

"Good heavens, no! Do you remember a character who used to appear a lot on the films in the old silent days? A chap called Chester Conklin?"

Travers smiled. "Of course I do. He looked a kind of harassed, dear old bungler."

"Well, he's the very spit of this chap Wharton." He smiled tolerantly as he shrugged his shoulders. "Still, I suppose he must have brains somewhere, or they wouldn't have made him one of the Big Five."

Travers frowned. "I don't know. There's influence in all things. You know what I mean. And whatever he is, he doesn't seem to have made very much of this particular case; at least, I don't think they've solved it yet, have they?"

"And they never will, if you ask me," said Rennyet, and smiled cynically.

"But it's intriguing." Travers screwed up his features into profound thought. "Somebody must have done it—unless he committed suicide and the police took it for murder. I believe that's happened once or twice. You've got no ideas yourself?"

"Where the professionals fail you'd hardly expect an amateur to come in."

"True enough," said Travers. "All the same, I've got an idea that you could do as well as the professionals—given the same chance."

"You flatter me," said Rennyet, but his face showed no displeasure. "But you're not going already?"

"Indeed I must," smiled Travers. "There are some people I must call on before dinner. And when can you come to lunch with me? To-morrow? The day after?"

"The day after, if I may," said Rennyet. "I'd be absolutely delighted to come. You'll be comfortable at the Red Anchor, by the way."

"If I'm not, my man's a good forager," said Travers.

"You had him long?"

"He was with my father when I was born," smiled Travers. Then he smiled at Meek, who had helped him on with his overcoat, and out in the hall he smiled at the lovely bronze pestle and mortar that stood on the low chest.

"That's a charming piece. Crested, too. Mind if I handle it?"

"Do, please," said Rennyet, and Travers fingered it, and thought it was early seventeenth century.

Then he smiled at Rennyet yet once more, and at Palmer, who held open the door of the Rolls, and then with Palmer at the wheel the car drew out to the ridge road, below which the chestnut woods were all purple and madder in the luminous light of the April afternoon.

But Travers had not smiled as the car glided along that half-mile of quiet lane. He said no word to Palmer till he was in his room upstairs.

"Well, how'd you find them?"

"The Meeks, sir? Nice, homely people, sir. Quiet, well-spoken, clean, and very decent people, sir, indeed."

"The murder was mentioned?"

"It was, sir, but I don't like murders."

"Splendid," smiled Travers. "And now I'd like you to take a walk to the post office to post a couple of letters—as soon as they're written. And in a day or two I shall arrange to be out, and it might be just as well if you got so friendly with the Meeks that you could ask them round here. They're bound to have an evening off."

"Their arrangement is that they go out whenever they like, sir," said Palmer. "But I gathered they were quiet people, who don't care for Seaborough, and so they don't go out a lot. They have the wireless in the kitchen."

"That reminds me," said Travers. "I noticed the phone was installed. It wasn't in a month ago. Perhaps you could find out something about that."

"As a matter of fact, sir, something was mentioned," said Palmer. "From what I heard, sir, I took it that Mr. Rennyet had done without the phone because he objected to certain charges. Then apparently he decided, sir, that he'd have to pay, so he had the phone put in at the beginning of this quarter. As Meek was saying, sir, you can't really do without it in the country—not if you're anybody at all."

That evening after dinner, as Travers sat before the cheerful fire with a drink at his elbow and the wind howling sportively outside, he had a whole new series of problems to wrestle with. He wondered why he and Wharton had never taken the wireless into account as establishing Rennyet's alibi; why the phone had really been installed, and whether Rennyet had been as cynical as he had looked when he spoke of the case as likely to remain unsolved. Travers thought, too, of the mellow sound of Bicklesham clock as he had heard it at the hour of five, and his restless, inventive mind dwelt for a moment on that delightful pestle that stood in Rennyet's hall. More than once, too, Travers would give a dry, internal chuckle. That was when he thought of Wharton's face if ever he—Ludovic Travers—should relate in detail Rennyet's opinions of Conklin-Wharton, and the system of promotion at Scotland Yard.

CHAPTER XIII
SKIRMISHING

AFTER LUNCH the following day Palmer paid a visit to the Meeks. He had on a tweed jacket, a shooting hat and an old-fashioned pair of walking breeches, and with an ancient meerschaum to increase the effect, he looked for all the world like an Edwardian squire. But the great thing was that Palmer stood out, even in his unofficial garments, as something unique. There was no need for him to pose or act. One felt instinctively that but for the whims of fate, not only might Mr. Travers's man have been the master; he would, moreover, have been one of whom his own man could have spoken with pride.

Something of that, no doubt, was due to the way in which Palmer spoke of Mr. Travers. Already he had told the Meeks about the ramifications of the family, and Travers's father and life in the old days. With a natural pride he mentioned the reputation which Ludovic Travers had acquired, his enormous circle of acquaintances, and his almost scandalous disregard of the considerable fortune he possessed. And most of all he dwelt on his master's warm humanity, his sympathy and thought, and all those things, in fact, in which the Meeks themselves might be interested by comparison.

Part of that afternoon he spent with Tom Meek in the garden, where work was now in full swing. Rennyet came out for a bit, and was charmed with Palmer's deference. At first he had been disposed to treat him with some condescension, but like Tom Meek, he soon saw in him a something different that brought the three of them to one level of friendliness and interest. Rennyet could never have had the least suspicion of Ludovic Travers, and yet, had Palmer fitted less admirably the eccentric, lovable person whom he was pleased to serve, those suspicions might in time have arisen.

Rennyet had looked Travers up in all the books, and the gist of his discoveries was that there were an enormous number of things of which he himself—had he been Travers—might reasonably have boasted. Rennyet, then, was flattered at Travers's interest, and for all the casualness and flippancy that Travers had been pleased to display, he knew him for a man better in most ways than himself. And that was amazing for Rennyet, whose self-possession, self-confidence and jealous ironies were apparent to people of far less penetration that Ludovic Travers.

On the whole, then, Travers and his man were ideally placed for a first-class inquisition into the affairs of the Rennyet household. But Travers moved warily. His long association with George Wharton had taught him the value of occasional showmanship, and that day when Rennyet came to lunch, he chose to be quietly courteous and even avuncular. Without more than the barest suggestion, he created a vague atmosphere of patronage. It was as if he had said to himself, "I was far too free when I first met this man, whose uncle I'm more than old enough to be. I'll let him talk about himself, and without showing it, I'll cap his small experiences and doings with my own. He shall regard me as far more important than I am, and he may even pity me for not being aware of the fact myself."

Palmer waited at table that day, and did it with a magnificent competence. The meal was good; its trimmings spoke of unobtruded wealth and perfect taste. The conversation ranged from Pole to Pole, though Seaborough was shrewdly left out. Not until Rennyet rose to go—and it was then three o'clock—did Travers refer to what had been the main subject of conversation at their first meeting, and then he spoke with considerable reserve.

"I was extremely interested in that business we were talking about the other day," he said, "and I had an idea which struck me as rather clever. I sent my man in to Seaborough and got the files of the local paper. Last night I read all about the inquest. Amazingly interesting, I found it. A verbatim report, too."

"Yes," said Rennyet. "I haven't seen the papers much, but I was there myself."

Travers nodded, then looked away abstractedly "I really think my mind's made up. I really must have a shot at a murder mystery." He smiled. "Perhaps when I see you again the first chapter may be written, and after that nothing will stop me. Still, you don't want to listen to the babblings of an amateur."

He changed the conversation deftly round, and when his guest had gone, he wondered if the effort had been too apparent and the morning wasted. But it had not been wasted. Rennyet was intrigued, and he was definitely jealous. He told himself that if Ludovic Travers wrote a detective novel, he would do so with unfair advantages. All sorts of vague jealousies began to float in Rennyet's mind, and when two or three days passed and Ludovic Travers made no further advances, jealousy became dislike, and dislike fed itself on sneering, introspective ironies.

"I think I noticed what you told me to look out for," Palmer reported to Travers. "He was very short with me to-day, sir, when I was with Meek. Almost rude, you might have called it, sir."

"All right," said Travers; "we'll let him cool his heels a little bit longer. When we whistle him he mayn't come, but we've got to risk that."

"Don't forget that Friday's Good Friday, sir. He's very busy now with rehearsals for that play they're doing."

"Yes," said Travers, "he mentioned it when he was here."

"Meek was in the show last year, sir. I don't know if it's of any interest to you, sir, but I was told so by his wife. This year there don't appear to be enough parts to go round. Apparently he was to have been something, and then one of the local notabilities was left out, sir, and Mr. Rennyet asked Meek to stand down."

Travers smiled. "Nothing's uninteresting. However, you shall take a note round at once. I'll ask him here for breakfast on Wednesday."

"Breakfast, sir?"

"You heard what I said," smiled Travers. "Breakfast. Groaning sideboard. Help yourself to devilled kidneys, and all the rest of it. And sufficiently old-fashioned to be ultra-modern. Which reminds me. If you see Meek for a moment's gossip, let out that I've only just begun a book, and that on such occasions I'm always like a bear with a sore head."

Rennyet came. His jealousies, envies and bitter ironies all passed like morning mist in a summer sun. Travers laid himself out to be perfectly charming, and when Rennyet left it was with the certain knowledge that Ludovic Travers was the most like-able, unspoiled, generous and understanding person the world had ever seen.

But it was not till almost midday that Rennyet left. Over three hours had been spent in Travers's company, and they had passed all too quickly. While the meal was in progress, Travers had thrown his first delightful bombshell.

"I'm going to be utterly shameless, and throw myself on your mercy," he said. "I've had the temerity to draft out that detective novel and, frankly, I'm already in a muddle."

Rennyet smiled. "You mean with the plot? You see, I can't conceive of your getting muddled with anything else."

"That's very nice of you," said Travers. "But it does happen to be the plot—principally. May I tell you what I had in mind?"

"Do, please."

"Well," began Travers, with a humorous diffidence, "it's like this. That Seaborough case has got on my mind—chiefly, I admit, because you were connected with it yourself. It's like a murder at first hand, so to speak. However, it's intrigued me enormously. Not only that—I do feel that one ought to cater for the public taste. And it's all a kind of challenge, and I hate being challenged, don't you?"

"I certainly do," admitted Rennyet, who was finding it hard to follow Travers's mixed trains of thought.

"There we are, then," said Travers triumphantly. "The Sea-borough murder is a challenge to all writers of detective fiction. It's bang in the public eye—or it was; and a real good man can make it so again. What I've decided, therefore, is that unless I can write a book along the actual lines of that case, I shall not write one at all."

"You mean that you'd try to solve the case!"

"Good Lord, no! The law of libel stands in the way for one thing, if my lack of intelligence wasn't an obstacle far more monstrous. No," and he shook his head reflectively, "what I had thought of doing was to sail as near the wind as I could. I'd create a series of circumstances which roughly corresponded, and I'd suggest a solution which everybody would connect with the real Seaborough case."

Rennyet struggled between a new jealousy and a profound admiration. "By Jove! it'd take some doing. And if the publicity were handled well, it'd sell like hot cakes."

He was shaking his head with a kind of gloomy reflection when Travers came in with his suggestion.

"All that brings me to my unblushing proposal. What would you say if I suggested that you and I did that detective novel together?"

Rennyet stared. "You mean it?"

"Of course I mean it. It's gross impertinence, I admit."

Rennyet beamed. "But I'd be delighted. Under our own names would it be?"

Travers bowed slightly. "If you think fit."

Rennyet was rather dazed. That his name should appear on the title-page of a book side by side with that of Ludovic Travers, was something hard to contemplate.

"What I had in mind was this," went on Travers. "While I'm down here, we can decide on the plot and the essential details. Then we can settle individual shares. On one thing, of course, I must insist. You're the senior partner, and what you say goes."

"Nothing of the sort," smiled Rennyet. He shook his head bemusedly at the prospects the scheme unrolled. "You know, if we make a success of this—and we certainly shall—we might do a whole series."

"Let's tackle this one first," said Travers dryly. "When our hen has laid her first egg, then we can think about a poultry farm. But might I make another suggestion?"

"Make a hundred if you like."

"Well, I'll hear what you think first," said Travers, apparently changing his mind. "What, in your considered opinion, carries the main stress of a detective novel? What's the first essential, in other words?"

"Well, the plot."

"Yes, but what is the essential for the actual plot?"

"I'd say an alibi. Give me a perfectly good faked alibi and I'll write a murder story—of sorts—round it."

Travers beamed. "Now isn't that amazing? That's the very thing that struck me in this Seaborough case. Why did the police put the two Trenches in the witness-box? To let the public see their alibis, and hoping someone could come forward and point out a flaw. And, between ourselves, I shouldn't wonder if they had a furtive idea of the same sort about that doctor and his wife. Then there was that man Beece, who committed suicide. It seems to me that any of them might have done it, provided you—I mean *we*—can suggest a faked alibi—and show how it might have been faked."

"I know," said Rennyet, and as senior partner pursed his lips reflectively. "The trouble is, it sounds too easy."

"I know it does," said Travers. "But surely two people like our two selves aren't going to be stumped by a mere faked alibi. You're in no hurry, by the way? Splendid. Then let's draw up to this excellent fire and have a preliminary survey."

But all that emerged from the conference of the next hour and a half were the following main outlines:

(*a*) To save time over colour, the scene should be local. To avoid too close an identification, however, all names and strongly marked local features should be altered.

(*b*) A list of characters should be drawn up by each author, and be ready for discussion within twenty-four hours.

(c) The murderer should certainly be a victim of Lewton and Beece.

When Rennyet departed, Travers proceeded to exult, and the reason for his exultation was, paradoxically enough, the very fact that so little had really been done. Rennyet had dexterously avoided coming to grips with alibis. He had been strongly disinclined to place the murderer's home in Bicklesham. And, above all, there could be—as Travers expectantly saw it—only one reason for the unnecessary hesitations and delays which Rennyet had so cunningly fabricated. *Rennyet wanted time.* He wished to get away by himself and think things over. Only a fool would thrust his neck into a noose, and only a fool would refuse the offer of a novel in collaboration with an author with the reputation, and the sales, of Ludovic Travers. Rennyet, then, was between two stools. Without betraying himself, he still had to show himself a master of the craft by which he ostensibly got a living, and there was little time in which to do it. Ideas must be found at once. *And, with that desperate need for ideas, Rennyet might find it safe to divulge something of the truth.*

That evening Travers rang up Seaborough police-station and learned that Wharton was in the town. At nine o'clock they met in Tempest's house, and at Wharton's own suggestion, Travers said nothing about Bicklesham.

Wharton himself was following up a new scent. He had already discarded Carry's brain-wave following on the discovery that Howard Trench had had the chance of tampering with Juker's watch. Now, at Tempest's invitation, he was reconsidering the question of Dr. Hule, and from a wholly new angle. Given as basis the fact that the doctor's alibi depended on the evidence of a patient with whom it had been only too easy to tamper, Tempest had erected quite a hopeful edifice. Hule—a loose talker with a drink or two inside him—had said that if he ever cared to talk he could do good work in the blackmailing line himself. The fact was only too true about all doctors, but Tempest chose to see something special in Hule's use of it. Why should not Hule have parted with some of that information to Lewton, whose doctor he was? Might not the familiarity thereby arising between them have been the cause of the jocular advances which Lewton had made to Mrs. Hule over the phone? And finally, might not Hule have realized that Lewton knew too much?

Travers, who had been told all about it, ventured an objection. "A knife would be rather crude for a doctor, wouldn't it? Of all people who could commit murder and get away with it, doctors stand out alone."

"I was thinking of a quarrel and a sudden blow," said Tempest. "Even there I admit that it was hardly likely that Hule would have had the knife on him. And Trench swore there never had been one like it in the house."

"Hule's certainly worth another try-out," said Wharton. "He can't have much of a practice—at least, judging by their house and the general look of everything. Also Hule's a spender."

"And what about the slip, if he imitated Lewton's voice?" asked Travers.

"As we see it now," Tempest told him, "we think it wasn't a slip at all. It might have all been cleverly arranged. I admit it's rather involved, but look at it this way. We've said Hule couldn't have been the man who imitated Lewton's voice because he didn't speak to Mrs. Hule as Lewton would have done. Why shouldn't Hule have done that with deliberate intent? Why shouldn't he have anticipated the very course of events as they've actually happened? Dr. Hule would have known that Lewton would have been familiar with Mrs. Hule. But the man who imitated Lewton's voice was not familiar, as he certainly ought to have been. Therefore it wasn't Hule who imitated the voice. That's how Hule saw it, and he planned accordingly."

Travers smiled. "Well, in Wharton's own words, all that's left is to bust Hule's alibi."

It was ten o'clock before Travers could reasonably get away, and Wharton left with him. The General was most interested in Travers's doings, and not in the least supercilious.

"For the love of heaven, go steady," he said. "One single slip and you've lost him for ever."

"He's damnably clever and he's damnably conceited," said Travers. "I'm perfectly content to go on being a comparative fool. Those three points are the legs of my stool."

"Well, don't think I'm being too critical," said Wharton, "but there's just one point I'm going to put up to you. Suppose Rennyet does concoct a perfect alibi. The mere fact that it's perfect will mean that it can't be disproved."

"We shall have to concoct a flaw," said Travers. "Otherwise, how can the case be solved?"

"That's my point," said Wharton gloomily. "Rennyet may tell you just a little about his own alibi—always assuming, of course, that he's the man we're looking for. But I bet you every penny I have in the world that he only divulges what he knows can't do any harm. What's more, if I know that cynical devil rightly, he may even be laughing up his sleeve. Think of the ironical joy for a man of his type to confide in a fellow-mortal how a murder might have been done—and then still to be utterly safe himself."

"Yes, but the flaw?"

Wharton snorted. "The flaw be damned! How can he give you the flaw if there never was one? And if it's a question of mere invention, then any village idiot could make up a flaw. Still, we shall see. In any case, yours is a thundering good idea, and I wish you luck."

Thursday was Rennyet's busy day, and it was not till nearly ten o'clock that he called in on his way home from the village hall, where he had been supervising the final rehearsal. Travers—a late bird if ever there was one—kept him till past eleven, when Rennyet was unashamedly yawning. But the tentative list of characters was complete, and all that remained was to scheme an alibi.

It was just after nine the following morning, and Travers was in the act of lighting his first pipe, when Palmer announced Rennyet. Travers hopped up with a smile.

"Hallo! You're abroad early?"

"Yes," said Rennyet. "Something occurred to me last night in my sleep, and as soon as I woke up I knew it was what we're looking for."

"Fully armed from the brain of Jove, what?" said Travers fatuously. "And you mean to tell me you've got the alibi?"

"I have," said Rennyet confidently, and then with an assumption of diffidence, "At least, I'm hoping you'll think I have." He shrugged his shoulders. "Of course you realize that we shall have to manufacture a certain set of circumstances to fit in with it."

"Oh, naturally," agreed Travers. "And who's to be the murderer?"

"Well, I thought somebody like yourself. We can have him staying in the village at a furnished house. Take my house, if you like; it'll save all question of bothering over local colour."

"Why not?" Travers drew up a chair. "Now tell me all about it. I'm simply bursting to hear. Perfectly marvellous," he chattered on. "You've actually discovered how to kill our man and get away with it!"

Rennyet took the chair and a cigarette. "I know you'll be disappointed," he said. "But you do realize, don't you, that all an alibi is, is that a man should do something at a place where he can't possibly be?"

"Naturally," said Travers.

"And that that must involve some tampering with time?"

Travers nodded. "That's agreed too."

"Well, then," said Rennyet, "all we have to do is to alter the clocks in the man's house."

Travers stared at him blankly. "But, my dear fellow—pardon me, of course—but that's too obvious. Why, it's been done a hundred times!"

Rennyet leaned forward to him with a singular earnestness. "If you'll pardon *me*, that's where you're wrong. What I'm going to put up to you is admittedly hackneyed. It's so hackneyed, in fact, that nobody could have the temerity to suspect it. You remember Naaman the Syrian? '*Are not Abana and Pharpar, rivers of Damascus, greater than these?*' Jordan was too simple for him. This scheme may appear too simple to you, *and only because it's so utterly easy.*"

CHAPTER XIV
RETIREMENT IN GOOD ORDER

BUT WITH A hundred and one things waiting for him that morning, Rennyet could stay no longer.

"You think the proposal over," he said. "Don't look at it from the point of view of what I might call a lover of novelty. Look at it from the point of view of the police—and a jury."

Travers did look at it, and from all sorts of angles. And the more he looked, the more did his disappointment disappear. Suppose the alibi did depend on moving the hands of a clock; did the hackneyed simplicity of it matter, provided it worked? If by use of even obvious means a man gave himself an alibi which the police could nevertheless not break, then the scheme could not be called anything else but good.

But Travers had not the slightest intention of trying to work out such an alibi for himself. It was his role to be a fool in such matters. He would force Rennyet into patient explanation, and even perhaps exasperate him into outrunning his schedule of disclosures.

That afternoon, Palmer was sent to the performance of *Everyman*, and Travers took a walk. Palmer liked the show.

"I don't know if you'll understand me, sir," he said, "but it was the kind of thing that makes a man feel better for it. Very simply done, sir, but very impressive. Mr. Rennyet was specially good, sir."

"I'm glad you liked it," said Travers. "Anybody else there that you knew?"

"Only Meek, sir. Mrs. Meek has to lie down every afternoon, as I believe I told you, sir."

"You didn't tell me," said Travers. "What's the matter with her, then? Heart?"

"The stomach, I believe, sir. All I know, sir, is that the doctor ordered her to lie down of an afternoon. I think I'm right in saying it's from two-thirty to four."

On the Saturday Travers was still not inclined to force matters. When Rennyet called, he was out, and it was not till the Sunday morning that he walked the half-mile to Rennyet's place to convey his own apologies.

"If you can spare an hour, we'll get down to the book," Rennyet said.

They got to work on it, and in five minutes Travers was confessing his hopeless inability to cope with the task.

"I don't see how the police are going to be bamboozled. The first thing they'd think about would be altering a clock. Provided the murderer had a good enough motive, I don't think the mere fact that the hands of a clock were in a certain place would save his neck."

Rennyet began the patient explanation that Travers had anticipated. There were the rulings on the taking of evidence, for instance. Was Mr. Travers aware that if the police questioned a suspect, that suspect could refuse to open his mouth? A man could refuse to say where he was at a certain time, and what he was doing. If the police wished to prove that a man could have been in a certain place at a certain time, they had to prove it by means of their own devising.

"Now take my own case," he said. "Well merely suppose that I had some reason for killing Lewton, and the police were aware of it. I told you that the comic superintendent and the Seaborough Chief Constable came here to ask me if I could throw any light on Lewton's past. Well, suppose they'd come here to ask where I was at the moment Lewton was killed. I could have told them to find out. I could have previously instructed my servants to do the same."

"But they might have arrested you! I mean, it would then have been up to you to prove an alibi."

Rennyet smiled. "They'd have needed a case a hundred times stronger than that to have taken the step of making an arrest. However, in our book we don't want to keep back evidence in the way I've just outlined, because the reader would naturally feel himself swindled. No; we've got to make the suspect say that his servants are open to question, and himself, too. And when the police do ask questions, they know at once that the suspect has a perfect alibi. He was elsewhere at the time of the murder."

Travers was suddenly struck with an idea that illuminated his face with a kind of joyous bewilderment. "I say, I've just thought of something. I don't know any too much about modern publicity methods, but wouldn't it create a sensation if the public knew our book was written by a man who'd actually been questioned by the police in connection with the murder? I mean, we can still steer clear of the laws of libel, but it would be magnificent if we could create a set of circumstances to show how the murder might have been done."

"That's the very idea I've got in mind," said Rennyet. "Now this is a Tudor house, so we'll make it Queen Anne. It stands on a hill, so we'll have it in a valley. You shall be the murderer, because we can draw partly from life, and that will save time. We begin by imagining that you've hired this place for two months in the spring, and you've come down here with your man."

"But would I hire it in spring?"

"Of course you wouldn't," explained Rennyet. "Who'd want to live in a place like that in the spring? That shall be one of the very reasons why the shrewd detective has a suspicion."

"Very clever," said Travers, and nodded. "Very clever indeed. But just one other thing before I forget it. Suppose I alter a clock and swindle Palmer. Later, of course, I alter it again. Would the evidence of a man like Palmer—who's certainly biased in my favour—count very much? Oughtn't there to be two people swindled?"

Rennyet drew in his horns at once. "We don't want too many characters. They'd only confuse the issue—and the reader." He frowned. "I shall have to think about that. But any other objections before we go on?"

"To be perfectly frank, I can see a hundred. What time was Lawton—I beg his pardon; Lewton—killed? My memory's very unreliable."

"Ten-past seven is near enough."

"Right, then. I alter the clock at some convenient time. I ought to tell you, by the way, that I know a good deal about clocks. It's been a hobby of mine—old clocks principally."

Rennyet broke in there. "I'll tell you what we'll do. You take till to-morrow morning to make out a list in writing of every conceivable objection you can have, and of every possible flaw in that kind of alibi. I shall find it easier to think them out myself if I have them in front of me *en masse.*"

So they got to work on motive, and as that was bound up with the murderer, his character had to be manipulated. And so well did things work out that when Travers left, there seemed nothing to delay the writing of the opening chapters except the details of that alibi.

On the Monday morning Rennyet was sitting in Travers's room at the inn, and the list of objections was in his hand, (*a*) had already been disposed of. If Palmer's evidence was not sufficient, then a woman might have been hired in the village to come in and do housework.

"I think that meets the case," he said. "Now (*b*). *At least twenty minutes' alteration is necessary to allow me to get to Seaborough and back. How, then, explain the gap which may have been noticed?*" Rennyet looked up smilingly. "I suppose you refer to the fact that as the clock had been put back twenty minutes, Palmer might have wondered why the evenings had suddenly drawn out."

"That's one item," said Travers.

"I think I see the others," Rennyet told him. "And my answer's this. The time is chosen as the spring because the nights *do* draw out in the spring. As for the sudden gap of twenty minutes, there needn't be any. The clock or clocks could be altered several times, at five or more minutes a time."

"I see that," said Travers. "Now look at (c), which deals with the number of clocks . . ."

So the voices went on and on, and as Travers spoke, and listened, Rennyet became a terrifying fascination. Those white, immaculate fingers had held a knife. That forearm had stiffened as it was stiffening now, and had driven the knife home. Those arms had dragged a murdered man, and that voice had spoken in that dead man's voice. So Travers thought, and while he spoke it was sometimes like a man in a dream, so that he had deliberately to rouse himself from the dreadful obsession which Rennyet was becoming, and the awful urge to think of his voice as now the squeak of Lewton, and now the wheezy, gasping accents of old Trench.

Two days later, the objections had all been swept away, and the alibi was concocted. All that remained was to find a flaw.

Rennyet shrugged his shoulders. "That's child's play. We can let somebody see him. Too obvious you think? Well, he'd have to leave his car somewhere. Why not let a tramp or a gipsy steal something from it, and let the thief be afterwards caught on another job, and when the police make a search they find whatever it was on him with your name on it. They make inquiries, and the thief owns up and swears your car was at that particular place at a certain time. Then the milk is found in the coconut."

He waved his hand airily, but Travers looked flabbergasted.

"By Jove! Rennyet, you're a wonder. How the devil you think of these things beats me!"

But no sooner had Rennyet gone than Travers went up to his bedroom and prowled about like a man distracted. And when he sat down, something like terror again came over him. From the jumble of words which his mind reviewed, the face of Rennyet would emerge—amused, contemptuous, cynical. Travers would see the casual sweep of his hands as he removed a difficulty; the quick, alert pauses as he confronted a problem that came home to his very self, and the dexterity with which he shifted to safer ground.

But as Travers forced his mind to grapple with the whole problem of Rennyet and his connection with the murder of Lewton, the horror of it so seized upon him that a kind of brain-panic held him to his seat. Then, as the morning passed, he took refuge in the sanities of pencil and paper, so that the sheer hard facts which he noted down kept his mind from those ghastly, paradoxical bypaths into which his fertile thoughts were only too ready to wander.

Lunch-time came, and his mind was made up. Rennyet had mentioned that he was going to Seaborough that afternoon, which meant most likely that Meek would go too, and Mrs. Meek would be alone in the house. So Palmer was sent ten miles the opposite way to dispatch a telegram recalling Mr. Travers urgently to town. With that telegram in his pocket, Travers set off at four-thirty for Rennyet's house.

Mrs. Meek smiled at him as she let him in.

"The master's out, sir. I don't know when he'll be back."

"I know," Travers told her. He was already by the study door. "He told me he was going to Seaborough, and I rather thought he'd be back at any time now."

"Perhaps you'll wait for a bit, sir."

Travers beamed. "Perhaps I will—just for a few minutes."

But hardly had Mrs. Meek gone than she was back again. "May I bring you a cup of tea, sir? I'm just making one for myself."

"That'd be delightful," said Travers.

His eyes roved round the room as he reviewed the insuperable difficulties of the case. Two clocks in the kitchen, one in the dining-room, and the grandfather that faced him. Others too, perhaps, that Palmer had not dared to hint at. Then there was the pestle and mortar, far-fetched enough in itself.

Mrs. Meek came in with a tray. "I've brought you just a little to eat, sir. Mr. Palmer told us you didn't take much tea."

Travers munched away at the cake and kept her in conversation. Mrs. Meek found herself telling him all about her complaint; her husband's illness; her dislike of Seaborough: how she had once been thin enough to ride pillion—and only a year ago at that. And then all at once Travers looked at her with the most comical dismay. He pointed to the plate. It was empty. Four pieces of cake had gone.

"It shows what an interesting person you are, Mrs. Meek," he said. "One piece of cake is my daily allowance. But it was a lovely cake. I don't know that I've ever tasted a nicer."

"It *is* a nice cake, sir—though I say so." She nodded. "It's a competition cake, sir. The *Seaborough Beacon* offered a prize for recipes, and this one won it, so I thought I'd try it myself. Everybody likes it"—she smiled—"though I don't always say where I got it from."

Travers looked at her roguishly. "But you'll give me the recipe, won't you? I'd like Palmer to have a try at it. One gets tired of ordinary cakes, you know."

She nodded and smiled. "I'll make you a copy, sir—if you'll wait."

Travers had already risen. "That'll be very good of you. But I daren't wait any longer." He produced the telegram and explained.

"But I shan't be more than a moment, sir."

She disappeared at once, and Travers hardly had time for one more look at that pestle and mortar when she was back again.

"I'd already taken a copy of my own, sir, and you'd better have the original. Just a moment, sir, and I'll find a big envelope. Mr. Rennyet won't mind. And I'm to say that you'll be down again in a day or two at the latest, sir."

Inside half an hour Travers had left Bicklesham, and his luggage went with him. In spite of what he had told Mrs. Meek, and the people at the inn, and Captain Rappway, at whose house he called, he knew in his heart of hearts he would never set foot in Bicklesham again. And the tremendous revulsion that had come over him still persisted long after the pleasant hills had been left behind and the outer suburbs were reached.

It was dark when the Rolls drew up before Wharton's house. The General was enjoying an hour before the fire, having recently been bitten with the cross-word puzzle craze, and Mrs. Wharton was reading in an easy chair that faced his own. Both looked up startled when the maid announced Travers, who came in with Palmer at his heels.

"Hallo!" said Wharton. "Found something out?"

The smile which accompanied Travers's greetings died away. "Yes and no, George. But I can't go on with it."

Wharton nodded knowingly. "Spying goes against the grain?"

"It's not that so much," said Travers, "though I grant you somebody's got to do the dirty work. No"—and he shook his head—"it isn't that I feel grubby. It's because I feel rather frightened."

"Frightened!" Wharton stared. "Frightened of what?"

"I'll try to tell you." He took a seat. "I've brought Palmer along to help me out. All the same, I don't think you'll feel quite as I did when it came home to me this morning. You remember what you said, about Rennyet letting out only what he knew was safe? Well, that's what he's done. He's shown me how the murder could have been worked."

"By himself?"

"By himself," repeated Travers. "And the thing that appalled me was that he made few bones about it. There was he, a murderer—calmly sitting opposite me and letting out how it was done, and—this is the terrifying point—*knowing all the time that he was utterly safe.*"

"He didn't suspect you?" asked Wharton quickly.

"Lord, no!" said Travers, and smiled. "But he might just as well have told you what he told me. You'd have been helpless. He's got an alibi and no power on earth can even hint that it's faked, let alone prove it. If Rennyet killed Lewton—and I know he did—the law will never lay hands on him."

Wharton gave a prodigious grunt, then rubbed his chin. "I see. Like that, is it? Well, let's hear all about it."

"That's what I've come here for," said Travers. "But first of all I want you to understand precisely how the different pieces of information—disclosures, if you like—were given. When Rennyet and I were discussing various difficulties in the way of our plot, he'd take them for very real difficulties. He'd frown and nod and say they were things that had to be thought over. Then on his very next visit he'd come with the solution he'd pretended to have thought out. He'd say, 'Why, take my own case. Take what happens every day,' and so on. You see the point. He'd detach himself cleverly from all association with the book, and yet supply the actual thing that might have happened. And he did it so well that he could always claim it was sheer hypothesis."

"They were vital things?" asked Jane Wharton.

"Some of them. But you do see, don't you, that what he was ostensibly doing was to make his own house and its affairs fit in with *our* plot. It wasn't a case of making his house and its affairs fit in with the real Seaborough case." He smiled. "I'm afraid that's rather involved. We'll get to facts. What I'll do is to tell you how the murder was done. When I nod to Palmer, he'll fit in the information he gathered from the servants."

Wharton got up hurriedly for paper and pencil, and Travers ran an eye over his own notes.

"We'll leave out the question of motive," he began. "We'll merely begin with the premise that Rennyet determined to kill Lewton and get away with it. The time of year chosen was the spring, and for many reasons. In the spring there's gardening to do; the nights lengthen, and lengthen slowly as they always do, and their lengthening is often unnoticed because of the particular weather of a particular day. A dull day in March and it's dark at five-thirty. A fine, luminous day and it may be light till nearly seven. A person, therefore, may not connect the lightness or darkness of any particular evening with the actual time by the clock. You get that?

"We come to what happened on that particular day. Rennyet, if you remember, worked out of doors all the afternoon at making a pergola, and Meek was with him. The first thing to do was to dispose of Meek's watch, which had a trick of falling out of his waistcoat pocket when he stooped."

"I've seen the watch, and it's all dented," said Palmer. "Mrs. Meek told me that the last time it was dropped it fell on some concrete."

"You see," went on Travers, "that even if Meek didn't drop his watch so that it stopped—or Rennyet could stop it—it would have been easy for Rennyet to have sent Meek to the house and then taken the watch which was left hanging either in the coat for safety, or on the wood of the pergola. But that's a small point. While the two men worked out of doors, Mrs. Meek was asleep on her bed, as Palmer will tell you. She has an alarm clock up there, and Palmer has seen it."

"Quite a common metal clock, sir. You can buy them for three or four shillings at any jeweller's shop."

"There I offer two solutions," said Travers. "Mrs. Meek mentioned that hers was a very reliable clock and had stopped only once. Palmer didn't press the point, but by shrewdly hoping that it hadn't been on an important occasion, he learned that it was during an afternoon, *and about the time of the murder*."

"Carry on," said Wharton quietly.

"Then this becomes the solution. The clock is a nearly new one. It is of standard pattern. Rennyet had one up his sleeve, which he allowed to run almost down. It had been substituted for Mrs. Meek's clock, and it stopped while she slept. Later on, Rennyet changed the two alarm clocks over again.

"In the meanwhile Rennyet kept Meek at it in the garden, and himself went into the house and changed every clock. The grandfather he had to stop altogether, and that made two visits necessary. He and Meek went on working till half-past four, when tea was ready. In the meanwhile Mrs. Meek woke up and found her clock stopped. She got up quickly and went downstairs. Perhaps she wondered about it being so early, but as all the clocks were the same, she couldn't think one was wrong. And suppose Meek had made a remark—well, you can't call every clock a liar, and Rennyet might easily have made some retort about the time not having gone so quickly as he had thought. You've got all that?"

"I have," said Wharton. "But what about Bicklesham church clock? Suppose Mrs. Meek had heard that?"

"She never does hear the clock, sir," said Palmer, "except on an exceptionally favourable day. I've tried that out, sir."

Travers nodded. "That night when she was supposed to hear the clock strike eight—in unison with the two grandfathers that also struck about then—it might have been Meek who said by accident that he thought he heard the clock, and she'd naturally agree. I admit I can't fit in Meek himself. If the clock went, he might have heard it. Perhaps it had become part of life's daily sounds with him, and he didn't notice it. Or there may be another solution, which I'll suggest later."

"Tradesmen calling?" asked Jane Wharton laconically.

"They don't call except in the mornings," Travers told her. "One reason for that is that Mrs. Meek lies down in the afternoon. Also, that particular day was early closing in Bicklesham as well as in Seaborough. Not only that. If a tradesman called, why should he see the kitchen clock and comment on it?"

"I'm sorry—"

"For the love of heaven don't apologize," Travers told her. "It's only by finding the holes that you can cover them up. But now I would call your attention to this. Rennyet had till six-ten by the clock. If anything had been discovered before then, he could have explained it away—in his capacity of detective-novel writer—as an experiment. But six-ten came, and he was safe. That was when he set off for Seaborough, having announced that he had a very special letter to post."

"What about the wireless?" asked Wharton.

"The wireless, somewhere about that time, was out of order, sir," Palmer told him. "It was an old-fashioned set, sir, and Mrs. Meek knocked it over when dusting. Mr. Rennyet tried hard to get the spare part and couldn't, sir. He sent Meek in to Seaborough, and in the end, sir, he bought a new set. Mr. and Mrs. Meek told me all about it when I admired the new all-mains set, sir."

"Mrs. Meek broke it," said Travers, and smiled suggestively. "How easy to arrange things so that she couldn't have helped the breakage! Still, to get on with that evening. No friends called, because the Meeks hadn't any that were likely to call at that particular time. Meek would be tired, or he would help his wife get the meal ready. Then just before seven by the clocks, having committed the murder, Rennyet returned. Thereafter life was normal, except that Rennyet called in his two faithful servants, and on the excuse of a birthday, treated them both to a glass of special port. I'd say it was special because it was doped. It made them both sleepy and it made them sleep. They slept so soundly that Rennyet, if he liked, could have walked into their room and changed the alarm clocks again. Also, next day, both Meek and his wife felt the effects."

Wharton nodded solemnly. "I see. And what was that you were going to add about the Bicklesham clock?"

"Oh, that." Travers smiled. "That's a family joke. You know my sister Ursula, and you know my young niece and nephew.

Well, in her hall there's a pestle and mortar which they use for a gong. Well, one day the boy was imprisoned in the dining-room, where his mother was, as a kind of punishment, and he was not to go out till three o'clock. His sister actually imitated the sound of a clock striking three, only Ursula got suspicious and nipped into the hall and caught her manipulating the pestle. Neat, wasn't it?"

"Rather too neat," said Wharton dryly.

Jane Wharton laughed. "You're not the only ingenious one in the family."

"But it isn't so frightfully ingenious," protested Travers. "You've got an old brass mortar in your spare room. You try it and see if it doesn't ring like a bell. Rennyet could have experimented and made Bicklesham clock strike when and how he liked. Not that our case stands or falls by it."

And then Travers went on to the proposed flaw by which the book murder was to be discovered.

"Exactly what you told me, you see, George? His own case hasn't any flaw. He's got a hundred-percent alibi. Why, suppose you were such a preposterously, hopelessly insane idiot as to bring a charge against him, and to shove me in the box. His counsel would say, 'Why, Mr. Travers, isn't all this hypothetical rubbish you've just been telling us, merely things suggested to you by defendant himself to fit in with a book you and he were proposing to write?'"

"*Yes,*" said Wharton. "Even if Rennyet walked in that door now and put his tongue out at me and his fingers to his nose, and told me what you've told me, and dared me to prove it, I'd be utterly helpless."

Travers got to his feet. "Well, there we are. I'm dog-tired of Rennyet. I shall see that face of his in my dreams. I don't know that Palmer and I won't also have some special port to-night."

"Well, you've put up a damn good show," said Wharton.

"But all for nothing," said Jane Wharton, with a pout.

Travers suddenly smiled dazzlingly. "Lord, no! I've forgotten something."

He felt in the breast pocket of his overcoat and found the quarto envelope in which a newspaper was neatly folded. Then he told her about the famous cake.

"Here you are," he said. "Here's the recipe. You shall make it and solace George's heart. You shall re-christen it the 'Rennyet Cake' for a lasting remembrance."

"If it's as good as you say, I certainly will try it," she told him.

"Where are you going now? Home?" asked Wharton.

"That's it," said Travers. "There ain't no roses round the door, but there'll be no Rennyet."

But exactly five minutes after Travers had drawn up his special chair to his own fire, the telephone bell went. It was Wharton.

"Where'd Mrs. Meek get that paper?" he snapped.

"Wait a minute. Don't bully me," said Travers. "She got it from Rennyet's study, where she found it. She took it because she took all papers by routine, and she kept it because of the recipe."

"You're not in bed?"

"Good Lord, no!"

"Then have that car of yours at Westminster Bridge in half an hour," said Wharton. "You and I are going down to Seaborough."

Travers stared. "What, now?"

"Now!" said Wharton curtly, and hung up.

CHAPTER XV
THE MIRACLE MAN

IT WAS ALMOST seven o'clock the following evening before Wharton's plans had been completed. Now Rennyet was on the way from Bicklesham to Seaborough police-station, and in the Chief Constable's room a party of four were waiting.

It was a setting designed to put Rennyet at his ease; a setting in harmony with the telephone conversation Wharton had made. He had said, for instance, that something really remarkable had turned up which would interest Mr. Rennyet as a writer of detective novels. If he cared to be present, Wharton could promise him some fun. Tempest's room, therefore, was more like a smoking-room than an office. An east wind was biting cold outside, but in that room a fire was blazing, an easy chair or two had been imported, and there were cigarettes and ash-trays on a couple of small tables.

"You will remember that I don't want to see him under any circumstances," said Travers. "There'll be heaps of time for that if I ever have to give evidence, which I shan't. I never want to see him again, and I'm terrified even at the thought that I'm bound to get a letter from him."

Wharton waved his hand. "Now don't panic. You'll be in that room there, and there's a door that opens to outside." And then not being able to resist the temptation to pull Travers's leg, he looked over at Tempest. "You know, what Mr. Travers is worrying about is having lost the chance of writing that detective novel."

"I dare say they'll give Rennyet facilities in jail," said Tempest dryly. "About time we grouped ourselves, isn't it?"

There was a gas fire for Travers in that inner room, and the others now gathered round their fire with pipes going, and a pleasant haze of smoke made a companionable mist. And when a knock came at the door to warn of Rennyet's approach, the three voices began a babble of argument, so that Rennyet must have thought he had entered by error the card-room of a local club.

He smiled round. "Quite a family gathering, what?"

"Yes," said Wharton, removing his antiquated glasses. "Come and join it."

Rennyet gave him a special smile. "You're down here again, then, Mr. Ward." An ironic smile. "I beg your pardon—Mr. *Wharton*."

Carry he had met before, and the four sat down. Rennyet refused a cigarette. A slight soreness of the throat, he explained, after taking part in a dramatic show.

"Well, I don't think you'll regret your visit," Wharton said. "You'll be interested to learn that we've discovered something at last about Lewton's murder."

"Really?" He was still smiling, and if ever a man was certain of keeping the hangman at arm's length it was he.

"Yes," said Wharton.

It was strange how Rennyet's mere presence irritated him. He hated that superior, affable smile, and the little gigolo excrescences of hair that hung by his ears. But Wharton took some little time over a refilling of his pipe, and when he spoke again, he was sure of himself.

"Now you were in Seaborough that famous night," he said, "only you were away and gone long before Lewton was killed. Now here's where the interesting point comes in." His voice changed to the completely casual. "Oh, by the way, you bought a paper that night when you were in Seaborough, didn't you?"

Rennyet's eyes narrowed slightly. "Did I?"

"Well, I suppose you did," said Wharton, apparently surprised. "I mean, most people do. My wife's always grumbling at the amount I spend on evening papers. Still, that's neither here nor there. You bought a paper, didn't you."

Rennyet said he did. Wharton's had been no question, but a casual statement of an obvious fact.

Thereupon Wharton went off at an inexplicable tangent. "Curious what shrewd business people you get in the provinces," he said, taking the circle into his confidence. "Look at the proprietors of the *Seaborough Evening Beacon*, for instance. They tell me that before the advent of wireless, they used to get out a seven o'clock edition. Now they find it doesn't pay. But they still do it in the summer, because the wireless news is at six, and it doesn't give the close-of-play cricket scores. The same with Saturdays in the winter. They get out a special edition which they call the *Football Beacon*. All the other weeks of the winter, their final edition is on sale at six o'clock. That's bought very largely, I understand, by betting people, because the wireless doesn't give the prices of the winners it announces at six o'clock. It only gives results." He beamed amiably round the circle.

Carry took up his cue by asking what all that had to do with Mr. Rennyet.

"I thought he'd be interested," said Wharton. "Still, to get on. That Wednesday night when Lewton was murdered was noteworthy for something very different. That night—or rather afternoon—our local idol, Captain Moile, did his famous feat and incidentally won ten thousand pounds. Seaborough was interested, and the proprietors of the *Beacon* were naturally interested. *Although the news reached them after the publication of their last normal edition, and most of the staff had gone, they nevertheless printed the news in the Stop-Press corner of all stock on hand and rushed it out on sale by seven o'clock.*"

"That's right," said Tempest. "You and I were having a drink at the time, and I slipped out and bought a paper."

Wharton nodded. "Of course Mr. Rennyet didn't have the chance of buying that edition. He had to be content with the ordinary one. Now here"—while talking he was moving across to the desk and putting on his glasses again—"we happen to have the very identical paper that Mr. Rennyet did purchase that night, and as you see—"

He stopped so dramatically that all eyes were on him, as he intended. He pretended to stare. His finger pointed to the Stop-Press column. He glared. His voice became grimly official.

"Mr. Rennyet, how do you explain that you were having your dinner in Bicklesham at seven o'clock that night, and buying a paper in Seaborough at the same time?"

A smile that was as grim as Wharton's flickered across Rennyet's face. He turned idly towards the table.

"I think I will have a cigarette after all. I have a match, thank you."

He lighted it with steady hand, blew out a long, slow puff—and frowned.

"It does seem rather strange, I admit. Only, you see, I didn't buy that paper. It was brought to my house the following morning."

Wharton tossed the paper contemptuously aside. "I see. We're going to prevaricate, are we? Then let me tell you that we can put on the stand a witness who can prove that that paper was brought home from Seaborough by you, left in your study, and taken out before it was properly light the following morning."

"Really?" He frowned once more, then suddenly smiled. "Do you know, I shouldn't be surprised if you're right!"

"You know we're right," snapped Wharton, irritated beyond bearing. "What we're asking you to do is to explain how you could be in two places at the same time."

"But that'll be a long story," protested Rennyet. "I admit it's childishly easy, but it's going to take a long time."

"Take a week if you like," Wharton told him curtly.

"Yes, but you don't understand," said Rennyet. "I came here to-night and put my people to some inconvenience. I also promised my housekeeper I'd be back at eight, and she knows me sufficiently well to have the dinner on the table." He smiled at Wharton in the most friendly way. "Now if I might call her up, I wouldn't mind how long I stayed—in reason."

"Here's the phone," said Wharton. "Help yourself."

Rennyet took a seat at the desk. His manner was as unruffled as if he had been in his own study. He smiled at the ceiling till his number was through.

"Who's that speaking? Oh, it's you, Helen. About dinner to-night. Don't put it on till I actually get back. You understand? . . . And say the car will be wanted. . . . That's right. Say the car will be wanted. . . . Good-bye."

As he was hanging up, Wharton was all at once seized with a spasm of coughing. Something had gone the wrong way, and he gurgled and wheezed so alarmingly that Tempest patted him on the back in the approved style. The tears streamed down Wharton's face, but he got over it. Rennyet stood watching till the General was himself again.

"Now I'm at your service, gentlemen."

"You're wrong," said Wharton, still panting somewhat. "It's we who're at yours."

"As you like," said Rennyet. "The main point is, you think you've got me."

Tempest gave him an official stare. "It certainly looks like it. If you wish to make a statement—"

"You'll warn me and press the button for a stenographer," Rennyet cut in, smiling. "What you're inviting me to do, in fact, is to confess that I killed Lewton."

Wharton peered at him over the top of his glasses.

"Do please stop those theatricals," said Rennyet. "They're really most disturbing—and very unnecessary. I take it, Major Tempest, that you want to know where I actually was at seven o'clock on the night when Lewton was killed."

"From seven o'clock till seven-fifteen would be more comprehensive," Tempest told him.

"Well, I can do that easily enough. By a stroke of luck, I can do it in two or three minutes. All I ask you to do is to have fetched in here a thin, undersized man of about forty, who sells papers on the memorial steps. He's known as Charlie."

"I know him," said Carry.

Tempest caught Wharton's eye, and Wharton nodded.

Not a word was spoken in the room till Carry came back. With him was the man that Rennyet had described—a shrivelled-up specimen of four foot six, but with all the quaint alertness of a sparrow.

"Would you mind if I did the talking first?" asked Rennyet, and at the sound of his voice the new-comer gave him a sudden interested look.

"Why not?" said Wharton, and Rennyet swivelled round in his chair.

"Now, Charlie, you remember the night when the murder took place at Seaborough? The night when Captain Moile landed in Ireland?"

Charlie tried a furtive grin. "Of course I do, sir."

Rennyet smiled. "That's good. You also remember that that night I called your attention to something. Tell these gentlemen, will you, what it was, and just what happened that night as far as concerns you and me?"

"Well, sir, it was like this here. You give me a bob and asked for a paper, and while I was fumbling for the change, you said

I was to keep the change. Then you asked me what the time was. 'Blimey, guv'nor,' I said, 'ain't you got no eyes?'" He looked round at Wharton. "You see, sir, there was the clock right over his head!"

"And what was the time by it?" asked Wharton.

"Five minutes past seven, sir."

"Who said so? This gentleman, or you?"

"Why, both of us, sir. We both see it was five-past seven."

"All right," said Wharton. "Get on with what happened."

"Well, sir, I laughed and this gentleman laughed, because of him asking me the time—see? Then he says to me as how he was expecting a young lady in a red dress, and he was going to look out one way and I was to keep my eyes open the other, and if I see her I was to let him know. And there he stopped, sir, till a quarter-past, when he said he couldn't wait no longer, and that was the last I see of him till the other night when he come up and spoke."

"But how'd you know this gentleman was standing there from five-past till a quarter-past?" asked Wharton. "You were doing a roaring trade—"

"Not so that you'd notice it, I wasn't," broke in Charlie. "A good few there was, but not like if it hadn't been early-closing." He appealed to the room. "Why, blimey, if it'd been an ordinary night I'd have got rid of them lot what I had inside five minutes."

"What you're trying to tell us is that you had this gentleman under your eye all the time."

"In a manner of speaking, so I did."

"He couldn't have slipped away without your knowing it?" asked Tempest.

"Well, sir, he kept looking up at the clock, sort of wondering if this young lady was coming, and I kept an eye on him and I was looking out for her too, thinking I might be on another bob."

"Anything you'd like to ask?" said Wharton to Rennyet.

"Nothing else whatever," said Rennyet, and with the least suspicion of a bow, "Gentlemen, the witness is entirely yours."

There was silence for a moment or two.

"All right, inspector," said Wharton. "Let him go. And see he doesn't lose anything by his absence. Here, take this too," and he handed over a shilling.

Rennyet watched amusedly the shepherding out of Charlie. Then he smiled over affectionately at Wharton.

"Do you know, I should never have suspected you of such kindness of heart. Not that I wouldn't have given him a tip my-self—only you'd have been bound to misinterpret it."

"Don't you distress yourself about me," said Wharton. "You'll need all your energy to explain what you've got to explain." He smiled. "A miracle worker, eh? I've heard of alibis in my time—double ones principally—but yours caps all. Three places at the same time! Having your meal at Bicklesham, waiting for a young lady, and disposing of Frederick Lewton!"

"I don't think I'd say that last if I were you." Rennyet's eyes narrowed again. "And while I'm at it, my last word is this: Do what you damn well like. Lewton was killed between five-past seven and a quarter-past, and you've just had in this room an independent witness who'll prove that I couldn't have done it. And he's a witness you'll never shake."

"Well, I'm holding you for a bit in any case," said Wharton off-handedly. "If, however, you care to explain the details of that false alibi you gave us—"

"False!" He assumed a tremendous surprise. "Who says it was false?"

"That'll do!" broke in Tempest sharply. "Don't waste our time over nonsense. You don't think we're fools? Miracles are done for nowadays. You're not going to stand up in court and make out you were in two places at the same time! Tell us how you faked that alibi."

"Just a moment," said Rennyet. "You say you're not a fool. Neither am I. You've no right to question me. If I care to volunteer any information—"

"Does it matter?" Tempest smiled wryly. "Let's get down to hard facts. We can now prove through Charlie that you were in a certain place at seven-five. We can prove, therefore, that your original alibi was false. That alone is enough to hold you on."

"Please, please!" Rennyet was holding up his hand. "I've never made an official statement yet. Still, if you want to arrest me, all I can say is that you'll never do anything that'd please me more. You'll give me the finest free publicity I could ever dream of, and you'll cut your throats at the same time."

The door opened and Carry came in with a sheet of paper. He made a bee-line for Wharton and thrust it under his nose. Wharton read the message, beamed, and then frowned. Then he got to his feet.

"Mr. Rennyet, the comedy is played. You've been sparring for time, but you didn't know that I'd been doing the same thing. Now we must ask you to wait."

"Wait? For what?"

Wharton shook his head in playful reprimand. "Still playing for time? You ask what you're to wait for? Well, I'll tell you. *You're to wait for the man round whose neck you've just put a rope!*"

Rennyet stared. There was no flippancy now. "What do you mean exactly?"

"You know who I mean," said Wharton. "I mean the man with a motor-bike. The man whose alibi was bound up with yours. The man who hated Lewton like hell. In fact, I mean your man—Tom Meek!"

Rennyet shrugged his shoulders. "You're talking utter nonsense. Meek's got a first-class alibi."

"Has he?" said Wharton, and smiled. He took a seat. "The bother with you, Mr. Rennyet, is that you give nobody credit for possessing brains but yourself. Take this whole evening's talk. It was obvious, once we knew about the newspaper, that either you'd used Meek for your own ends, or else he was a confederate. We got you here at this particular time because it would interfere with your meal, and you'd probably make it an excuse to ring up your house, once you saw which way the cat jumped. I intended to have Meek here, in any case, as soon as I knew which way the same cat jumped. As soon as you rang up your house—on the telephone you'd had installed for that very purpose—I had a nasty fit of coughing. That was merely a signal for those outside there to ring up the sergeant and man who were waiting at Bicklesham and tell them to collect Meek and bring him in. *Then* I wanted him as a witness; *now* I want him for murder. This message tells me that he'll be along very soon. They're just having some little difficulty in collecting him—that's all. Meek appears to have recognized from your message that the game was up. You don't believe me? Well, there's the phone. Ring up your own house again and hear the latest at first hand."

For a moment or two Rennyet sat looking at him; then he went over to the desk. Wharton began another filling of his pipe, and Rennyet's voice came curiously incisive in the stillness of the room.

"Hallo! Hallo! . . . Hallo! who's that? . . . Who is it? . . . I say, do say something for the love of heaven. . . . Who is it? Say something, can't you?"

His eyes were straining across the room, then all at once he spoke.

"She's crying! She doesn't seem able to speak."

"No wonder," said Wharton calmly. "They've just taken her husband away. Maybe they've told her why."

But Rennyet's face was undergoing a subtle change. He was speaking again, regardless of Wharton's grim irony.

"Who am I? Oh, I'm Mr. Rennyet. . . . From the police-station, of course. . . . Yes, I'll give a message. . . . He's what? . . . *Cut his throat!* . . . Oh, my God!"

Wharton was over in a flash and snatched the receiver from his hand. But it was true, and Wharton hung up again.

Rennyet still sat hunched in the swivel chair. He glared. "So you drove him to that, did you?"

"We didn't drive him," said Wharton quietly. "He drove himself. Maybe he drove you, too."

"Yes," said Rennyet slowly. "Maybe he did."

CHAPTER XVI
CUT-THROAT CAKE

"IF YOU CARE to tell us all about it," said Wharton, "you can do so without prejudice. We're all men of honour here—at least, we hope so."

Rennyet shook his head. "I don't know. It doesn't seem right somehow, with him—" He broke off there, and from the wince Wharton knew his mind had seen that slit across a dead man's throat.

"Get it out of your system," he said. "You've been trying to keep him alive; isn't that it? And now he's let you down."

Rennyet said nothing. His body still sagged in the chair, and his eyes stared unwinking beyond the desk at the red glow of the fire. Then all at once he shook his head and seemed to rouse himself.

"I think, perhaps, I will tell you. Where'd you like me to begin?"

"Where you like," said Wharton. "And have a cigarette. It'll steady your nerves."

"My nerves are all right," said Rennyet impatiently, but he took the cigarette all the same.

"Come and sit here," said Tempest, pushing the easy chair forward again.

Then Rennyet came over, sauntering abstractedly and moistening his lips. "Did you know about Meek's sister-in-law?"

The angle of approach was so unexpected that the three looked surprised.

"We knew she committed suicide," Tempest said, "and that's all we did know. Meek never knew any more than that. That's what brought on his illness. If it hadn't been for that, he'd never have left us. He was a good man. I might say an exceptional man."

"I liked him as soon as I clapped eyes on him," Rennyet said. "He wasn't in very good shape even then, but I took to him, and I liked his wife. Tom did well for himself with me, as far as health goes. Though I say it, it was I who got him on his feet. I got him interested in all sorts of things—his work, my work, our little dramatic society and heaps of other things. He was a great help to me—in my writing that is. He saved me many a hunt for local colour. You wouldn't believe it, perhaps, but he soon was as keen as mustard. I think he liked me too—so did his wife. Then he discovered the letter."

A moment or two's pause and Rennyet went on again. "You see, he sold his home and most of his things when he came to me. There were some of his sister-in-law's things, too. They kept some of her stuff and some of their own and furnished an empty room I had. It was when they were doing something to that, and turning things out, that they came across the letter, the one the sister-in-law left behind.

"Mind you, I don't know quite where she put it, or why she put it where she did, but she evidently meant it shouldn't be found till she'd done herself in. It was the usual letter a suicide leaves, only a little longer and a bit more pathetic. It rang absolutely true as far as I could see, and it explains a lot of things.

"She was a nursery-governess—but perhaps you know that. She'd been out of a post for a bit, and she got a job through Beece's agency. Beece hinted that he could use any information she could give him, and she didn't understand him. Then when she'd been in the job for a bit, Beece approached her again, as apparently there was some scandal afloat about the young widow she was with. That time she knew what Beece was driving at, and she told her mistress.

"What happened then was that the mistress came down to see Beece in a thundering rage, and threatened him with the police and so on. What did Beece do but produce Lewton as a man who'd been present when Miss Mallow had herself offered to supply news about her mistress—an offer which Beece said he had rejected with the utmost loathing. Lewton was his witness all through. The result was that Miss Mallow got the sack, and her employer only refused to prosecute at Beece's request, and because she didn't want to ruin the girl for life. Miss Mallow kept her mouth shut because she knew she'd never be believed. Her employer kept her mouth shut because she'd promised Beece, and she didn't want to harm the girl any more. The rest of that story you know."

"I see now," said Wharton. "That was one of the safeguards Beece and Lewton had. If ever they were double-crossed, they could do some double-crossing themselves. Still, go on, Mr. Rennyet."

"I hardly know where to go on," Rennyet said. "Perhaps I'd better tell you about Meek and myself. I was doing a story which depended on impersonation. It was to do with a Canadian, and I wanted just a little colour to give verisimilitude. Then Meek suggested that I should see Lewton, whom he knew through Trench. Meek had laid for Trench and got into conversation with him at a cinema, and it wasn't long before he was dropping into Homedale the back way. But that's anticipating a bit. I went to see Lewton as you know, and with the results that you know.

"In the meanwhile Meek approached me with an idea. I may say that I'd offered him—as I offer all my friends—a fiver for any idea round which I can write a book. He came to me a week or two before the murder with an idea for an alibi, and it turned out to be merely the altering of the hands of clocks. I laughed at him, of course; told him it'd been done to death, and it was too obvious and so on. Then he began to explain, and I don't mind saying he got me really interested.

"His wife was the pivot of the thing. If we got our alibi past her, then we could get it past anybody—I mean for book purposes. Finally we decided to try the idea out seriously, and it was fixed for that Wednesday. It was a cold, dullish day if you remember, and tampering with clocks wouldn't be noticed. I did everything myself, because in the book I should have to deceive Meek too. The time came for me to go to Seaborough, and Mrs. Meek was utterly unaware of what the real time was. About the details of that—"

"You tell us those later," said Wharton.

"Well, I went to Seaborough. That had been decided on as the scene of the murder. We hadn't decided who the murdered man was to be or the motive for murdering him, because that could easily be worked out once the alibi proved correct. Also I had the idea that it would be remarkably good publicity to give it abroad when the book was published, that the alibi had been worked out as printed. However, I went to Seaborough, driving myself, and I posted my letter. Then—I don't quite know why— some perverse strain in me made me after all give myself another alibi; an alibi against myself, so to speak. I thought it would be damn good mystification, and I had a vague idea of using it in the book, though I hardly knew how. You see, I had so much time to spend—to fit in with the alibi we'd planned—so I thought I'd spend it there by the memorial. That's why I did that business with Charlie. Then I got home just before seven by the clocks, and Meek reported everything as still correct. Later on, when the Meeks had gone to bed, I put the clocks right again, and I'd also done something which made them sleep sound. But I'll explain all that when I come to the details of the alibi. We'll go right on to the following morning, when you called to see me."

He paused for a moment, as befitted the climax at hand. The cigarette had gone out, and Wharton unobtrusively passed the box again, and Tempest held him a light.

"I'll never be able to tell you what a shock it was when you told me about Lewton's murder. I got the idea that somehow I was caught in a trap, and that things were going on behind my back, and—well, I can't tell you how I felt. But as soon as you'd gone, I began to put two and two together. I began to see certain things in a new light. I remembered, for instance, that recently I'd seen Meek get out his old motor-bike again. He'd stood it by for the winter to save tax, and Mrs. Meek was getting a bit too heavy to do any pillion riding. But that was only one of the things that occurred to me. Then all at once I decided to send for him.

"I told him very quietly to sit down. Then I looked at him as I might be looking at you, and I put my hand on his shoulder like that. I said, 'Tell me, Tom. *Why did you kill Lewton last night?* And you wouldn't believe it, but he started right in and told me, just as if we'd been talking about the weather or what we were going to do in the garden."

Rennyet looked round challengingly. "Now I'll tell you something, gentlemen. When Meek had finished his tale I almost shook hands with him. I didn't—but I still feel I ought to have done, and I'll always be sorry I didn't. You see, there wasn't only that true story about his sister-in-law; there was also something about myself. To make dead sure of his men, he had suggested to Trench that he had information to give about *me*. Trench was delighted, and took him into the dining-room to see Lewton. Then Meek made all sorts of vague charges against me, which we needn't go into now, and Lewton promptly bit. That was probably when he jotted my name down lightly in his book—so lightly that I didn't see it myself. Moreover, Meek had already induced me to see Lewton, and he'd pretended to Lewton that I was coming so that he could run an eye over me. Then Meek also was clever enough to bring Beece in, and if he hadn't known it well enough before, he then knew that everything his sister-in-law had written was perfectly true. The rest, I think, you can fit in for yourselves. That motor-bike of his can go half as quick again as my car. There's a slope downwards from my house, and there's a slope downwards from Homedale, so he got away at both ends without having to start off his engine. I may say that he was under the window and heard Lewton and Howard Trench talking, but he tells me he had thought of implicating both Beece and old Trench long before that."

"And what'd you do after Meek confessed?"

"Still without prejudice?"

"Still without prejudice," gravely repeated Wharton.

"Well, I said I'd stand by him, though he hadn't treated me right. I asked him what he'd got out of the safe, and he said he'd got enough evidence to justify what he'd done, but he'd burnt it all except Lewton's note-book. I made him give me that, and I had a good look through it; then I gave it back and told him to burn it too. When you came along to see me again and you showed me that book, I was flabbergasted. I had Meek in afterwards, and he owned up he sent it. That was when I began to get rather afraid of him. There was a look I didn't like. He said he'd sent the book so that you could get Beece, and if you didn't get him, he'd get him himself."

There the station-sergeant knocked on the door and stuck his head inside. "They're ringing up again from Bicklesham, sir, and want to know what to do."

"Tell 'em to stand by," said Tempest. "We'll be along shortly—and Mr. Rennyet too."

Rennyet went on with his story. "I think I've already told you I gave my word to Meek that I'd stand by him. I told him he was safe if he didn't lose his head. So first of all I made him take that motor-bike far enough away and sell it, and in case there might be the slightest suspicion of his ability to imitate those voices, I stood him down from the dramatic show we were doing. I got him out in the garden, and I got a fine new wireless set to take the place of the one we'd bust up for the sake of the alibi. I got the telephone rushed in, in case I wanted to communicate with him suddenly—or he with me. I also arranged for him to go to a brother of mine up North if ever he had to bolt. But to-night I felt in my bones that something had gone wrong. I didn't like that excuse you gave to get me here. I didn't want to warn Meek for nothing, but I did tell him that if I should ring up to say the car would be wanted, he'd better make his getaway till we saw how things stood. That I think's the lot."

"And lot enough," said Wharton grimly. "But tell me as a matter of interest. Did Meek phone Beece?"

"Oh, no. As soon as Meek was let in by Lewton—who expected him at about seven because Meek had dropped him a discreet line to tell him so—he told Lewton he'd got some splendid news for him about me, and on the strength of that he got Lewton to send for Beece at once. As soon as Lewton rung up, Meek killed him. He said he took a second or two to die, and as he lay there, Meek told him all about it."

"Meek'd have had him, alibi or no alibi," said Carry.

"Yes," said Wharton, "I think perhaps he would. And that reminds me, Mr. Rennyet. Did you know anything about an anonymous letter that was sent to old Trench?"

Rennyet knew nothing, and Wharton gave details.

"I expect he sent it," Rennyet said. "I know he didn't blame old Trench as much as the other two—though he was bad enough. You see, Trench didn't have anything whatever to do with that affair of Miss Mallow."

Wharton nodded. "And what about the actual knife?"

"We have some like it in the house," said Rennyet. "They're a common enough type, as you know. I never asked him about that." He smiled curiously. "It was queer how impersonal those talks of ours used to be. It wasn't a murderer and myself—it was just Tom Meek talking to me. I do know, though, that he used ordinary rubber gloves. He's always getting those at Woolworth's for his wife. She uses them for her hands."

Wharton grunted, then wriggled in his chair. Rennyet took the hint and got up.

"Well, you'll not be running away, Mr. Rennyet," Wharton said. "If we want a confidential statement, no doubt you'll be good enough to supply it. We'll keep you out of the inquest if we possibly can."

"That's very good of you." He looked down, and his foot scraped the floor uneasily. "May I ask you just one question?"

"I think you may," said Wharton.

"Then, about that paper. How'd you get hold of it?"

Wharton frowned. His hand went out to Rennyet's shoulder, and he gave it a paternal pat.

"Meek's dead, isn't he? Then let him rest. If he committed an indiscretion, you don't want to know what or how it was, and go blaming him for the rest of your life?"

"Something Meek did, eh?"

Wharton broke into his ruminations with a pretence of enormous surprise. "I knew there was something I had to mention. You'll pardon me for saying that we've had you under observation for some time now."

"Really?" Something of the old irony had flashed across Rennyet's face.

"Yes," said Wharton. "And we found that you've been very friendly recently with a spindle-shanked sort of fellow who's been staying at the Red Anchor."

The four were now across the room and by the door. In the mirror above the desk Wharton saw another door carefully open—the door of the room in which Ludovic Travers had spent a solitary hour. Wharton's hand went out again and he held Rennyet back.

"An author fellow we understand he is—though he doesn't look like it."

"He's a very famous author," said Rennyet, with some considerable dignity. "Ludovic Travers his name is."

Wharton frowned. "Weird name; still, he looked a weird sort of bloke. And he wasn't mixed up with Meek in any way?"

Rennyet laughed. "Heavens, no! He and I had been thinking of collaborating over a book—a detective novel."

Wharton's pretended thought was followed by a quick alarm. "Not about this case, I hope?"

Rennyet was silent for a moment, and then he shook his head. "It might have been—but not now. Somehow I don't feel like writing detective stories for a bit. I'll drop him a line."

"I would if I were you," said Wharton, and his hand went out and opened the door.

The voices trailed away, then ceased abruptly as the door was shut. Then the other door opened and Ludovic Travers emerged. A sheepish look stole over his face, and with it was a kind of amused chuckle. Spindle-shanked—and a weird sort of bloke! Maybe Wharton had better be told after all what Rennyet's word-portrait of himself had been.

Then Travers's face straightened as his thoughts ran on. Rennyet was going back to Bicklesham. There was what he would find—in a bedroom maybe, with the door smashed in. There would be blood on the floor, and a sobbing woman at the foot of the stairs. A woman who had created her own tragedy from the kindness of her simple heart.

Wharton came in and closed the door behind him. Travers was polishing his glasses and he blinked up as the General came over.

"You got me out of that hole with Rennyet, George. Now there's something else I'd like you to do. Tell Mrs. Wharton to throw that damn recipe on the fire."

Wharton raised his eyebrows. "The cake, you mean? The Rennyet Cake?"

"Don't call it that, George. Cut-throat cake is how I'll always think of it." He made as if to replace his glasses, then kept them in his hand. "You're satisfied about Rennyet?"

"Why, yes," said Wharton, and with a quick look, "Aren't you?"

"I don't know," said Travers slowly. "He might have done the murder with Meek on condition that Meek did the actual killing. It was curious, you know, that he should have given himself that alibi at the memorial."

Wharton grunted. He frowned prodigiously. Then he began a prowl of the room.

"I see what you're getting at. But we'll never prove it now." He came over to Travers again. "Funny we didn't concentrate on Rennyet before. He had just that little something the others hadn't got. He's clever—my God, he is! That cynical way he looks at you, as if he didn't give a damn." Travers hooked on the glasses. "As you say, George, we'll never know. Rennyet may have thrown Meek overboard to save himself. And he'll still have that little something Meek hasn't got."

"You mean, he'll be alive—and walking about."

"Yes," said Travers, "and with a hundred-percent alibi. And this time it's one you'll never break."

THE END

CPSIA information can be obtained
at www.ICGtesting.com
Printed in the USA
LVOW03s1808080418
572690LV00032B/1973/P